A Wedding
at the
Chateau

Annabel French is a bestselling author of several contemporary romantic fiction stories for HarperCollins. Based in southeast England with her family, when she's not busy locked in her study writing, or daydreaming, she can be seen in the great outdoors, running after her two dogs, Wotsit and Skips. This is the third novel in the chateau series.

Also by Annabel French:

Summer at the Chateau

Christmas at the Chateau

A Wedding at the Chateau

ANNABEL FRENCH

avon.

Published by AVON
A division of HarperCollins*Publishers*
1 London Bridge Street
London SE1 9GF

www.harpercollins.co.uk

HarperCollins*Publishers*
Macken House, 39/40 Mayor Street Upper
Dublin 1, D01 C9W8

A Paperback Original 2024

1

First published in Great Britain by HarperCollins*Publishers* 2024

Set in Birka by HarperCollins*Publishers* India

Printed and bound in the UK using 100% Renewable Electricity by CPI
Group (UK) Ltd

*To my amazing niece Jess,
I'm so proud of you!*

Prologue

13 Years Before

The balmy evening breeze brushed Olivia's sun-kissed skin, cooling it against the heat of the setting sun. Let's be honest though, sunburnt was probably more accurate than sun-kissed. That was the trouble with being a pale-skinned redhead travelling around some of the hottest countries in the world, but Nico had promised she looked more bronzed than pink today.

When they'd first started travelling six months ago, her fair skin had reacted to the heat with giant red welts and prickly heat. Not a good look when you're trying to be an adventuress and cool and less like your elderly grandma constantly sitting in the shade. She was here to live life to the full before starting university and boy was she determined to squeeze every last memory out of it. Travelling wasn't the most original thing to do in a gap year, but when Nico – her best friend – had suggested it, she hadn't been able to refuse.

As the months had gone by, her skin had adapted somewhat, though she'd still liberally applied sunscreen while Nico giggled. It was all right for him with his olive skin, dark hair and dark eyes: the benefit of an Italian heritage. From the corner of her eyes, she admired his square jaw, studded with stubble. He was smiling as they sat on the beach, staring out to sea, listening to the tide gently lap the shore.

How nothing had happened between them, she didn't know. Neither of them had met anyone else – only fellow travellers who'd become friends – and she was certain attraction bubbled beneath the surface. It did for her anyway, just as it had as they'd grown up together. There'd been a few fleeting moments over the years and more so on this trip when it had felt like the ground was shifting and they were on the cusp of something new. She'd caught him watching her a few times, putting his arm around her when guys had chatted her up. Something territorial and protective that had stirred butterflies in her stomach and filled her with longing.

She scooped a handful of white sand, letting it fall through her fingers like a sandglass counting down the hours and minutes until they had to return home. Bali really was an island paradise. The turquoise sea ebbed and flowed in front of her, tiny white horses foaming on the shore, and behind her, mountainous rocky outcrops softened with bright green shrubs hid them from the rest of the world. The sun was setting, the sky a mix of bold and beautiful colours: pinks and oranges slicing across the horizon and above them, a thick, velvety darkness rolled down as if gobbling them up. Every star seemed brighter than they ever had at home, shining overhead and begging her to make a wish. If she did, she knew exactly what she'd wish for.

'I can't believe we go home tomorrow,' Nico said.

Though his family were from Italy, he'd been raised for most of his life in England and there was still a slight hint of an accent in the way he rolled his r's. He too pressed his fingers into the sand, raking lines with his fingertips.

'It's gone too quickly,' Olivia replied, aware, as she always was, of his presence.

Was she the only one who felt like something was pulling them together? Like an invisible hand was edging her physically closer to him? After being friends for years, since they were both at primary school, Olivia had hoped that being away from home, from his family and hers, travelling alone together, he'd come to see her as she'd grown to see him. That he'd appreciate she was now a young woman about to start university rather than the snotty-nosed sidekick she'd been at school. Their friendship had changed as they'd both navigated school but there were times when she was sure he saw her as his childhood friend and not as a young woman with curves and hips. She sighed and looked out to sea again.

After partying with everyone else, they'd snuck away from the crowds, preferring a few minutes alone before their lives changed when they returned home.

'Back to reality, hey? Back to boring,' Nico said before taking a swig of beer and then adding it to the empty bottles stuck in the sand at their feet.

'You're off to Oxford, clever clogs! It won't be boring there.' She was slightly jealous though not surprised he'd made it into such a prestigious university. He was one of the cleverest people she knew.

'And you're off to Reading. I've never been there before. Dad said it's a beautiful city.'

Olivia laughed. 'I can't believe you're sat on a beach in Bali after travelling around Thailand and Singapore and you're going on about Reading being beautiful.'

He chuckled too, opening another beer. 'You were more impressed with the bars than the course I seem to remember.'

'So? They're important things to consider too. Plus, it's cheaper than London.' The bottle she'd been holding had grown warm, tepid lager tingling her mouth. 'Just don't get a new best friend, okay?'

4

'I wouldn't dream of it.'

'And don't go making marriage pacts with anyone else either.'

When they'd been in Thailand, sat in the bar, they'd drunkenly agreed that if they were both still single at forty, they'd marry each other. It had been a joke, but she'd also secretly hoped that when they reached thirty-nine they'd be able to make it happen. She chastised herself for being stupid. He'd never even kissed her and apart from a few flashes of possibility, nothing had happened between them in all this time.

'I won't, I promise.'

'I'll hold you to that.' There was no chance he wouldn't be married by forty. Girls had always fallen for Nico. Quite a few even threw themselves at him, some with as much force as a circus performer fired from a cannon. She remembered a blonde, bikini-clad model-looking girl who'd done so only the day before. Yet, he never left her side. That had to mean something, didn't it?

Nico wrapped an arm around her, resting his head on her shoulder. She could feel his dark hair tickle her neck. 'I'll miss you, Olive.'

He was the only one who was allowed to call her that. She couldn't even remember how the nickname had come about. Something about the first time she'd tried olives round Nico's house. His dad laughing as she screwed up her face at the odd taste. She hated the name Olive when anyone else said it. If they tried, they got the death stare because it was usually said as a taunt. Nico had always said it reminded him of home. Of Italy.

'Miss me?' Olivia replied, tilting her head to try and look at him but only seeing the chestnut curls on his head. 'Don't be daft, we'll only be an hour away from each other and you'll come to visit me, won't you?'

'Sure. Of course.'

She sensed something in his uncertain tone. He straightened up and she turned to him. He had never been as close to her as this, and there was something in the air. An electricity, a sense of something significant about to happen. He didn't move away. Instead, his eyes were flitting over her features, studying her eyes and coming to rest on her mouth. Her heart pumped and she was suddenly aware of her lips, her mouth, her eyelashes.

Was this it?

Was this the moment she'd been waiting six months – no longer – for?

Her heartbeat sped up as his head tilted slightly, his mouth moving closer to hers. Her body began to tingle with anticipation and hope. She closed her eyes, waiting for his lips to touch hers, unable to believe this was actually real. She thanked the stars for making her wish come true. When nothing came, she leaned forwards towards him, eager to find his mouth with her own. Then she felt him shift, sand sliding and covering her hand.

When she opened her eyes, he'd moved away and his expression had changed to fear.

She immediately thought she'd done something wrong. She shouldn't have eaten those garlic prawns for dinner, but it was her last night, and they were her favourite. She cursed her appetite. But then his words floored her.

'I'm not going to Oxford.'

'What?'

He pushed a hand into his hair and leaned away from her, pushing himself to standing. 'I'm not going to Oxford.'

She stood too, the soft sand reaching in between her toes, sucking her into the ground, which is where her heart was. 'What do you mean? You've got a place. You—'

'I've changed my mind. I'm going to the University of Florence instead. I'm moving back to Italy.'

His words were absorbed into the hot and heavy air, into the thick, dark sky creeping around them. The splashes of colour were virtually gone now, fading to pale yellows and damask pinks, and the tide was coming in, soaking her sandals. Nico took a step to the side and Olivia pinned him with her eyes.

'When did you decide this?'

'Before we began travelling. I was going to tell you. I just couldn't find the right time.'

'You've known all this time and you didn't say anything?' Anger and hurt surged inside her. He'd never

7

kept a secret like this from her before. Not in all the years they'd been friends. She'd always been the first person he talked to, and he'd always been there to listen to her. For years they'd confided their secrets, their hopes and dreams, their fears and worries. 'All the time we've been travelling, you've been keeping this a secret from me?'

'No – yes, but, Olive—' He reached out, but she wouldn't take his hand. His dark eyes implored her, but anger had set her jaw firm, and she wouldn't move. 'It's not like that, Liv. You know how much I've missed my mum, how much I've wanted to get back to my roots. She and Dad grew up in Italy and I thought if I could go there and—'

'I thought you meant going on holiday to Tuscany not moving to Florence! That's—' She threw her hands in the air, finally stepping out of the water. 'That changes everything!'

'We'll still be able to keep in touch. We can still visit each other.'

'Oh really? You're just going to hop on a plane and fly back to England during the holidays. Or am I going to do that? How am I going to afford it on my student loan?'

'I'll be coming back to see Dad, and my brothers, but since Mum died, I've wanted to know more about her family. To see where she came from. She always said it was the perfect place to live – to grow up. Like heaven on earth.'

Knowing that everything Nico said was true, and that his

mum's death five years before had affected him deeply, her heart gave a little, but she couldn't help feeling betrayed. 'Are you only telling me this now because you're drunk?'

'No! I've been drunk a lot on this trip and I've been wanting to tell you ever since I made the decision but I just couldn't say it. I didn't want to ruin everything.'

But he had, and she wasn't sure how it could be repaired. Every night they'd spent together these last six months, talking about the future, laughing, joking, supporting and encouraging each other, he'd known something so monumental and hadn't told her. Her heart seared with pain, and she couldn't help but wonder if she wasn't as important to him as he'd always been to her.

He came towards her, his voice softening as he spoke. She could hear the tension in his throat, the words wavering as his voice cracked. 'You're my best friend, Olive. One of the most important people in my life. You always will be.' He took her hands, holding them firmly. 'We'll stay in touch, visit each other all the time. Nothing will change. Not really.'

She desperately wanted to believe that what he said was true, but doubt lingered in the back of her mind. 'Promise?' Olivia asked, her voice wavering as she gripped hold of her emotions, looking into his eyes, reading his face for any sign he didn't mean it.

'I promise.' He pulled her close, wrapping his arms tightly around her and squeezing her in. He'd always been taller than her. Long and gangly, like he'd been stretched out a bit too much. That first night in Singapore, he'd struggled to get comfortable in his sleeping bag because he'd been too tall for it. They hadn't stopped laughing about it but now all those happy memories were tainted with hurt. Her head nestled just under his chin and she squeezed her eyes shut to stop the tears from falling.

'I'll always be there for you, Olive. No matter how far apart we are. I swear.'

She breathed him in, a mixture of salt where they'd swum earlier and the body spray he wore, believing his words but feeling as though she'd already lost him. When they separated, silence abounded. The only sounds were the lethargic twittering of birds, the lazy flowing of the tide and the rustling of the palm trees.

This wasn't how she'd wanted this night, this holiday, to end. It felt like a part of her life was suddenly over or had taken a new and unexpected, unpleasant route. The air felt suddenly colder and she shuddered, closing her arms over her chest. Everything she'd thought was to be, suddenly wasn't. He made it sound so simple, but she was abruptly and piercingly aware that the life she'd imagined wasn't to come.

Her heart broke, a piece falling away and washing out to sea. And to think only moments before he had nearly made her dreams come true and kissed her.

Chapter 1

Present Day

'Jacob!' Olivia pressed her hand into her forehead as she stared at what had once been a neat and tidy kitchen. Well, mostly neat and tidy. She wasn't exactly Marie Kondo and anything that didn't 'bring her joy' went in a cupboard under the stairs. But the small kitchen of her equally small London house now resembled the set of *Supermarket Sweep* after the contestants had gone on a particularly mad shopping frenzy. Irritatingly, she could also feel the wrinkles that now marred her brow. Were they deeper than they'd been yesterday? She was absolutely sure they were. Wrinkles sounded too nice. Ravines would be more like it.

Cereal covered the kitchen counter where her thirteen-year-old son's aim was apparently worse than in the bathroom, and the remains of a loaf spilled out of the plastic wrap where she'd made lunch for him and herself some toast. A knife stuck out of the open tub of butter as if it was a murder victim and splashes of milk and orange juice puddled the surfaces. Olivia turned her back on it and frantically brushed her hair before tying it into a messy bun while simultaneously trying to slip on her shoes.

'Jacob! Have you brushed your teeth?' No reply came and she moved to the bottom of the stairs in a lopsided walk because one shoe had cooperated while the other lay on its side half under the sofa. 'I swear, boy, if you're on that iPad again, I'll—'

Jacob, all wide-eyed innocence with toothpaste foam around his mouth, stood at the top of the stairs, dabbing at his black school tie. 'I was trying to get this off.'

She gestured for him to come downstairs. 'This is why I want you to brush your teeth *before* you get dressed. Come here.'

'But then I'm too minty for my breakfast.'

'One of life's conundrums,' she replied with a smile as she pulled out his tie and licked her thumb.

'Ewww! Don't use spit! That's gross.'

'I used to clean your face like this when you were little.'

His mouth curled. 'That's disgusting.'

Feeling suddenly mischievous as love for her son rushed over her, she yanked his tie just as the boys at school did to each other. She'd seen it many times as she dropped Jacob off at the gates. It seemed more of a teenage greeting than anything else.

'You peanutted me!' Jacob declared in horror. 'You actually peanutted me!'

'Serves you right for making us late.'

He still hadn't brushed his dark blond hair, the same colour as that of his roguish but ultimately useless father, and he pushed his hand through it before wiggling his tie, not really fixing it at all. That was unfair, Olivia thought to herself. Though Jack had started out about as useful as a chocolate teapot and marriage clearly wasn't his forte, he had stepped up to the plate as far as Jacob was concerned.

'I can't believe you just did that,' Jacob grumbled, adjusting his tie.

'Come on, let's go. I don't need your teacher giving me another telling-off via email, or worse, ringing me during the day so I look like a five-year-old in front of my team.' She hobbled to the sofa and slipped on her rogue shoe.

As she grabbed her bag and car keys, leaving the kitchen mess for later, she checked off all the things Jacob needed for his day: PE kit – yes, lunchbox – yes, water bottle – he ran back and got it, locker key – yes. Head down at his phone, Jacob made his usual grumbling noises as he got into the car, moaning about something on Snapchat, about a kid at school, about his mouth still being minty, but Olivia ignored it. They'd had quite a nice morning for once. She'd only had to raise her voice at the end and, even then, she'd managed to do so comically, and she didn't want to spoil it now. Goodness knows calm mornings were rare enough when you had a hormonal boy-monster roaming around the house.

She glanced at him remembering the tiny, unexpected baby he'd been. 'Love you, son.'

'What?' He looked up from his phone in unconcealed disgust, then his eyes softened and the boyish grin that hadn't quite faded under teenage coolness lifted the corners of his mouth. 'Yeah, you too.'

As usual, the traffic was awful and while Jacob blasted music that couldn't really be called music from the car speakers, she cussed under her breath.

'All right, road rage,' Jacob said coolly as equally impatient drivers battled their way past each other and through traffic lights that were just about to turn red.

Olivia was sure she hadn't gone above fifteen miles an hour on the whole journey to school and every set of traffic lights had stopped her. Her eyes ran to the dashboard clock. It was way too late again.

After dropping Jacob at the school gates, Olivia made her way to her office, fighting through heavy, uncooperative London traffic to the small events company based in Primrose Hill. Whilst stuck in various queues, she'd managed to apply some mascara and hoped that her complexion looked dewier and more youthful than sweaty summer in the city. And though the day was starting out warm and dry with blue skies and fluffy cotton-wool clouds, the forecast was for drizzle later in typical British summertime fashion. She glanced at the back seat where her bag was splayed half open. In true Olivia fashion, she'd been so busy getting Jacob ready that she'd forgotten her coat. Wonderful.

Olivia entered the open-plan office and raced to her desk.

'Pssst,' the receptionist said as she bustled past. Olivia turned her head to see her pointing then miming something. Olivia frowned, trying to understand what the sign language was all about. 'Your shirt's done up wrong.'

Olivia glanced down. Not only were her shirt buttons fastened incorrectly, they were so wrong that even a toddler would have done a better job. How had she not noticed? Not only that, she had a toothpaste mark on her left breast and part of her skirt was tucked into her knickers. She quickly tugged down her skirt and redid the buttons as Portia, her beast of a manager, walked past, her skyscraper heels denting the thin carpet tiles.

'Late again, Livvy?' Portia crossed her arms over her chest, her long red nails standing out against the black of her shirt as she drummed them.

Olivia checked her watch. 'Am I?' She tapped the

face like it was some nineteenth-century pocket watch, pretending it was wrong and that she hadn't known she'd arrived fifteen minutes late. 'Sorry. It must be slow. And the school-run traffic was horrendous this morning. As always.'

'Again?'

'Yeah, sorry. School-run traffic does tend to be awful when it's, you know, term time.'

'It's not a good enough excuse though, is it. If you know the traffic's going to be awful, you should leave earlier to compensate.'

'I can't leave too early or Jacob will be waiting at the gates. They don't unlock them too early.'

'Not my problem.'

'Do you have kids, Portia?' Olivia asked lightly.

'Can't abide them. Just make sure it doesn't happen again, all right?'

'Will do.' Olivia nodded, knowing full well it was going to happen again and lots more times after that. That was the problem with being a single mum to a laid-back teenage boy. Alarm clocks didn't work, shouting up the stairs didn't work. She'd even once tried firing a water pistol at him, which had put him in an outstandingly terrible mood, and smacking a saucepan with a wooden spoon hadn't gone down well either. All that had done was earn her a telling-off from the next-door neighbour who'd used more swearwords in five minutes than she'd heard in most of her life. It hadn't been a good day.

With a tut, Portia walked on, and Olivia turned her chair back to her desk to find Ian, one of her events team, giving her a sympathetic smile.

'She's the worst, isn't she?' he whispered across the small divider that separated their desks. 'When I came in, she told me I shouldn't wear brown suits because they make people think of poo. She didn't even say good morning or anything. It was just: "Don't wear brown, Ian. It makes people think of turds." Then she cited some kind of study, but I don't think that can be true, can it?' He held out his arms, studying the dark brown fabric. 'It's not even a pooey brown colour. It's chocolate brown and everyone likes chocolate.'

'Hmm,' she agreed. 'I'm not sure it's chocolate, but definitely more chestnut than poo. I like it.'

'Thanks, boss.'

'So, where are we with the Holden 100th anniversary gala dinner?'

The question was directed at Ian, but Ava, who was sat at the desk diagonal to Olivia, popped her head up and began to answer, making Olivia jump and place a hand on her heart.

'Christ on a bike! I didn't know you were in yet!'

'I've got short purple hair. How could you not know I was here?'

It was true. Her deep aubergine hair had been styled

in short, sharp spikes and she'd changed her lip ring to a bar. Normally, Ava was very difficult to miss.

'Keeping your head down while Portia was here, were you?'

'Yeah,' she said and laughed. 'She always looks at me like I'm some sort of alien just because I like tats and don't dress the way she does. Who'd want to dress like a Nineties middle manager anyway? I thought shoulder pads and oversized suits were an Eighties thing.'

Olivia repressed a grin, trying to remain professional. 'So . . . Holdens?'

'We are T-minus three days to the event,' Ava said. 'And everything is arranged. The only thing I'm waiting on is their presentation for the night. I'd like to have it backed up to the Cloud and I'll take my laptop in case there are any problems with the memory stick or their laptop on the night.'

'Sounds like you've got it all under control. Great job. Is there anything you need me to do? Any last-minute chasers or running around?'

'Ahh, thanks, Livvy, but it's all good. You've taught us well. We won't let you down.'

Ian was nodding along enthusiastically.

'I know you won't,' Olivia replied, warming with pride.

Ian and Ava had joined the company a year ago and though it was Portia's job to train them, that responsibility had fallen to Olivia when Portia decided she didn't have time. Luckily for Olivia, they'd got on well and had soon formed a close-knit team. Managing events excited Olivia. She loved the organisation, fitting all the different pieces together like a jigsaw, but it hadn't all been plain sailing. She could argue with vendors and service providers till the cows came home but managing people had been a challenge. She found conflict with friends difficult and didn't enjoy having to tell people when they'd done something wrong. Somehow, she'd fudged her way through, settling into the role in a way she hadn't thought she would, and now they'd turned into friends, not just colleagues.

'And what about the Buffington-Smythe birthday celebrations, Ian? We're what . . . twelve weeks out on that?'

'Yep.' He looked down at his computer and clicked. 'Just waiting for them to confirm the music. I know we're cutting it fine, and I have chivvied them up today already, but they can't decide between the DJ who'll do all evening, or the band.'

Olivia nodded, making a note on her notepad. She still preferred pen and paper for some things. 'Shall I email Mrs Buffington-Smythe on Friday if we haven't heard anything?'

'Could you?' Ian tipped his head in relief. 'She frightens me a bit.'

'She's all right underneath the tweed and pearls. You

just have to know how to handle her. And she doesn't always mean to be rude, she's just . . . to the point.'

'You're the best. Shall I make tea then?'

'Actually,' Ava said, 'I'm about to do a coffee run. Any takers?'

'Oh, yes, please,' Olivia replied. 'I feel like I've done a day's work already and it's not even ten o'clock. Can I have a double shot latte, please? Okay if I get the next lot?'

'Sure thing.'

'Caramel macchiato for me, please,' Ian said. He had something of a sweet tooth.

She dashed away, earning a glance from Portia that they all ignored. Everyone did coffee runs to the café next door. She'd just have to get over it. No other team was as on the ball with their work as Olivia's was, or as successful, and – in her opinion – that earned them a few perks.

When Ava came back a few minutes later, Olivia settled down to work, enjoying her coffee. The caffeine hit was just what she needed this morning, and she savoured both the delicious flavour of the strong coffee and the thrill of ticking things off her to-do list.

'Don't forget you're in this meeting with Portia at eleven,' Ian said, glancing over the divider.

'Damn. I could really do without that today.'

'She does love a meeting about a meeting,' Ava replied, grinning impishly just as Portia strode to the meeting room followed by a few different members of staff. Olivia stood and followed them, grabbing her phone and notebook.

They settled in the room, the others eyeing her takeaway coffee cup enviously.

'Right,' Portia began standing at the head of the table and projecting a presentation from her laptop. She loved a presentation, even when one wasn't strictly necessary. Olivia sometimes thought that must be all she did every day, creating useless presentations no one was going to remember when a quick email would do the trick. Portia got underway and Olivia concentrated on the salient points, ignoring the waffle that went with it. She was just about to raise her hand to ask a question when her phone rang.

'Oh, I'm so sorry.' She silenced the call as Nico's face popped onto the screen. Her heart instantly swelled. Hearing from him always brightened her day, but it was unusual for him to call this early. He normally rang in the evenings so he could chat to her and Jacob. She knew she should stay and listen to the rest of the meeting but her curiosity, and a little concern, had been piqued.

'I'm sorry, Portia,' she said to her wide, disbelieving eyes. 'I really need to take this. It's my son's school.'

She edged out of the room to sympathetic smiles from her colleagues. One even said, 'I hope everything's okay,' instantly filling her with guilt. She went to her desk and took her seat, plugging in her headphones and accepting the video call before he rang off. She glanced up to see Portia through the glass walls of the meeting room, glaring at the poor people still trapped in there and gesticulating wildly. Rather them than her.

'Hey, you. What are you calling for? Bit early for our monthly catch-up, isn't it?'

Since he'd moved to Florence all those years ago, they'd spoken at least once a month. It had taken a while for the initial pain of their separation and her anger at his not having told her about switching universities, and countries, to subside. But once it had, they'd decided that the first Monday of every month was off limits to everyone but each other. She'd turned down dates so as not to miss a chat with Nico and still, rather foolishly, secretly hoped he'd done the same for her. She hadn't minded. Who wanted to go on a date on a Monday anyway? They were stressful enough without adding first-date nerves into the mix.

It hadn't always been easy to keep in contact. Their lives had changed so much through the years. She'd fallen pregnant with Jacob in her first year at university and married Jack, Jacob's father, only weeks before their son was born. The marriage had proved to be a mistake, but she wouldn't change it for the world. Thinking philosophically, as she'd learned to do from a young age, life with Jack had taught her what she wanted and, conversely, what she didn't want. And of course, she'd never trade Jacob for anything. Her baby – though he

22

wasn't a baby anymore – meant the world to her.

Nico had been more than a little shocked at her pregnancy and she often wondered if that was when he realised she was a woman and no longer his childhood partner in crime. And though he and Jack hadn't really got on at first, he'd been over the moon to become Jacob's godfather. It was a role he'd taken seriously, and now, he and her son were almost as close as she and Nico had once been.

'Do you have a moment to talk?' Nico asked. 'In private?' His voice was a little unsteady and she pushed down the mounting worry.

'Umm . . . Yeah, sure. Just give me a second.'

She stared around the light open-plan office. All the meeting rooms and tiny private 'pods' were taken. She edged to the furthest corner of the office where the team who were in with Portia normally sat. They really didn't look happy and Portia was now standing up and pacing while she shouted at them.

'What's up?'

'I–I'm getting married.'

'What?' She'd shouted so loudly, Ian and Ava both looked up, frowning in concern. She waved their concerns away and said, 'Nothing to worry about,' while inside her heart was racing and she felt slightly sick.

'My wedding?' Nico asked in confusion. 'My wedding is nothing to worry about?'

'No, I was talking to Ian and Ava, I— It doesn't matter.' The word 'marriage' hit the inside of her brain like a hammer shattering a pane of glass. 'So you're getting married?' She tried to sound pleased, happy for him, but as concern and not a little jealousy grabbed her, she worried she sounded bitter.

'I know it's quick, but Sofia and I were talking, and we decided why wait, you know?'

She did know. She knew from her own rubbish experience that that wasn't the best basis on which to make one of the biggest commitments of your life. She and Jack had lasted five years and that had been more than enough. They should really have called it quits after two before Jacob had known what was going on.

'Right,' she said, then as a tense silence descended, she added, 'Well that's wonderful news, Nico. Congratulations. When's the wedding?'

'In just under eight weeks.'

'Eight weeks?' She'd screeched again, and this time it wasn't just Ava and Ian who looked up. The rest of the office had as well. A sea of half-amused, half-annoyed faces glanced at her before returning to stare at their desks. She lowered her voice and turned towards the window, her back to the room. *Positive*, she thought. *Be positive*. 'Wow. That's not long, is it? But I suppose when you know, you know . . . you know?' What was she drivelling on about? *When you know, you know . . . pah!* But she

24

couldn't turn around and say, *'Nico, this is an absolutely terrible idea. Please don't do it.'*

'Exactly.'

But the niggling feeling that this was a catastrophic mistake nagged in her mind. She felt she should mention the warnings she'd given him before, when he and Sofia had just started dating. Six months ago, when he'd first mentioned Sofia, she'd worried that they weren't really suited. At that time, it had only been a few months since he'd split from his ex: A long-term girlfriend who he'd been with for a few years. Not only that, but Sofia was a social media influencer – a job she didn't really understand – and after some subtle social media stalking, Olivia had counselled against rushing into anything. She couldn't see what Sofia and Nico could possibly have in common. Apart from a mention on the company website (an architects' firm he worked for) Nico didn't really have social media. But all her warnings had been ignored. He'd thrown himself into the relationship with gusto (a gusto that had broken her heart) and now six months later he was getting married.

How could you know someone after only six months? You didn't! That was the answer. You didn't know them. Not really. Not inside and out. You didn't know their bad habits, only the good side of them they were showing because it was all so new and you didn't want to spoil the romance by farting in bed or burping after a curry.

25

Although if Sofia's social media profiles were anything to go by the woman woke looking amazing. With sexily ruffled hair, she'd spend the day in her Lululemon set, eating things like avocado on toast or something with kimchi.

Her feed seemed to consist of pictures of her, which, to be fair, if Olivia looked like that she'd take more pictures of herself too, but there just didn't seem to be anything else. She never posted about films, music, books, TV . . . not even food and she was Italian! Italians love food! No matter what she'd heard about her from Nico they didn't seem a particularly good match.

Olivia's stomach sank that he was making such a big mistake, not least because she'd never even met Sofia in the flesh and didn't think Nico's family had either. She mentally scanned their conversations. No, she was sure there'd never been any mention of a meeting with Nico's ebullient dad and tricksy band of brothers.

'Looks like you won't need our marriage pact after all,' she joked.

'What marriage pact?'

She drew her eyes to the ceiling and bit her lip against the pain of him not remembering. 'You remember the agreement we made when we were travelling. We said if neither of us were wed by forty we'd marry each other.' She kept her voice as level as she could.

It had only been a silly joke. She knew that. It shouldn't

bother her now that he hadn't remembered, but the pain still stung. It just went to show that even now her love for him was of a different type to his love for her.

'Oh, yes.' He chuckled. 'Now I remember. So . . . will you come?'

'To the wedding?'

'No to the farmer's market. Of course to my wedding! And bring Jacob. FaceTime is great but it's been nearly a year since I saw you both properly. He has to come. He is my only godson and we Italians take that duty very seriously.'

To be honest, Olivia didn't know where she'd have been without him. Jack had got better as he'd got older but despite staying at university to get a degree while she dropped out and raised their child, he hadn't really made much of it. He'd flittered from job to job, only lately settling into something he enjoyed and could stand for more than six months at a time. Who'd have thought that in England where it rained for ten months out of twelve, it would have been gardening. Because of Jack's flakiness work wise, Nico had often helped them out financially when requests for expensive school trips had come in and he'd never hear of her paying him back, saying it was his job as godfather. He'd even helped at Christmas and birthdays when things had been particularly hard, ensuring Jacob had the things he wanted. Things they wouldn't have been able to afford otherwise. Whether she approved of this wedding or not, and there had been times when Nico hadn't approved of her choices, she owed him a lot.

'Olive? You will come, won't you?'

The use of his pet name for her brought her mind back to the present. 'Definitely! We'd both love to come. Jacob will be so excited. Do you want me to tell him or will you?'

'I'll call him tonight if that's okay?'

'Of course. Just leave it till after six so he's done all his homework.'

'You're a good mum, Olive.'

Nico's kind words softened the blow of his news just a little. Over the years, she'd needed that from those around her. There were times it had been heartbreakingly hard. 'Thank you,' she said quietly. 'Well, congratulations, and to Sofia too. She must be so excited.'

'She is. More than I thought possible.'

'I'll speak to you later then.'

They said their goodbyes and Olivia hung up, turning back to face an office that seemed to know something had happened. They kept their heads down. Even Ian and Ava were typing and staring at their screens like their lives depended on it.

Olivia made her way to her desk and took out her headphones, returning her phone to the little spot she always kept it on the corner of her desk. She adjusted it, making sure it was absolutely straight, aware of Ian and

28

Ava glancing over the divider and then looking at each other.

'Is everything all right?' Ava asked tentatively. 'Do you need another coffee?'

'No, thanks. I'm fine – everything's fine. A friend of mine is getting married.' She forced her voice to lift at the end as though excited at the news even though deep down she felt her heart tearing apart.

Nico was getting married.

And a little voice she'd never been able to silence told her it should be to her. If things had been just a little bit different, it could have been her.

'I'm just going to nip to the loo,' she said breezily. 'Back in a tick.'

But as soon as she locked the door to the cubicle and sat on the closed toilet lid, all she could do was cry, removing the mascara she'd applied that morning and, with it, any stupidly remaining hopes that somehow, someway, she and Nico would end up together.

Chapter 2

Five weeks later, Olivia attempted to stop her lip from wobbling as she lugged her suitcase down the stairs ready to depart for Italy alone.

In the weeks since Nico had called, he, and her friends at work, had convinced her to take a break from events, life, motherhood and everything else and have a couple of weeks sunning herself and catching up with Nico before Jacob and Jack joined her for the wedding.

Being a single mum from such a young age, she hadn't had a chance to take holidays and even when Jacob had gone to his father's for the weekend, she'd preferred to stay at home in case anything happened and Jack had to bring him back. It hadn't happened often. Jack was a lot of things, but he wasn't an absent or lazy father. He'd taken a while to get his head around such a huge change to their lives, and he hadn't been great when Jacob had been sick, panicking in a way that had always made her smile, but it had always reminded her that no matter how irritating he could be, he was a good man at heart.

He had, however, always been one of her life choices Nico had not approved of. When Nico had first heard Olivia was pregnant, he'd wanted to meet Jack and it hadn't taken long for his disapproval to show. Jack had always been a bit of a lad. He liked football and rugby, and a drink with the guys. Nico was more of a reading and hiking kind of guy. He liked architecture and history and culture. Those first few years with Jacob as a small baby had been particularly tense. But as they'd all grown older, things had become more civil, to the point that both enquired after the other and the relationship could now be defined as amicable acquaintances. Jack had been thrilled to hear Nico was getting married. He'd been even happier when Nico had extended the invitation, and it was agreed that Olivia would fly out ahead and they would join her a week before the wedding.

Now, as she stood looking at her son, whose lip, she was sure, was wobbling as much as hers was, she wished she wasn't going anywhere. Not only did she not want to watch Nico marry someone else – someone whose most

31

recent post had been about the latest teeth-whitening gel she'd been gifted – but how would she cope without seeing Jacob every day? She loved hearing about his day and savoured the fact he was a lot more communicative than some boys his age. When they sat around the table at night having dinner, he'd always tell her about the things that had happened at school to him and his mates. She savoured it and no matter what, he always had her full attention and she his.

It's only for two weeks, she reminded herself. *Stop being a wimp.*

'Right then,' she said with fake cheer. 'My taxi should be here any minute. Give us a hug.' Her voice cracked and she quickly squeezed her eyes shut to stop the tears falling. Jacob wrapped his arms around her and she took a second to sniff his hair, just as she'd done when he was a freshly washed baby. Unfortunately, despite her requests, it was clear he hadn't showered for a couple of days and instead of that wonderful baby shampoo smell she'd loved, all she got was a disgusting whiff that dried her tears almost instantly.

'I thought I told you to have a shower?'

'Uh, Mum, don't start. I did.'

'Well, you didn't wash your hair.'

'Hey!' came Jack's voice from the kitchen where he was making himself a coffee. 'Leave him be. He's all right. I couldn't smell anything when I hugged him.'

'That's because he smells the same as you do. You were always rubbish at showering daily.'

Jack gave a cheeky grin. Still in his early thirties like her, his blond hair hadn't turned even the slightest bit grey, though he had developed a little bit of a paunch from too many Saturday nights in the pub. He was still an attractive man, though he didn't stir any sort of romantic feelings inside her anymore.

He tossed the last bit of biscuit into the air and caught it in his open mouth. 'You're only saying that because you're going to miss us.'

'Him,' she replied, pointing at Jacob. 'I'm going to miss him.'

'Don't be weird, Mum.'

'It's not weird! I love you. I'm going to miss you, that's all. We've never been apart for this long.'

'So?'

She should probably be grateful, she realised as the stinging in her nose started again, signalling tears weren't far away. It would be much worse if he was crying and begging her not to leave.

The sound of the Rolling Stones blared from Jack's pocket and he answered his phone quicker than she'd ever seen him do so before. He turned his back and walked back into the kitchen.

'Now, be good for your dad. It's summer holiday so you don't need to worry about homework, but please remember to brush your teeth and have a shower every other day at least.' She ruffled his hair, feeling the need to touch him, then remembering what a bad idea it had been as the same smell from earlier drifted towards her.

Jack's mumbled voice carried from the kitchen. 'It's all good. Honestly. Yeah. No, we're still on. Promise.'

Olivia felt herself scowling before she realised she was probably making her ravine-like wrinkles worse by frowning so hard. Jack hung up and walked back into the living room. 'Everything all right?'

'Yeah fine. Brilliant.'

'You're not doing anything dodgy are you?'

'Me? No. Course not.'

A car horn blared outside and she took a deep breath. 'Right, that's my taxi. One more hug.'

Jacob edged forwards. 'Fine.'

'I love you.'

'Love you too.'

The tightness of his squeeze told her that despite his bravado, he'd miss her too. She took one last sniff of his whiffy hair then let him go. 'Right then.'

'Got your passport?' Jack asked, stirring his coffee. He'd been watching on from the kitchen and the smile he gave her was kindly. He knew how difficult this was going to be for her, and this was his way of taking her mind off her sadness.

34

'Yep. In my handbag.' She looked around for it and Jacob handed it to her.

'Got your bikini?'

'I think my bikini days are over since having this one.' She nodded at Jacob. She'd never quite managed to shift the roundness a baby belly had produced, even though it had been over a decade. Sofia had a stomach you could bounce protein bars off. Olivia shook the thought of trudging around the pool in front of her away. She'd cross that bridge if she came to it. Nico had told her to bring swimming gear, so she'd done as she was told.

'Nah, you're still a cracker.'

'Thanks.' She chuckled. 'I've got my swimsuit. Two in fact. Both with a little bit of tummy control for extra confidence.'

'You don't need that! I do though.' He patted his rounded belly.

This was Jack through and through. He was the ultimate cheeky chappy, flirty at times. That was another thing that had undone them: his roving eye. An eye that still roved even now, which was why he was still single. The women in Jack's life didn't often last long enough to meet Jacob, which was one thing Olivia was grateful for. No matter how hard things had been with Jacob splitting his time between his mum and his dad while other families went home from school to have weekends together, there hadn't been a succession of other men or women in her son's life. She'd only had a couple of one-off dates and one very short-lived relationship.

'Have a great time. You deserve it.'

The car horn beeped again. 'Be good, you two. Don't eat pizza every day and try to eat some fruit and veg.'

'We will.'

'No, you won't.' She chuckled as she opened the door and, taking hold of her case, began to wheel it down the path to the waiting taxi. 'But that's okay.'

'Have fun, Mum.'

The taxi driver placed her case in the boot, and she climbed into the back seat, winding down the window. 'I will.'

But would she?

It took everything she had not to let the tears escape. Waving goodbye to Jacob was proving the hardest thing she'd ever done. She knew it was only a matter of weeks until she'd see him again but it didn't stop her heart from hurting. The bond that tied them together as mother and son was being stretched in a way she'd never experienced before. Not even when he started school or secondary school or went to friends' places for sleepovers. This was horribly different.

As Jack ushered Jacob back into the house and she turned to face the driver, she tried to remember that she'd at least be seeing Nico for longer and they'd be spending longer together than they had in ages. Not only that, she was going to Italy, and who couldn't be happy at the idea of that?

***

Before long she was sat on a plane next to a newly married couple who couldn't stop giggling together. She turned her attention to the window and as her favourite songs played through her headphones, she watched the clouds pass by.

The last time she'd seen Nico in real life had been around eighteen months before when he'd come over to see his father's side of the family. They still lived in London, though a few of his brothers had moved a little further afield. She and Nico had video-called of course, just as he had with Jacob, but she couldn't help remembering what it felt like to hug him. It had always warmed her from inside, the unmistakable comfort of feeling like home. Even on that last night on a Bali beach when they'd hugged after he'd told her about moving to Italy, his arms around her had given her a comfort no one had, as yet, been able to beat. She wondered if that's what it felt like for Sofia and grew slightly jealous at the idea of him stirring a similar feeling in her.

She pushed the thought away, wishing she could simply erase her feelings for Nico in the same way you deleted a text message. She had to get control of this envious streak inside her. It didn't often come to the surface, and she'd always been pleasant when he'd talked about girlfriends, just as he'd been when she talked of boyfriends. Not that there'd been many since she and Jack had divorced. But it had always been there, niggling away, and she had to kill it once and for all. He was getting married and no matter how much she'd loved him through the years, he clearly didn't feel the same way about her.

As the time ticked by, nerves began to grow in her stomach, tightening the muscles. Would she look stylish enough? Paris might have been the fashion capital of the world but Italy wasn't far behind. Italian women were just as sophisticated and elegant. Her mind flew to icons like Sophia Loren with their dark hair and confidence, knowing her pale skin, red hair and sunscreen obsession would never match up. Sofia's latest posts and videos (not that she'd been stalking her or anything) had been about the expensive *castello* they were getting married in, and in each and every one she'd looked flawless. Annoyingly, Olivia was sure she wasn't even using filters. She was witty and clearly intelligent too, which made Olivia feel old and frumpy beyond her years.

Deep down though, she knew that all this faffing was her mind distracting her from her fear of seeing Nico. As soon as she laid eyes on him, the feelings she'd been fighting for as long as she could remember would come to the surface, and she worried she'd say or do something she'd regret. She closed her eyes and tuned back in to the music, listening intently to the drums and guitar, hoping the lyrics would distract her.

The short flight passed quickly, and as she gazed out of the window, the clouds parted to reveal the snowy-topped mountains of the Alps. Before long, they too had passed and the beautiful countryside of Tuscany came into view. The sun shone down, highlighting the undulations of the hills and the rolling, plush green fields. The clear blue sky she was flying in filled her with joy and she found her worry subsiding and excitement growing in its place. There was a lot to enjoy about this trip: the food and wine, the coffee, the prosecco! She'd always wanted to visit Florence and see the Duomo and the Uffizi Gallery, to stand on the Ponte Vecchio and see the city spread out before her. In fact, it was one of the destinations on her bucket list so she might as well make the most of it.

And above all, if Nico was marrying someone he loved, she'd be happy for him.

She *was* happy for him, she reassured herself, because that's what best friends did. He'd done it for her, even though she knew full well he'd disapproved of Jack from the start. On her wedding day, he'd smiled and congratulated them both before returning, quite quickly, it had to be said, to Italy.

'Sorry if we've been annoying,' the young woman next to her suddenly said. 'We're going to Florence on our honeymoon.'

'I gathered,' she replied smiling. 'And you weren't annoying at all. I hope you have a wonderful time.'

'We chose it because it's known as the city of love. Did you know that?'

'I didn't. But it sounds perfect for a honeymoon destination. Congratulations to you both.'

The plane taxied on the runway and Olivia began the laborious process of getting off the plane, getting through passport control and collecting her luggage.

The city of love. It clearly had been for Nico; perhaps it would be for her. Perhaps she'd find a handsome Italian man to whisk her off her feet and remove Nico from the special place in her heart he'd always occupied. As she waited for her luggage to appear on the carousel, she texted Jacob and Jack, letting them know she'd got there safely and would call later. Jack replied with a thumbs-up emoji while Jacob texted back with 'kk' which she had learned meant okay. She didn't approve of the ridiculous abbreviation.

She'd taken a lunchtime flight, so it was now only mid-afternoon, and she was beginning to get hungry. What should her first meal in Italy be? Pizza or pasta? Her mouth watered just thinking about it. It was a good job her swimming costume had tummy control panels because she was planning on eating a lot of gorgeous Italian food.

As she passed through the final set of doors, she glanced around Arrivals for Nico, knowing he'd promised to collect her. She scanned the crowd looking for his still-lithe and gangly frame, the head of dark hair and chocolate-coloured eyes. Then she saw him and her heart beat a double rhythm. As his eyes focused and he realised it was her, his smile grew wide, lighting his eyes. And despite her earlier resolution, as he walked towards her – strong, tall and even more handsome than the last time she'd seen him on her phone screen – her breath hitched as a little voice in her head whispered: *You should have been mine.*

Chapter 3

'Olive!' Nico called, his arms spreading wide as his long legs made short work of the distance between them. His dark eyes blazed with happiness, bright against his olive skin.

She took a breath, holding it to try and gain control of herself, but her unruly and irritatingly disobedient heart skipped several beats. This was Nico?

How could he have changed so much in almost two short years? Seriously, there were clearly abs underneath that T-shirt. Abs! Six tiny mounds of muscle that would be more than a little fun to run her hands over. She swallowed and lowered her eyes. Where she'd grown a little rounder from too many Friday night wines and boxes of Maltesers, he'd grown . . . hotter! There was no other way to describe it, or if there was, her brain wasn't cooperating with words right now. He'd clearly been working out, which was great, but she also loved the slightly softer version of him too. It didn't stop her body fizzing in places it really shouldn't be as she met her best friend.

The gangliness he'd had until recently – arms and legs that seemed just a little too long for his body – had been transformed into sculpted muscular limbs. Biceps – actual biceps! – poked out from under the arms of his T-shirt. Even his forearms had definition, and she refused to even look at or contemplate the thigh situation, drawing her eyes to his face, which was just as handsome as it had ever been. Maybe even more so with the small lines spreading from the corners of his eyes as he smiled and the slight wrinkling of his brow, which aged him in the most attractive way.

But she wasn't shallow. It wasn't just his changed physical appearance that made her heart leap. It was the love and intelligence in his eyes, the decades of teasing in his smile and the confidence evident in his gait. He wasn't exactly swaggering, but his walk was purposeful and assertive. And she'd always been a sucker for a man who knew what he wanted.

'*Ciao, bella.* I'm so happy to see you,' he said, engulfing

43

her in a hug that took her breath away. 'You look wonderful. Happy. Are you happy?'

'Of course,' she replied, smiling, ignoring the feel of his rock-hard torso pressing against her. She *was* happy to see him; she just wished she could get a hold of herself.

'Say *ciao*.'

'No.' It had been established long ago that Olivia was dreadful at languages. And not just charmingly game but ultimately useless. She was categorically awful at them. She could never remember the right words for anything and her pronunciation was never anything other than southern and slightly common.

'Go on . . .'

'No.'

'For me? Just once?'

Seeing his eyes brighten she conceded, if only to take her mind off how gorgeous he was looking. 'Chow. There. Any good?'

'Do you know, it wasn't that bad.'

'Yes, it was, it was awful. I sounded like a sneeze had got stuck in my nose.'

He threw his head back and laughed and her insides somersaulted. She'd always loved being able to do that. 'I can't tell you how excited I am that you're here. And ahead of the wedding too so you can meet Sofia and we can spend some time together catching up. I want to hear more about work, and Jacob and his school. How is he doing? What grades is he predicted? Does he have to do work experience? Because, I don't know if he wants to be an architect, but he can come to me and—'

Olivia laughed. 'I'll tell you all about Jacob later. He's excited to come out and see you but before we do anything else, I need some food. I'm absolutely starving and I'm in Italy so I'm expecting great things.'

He wiggled a finger at her. 'You won't be disappointed. Come. I have my car. Let me take your case.' He took the handle from her, his skin brushing hers and sending shock waves through her body once more. She was in so much more trouble than she'd thought she'd be.

She'd known seeing him would stir things up again, but this was *Macbeth*, three witches' level of stirring. She wasn't so much stirred up by him as thrown in a blender, whizzed about a bit and then placed back on the ground and spun on the spot, blindfolded. She couldn't get her bearings, emotionally or physically. Coming to Italy early might have been the worst plan of all time.

He led them outside to the car park and when they stood by his car, Olivia couldn't help but stare in surprise.

'This? This is your car?'

'*Sí*,' he replied slowly, as if it were a trick question.

'This?'

'Why not this?'

'It's just . . .' She stared at the baby blue classic convertible Porsche. It looked like something from a Sean

45

Connery Bond film and she could just imagine him darting around the Italian countryside next to some impossibly glamorous woman in a 1950s headscarf and massive sunglasses. 'It's a bit midlife crisis, isn't it?'

'No, that's motorbikes, which scare me too much.'

'So how did you get this? I thought you were still driving that old Fiat Punto. What did you call it?'

'Speed freak.'

'Speed freak. That was it.' They smiled at one another, sharing a moment that only two old friends could. 'What happened to her?'

'She was getting old and unreliable. I needed a new car and when I told Sofia I'd always wanted something like this, she suggested I buy it for myself.'

Sofia had suggested it. Olivia didn't quite know what to make of that. It seemed far too flashy a thing for Nico. Something he wouldn't normally have bought, but he clearly loved it. Olivia decided she was likely being harsh on Sofia, seeing an ulterior motive that probably wasn't there. Probably.

'How much did it cost?'

'Does it matter? Life is too short to worry about tomorrow. Isn't that what you used to say?'

'Yes, and look at where that's got me.'

Nico scowled at her though he knew she was joking. 'Get in. We'll eat when we get to our destination.'

'Which is? You were quite vague on the phone. And

46

why wouldn't you let me book a hotel? I don't want to crash in on you and Sofia.'

The idea had haunted her dreams since he'd told her he was going to take care of her accommodation. It was just like him to want to pay for her to stay somewhere luxurious as she was coming out for his wedding, but then the image of her sleeping in their spare room, hearing them have sex at night through the thin walls, had popped up and it had been all she'd been able to think about. It had been horrific. She mentally crossed her fingers that wasn't the fate that awaited her.

'You'll see,' he said annoyingly and with a grin that melted Olivia into a puddle. 'Now, get in and let's go.'

She climbed into the low-slung car, which was surprisingly roomy though her large handbag, which she suspected was incredibly unfashionable, was crammed in by her feet. He turned the key and the car rumbled into life. Smoothly, he pulled away and she stared out of the window as the beautiful city of Florence was left behind. They set off through the busy streets, car horns honking. The area around the airport was industrial but she knew the beautiful city lay just beyond it and soon the roads had quietened, and she began to relax as the exhaust fumes and noise were left behind.

'Don't worry,' Nico said, glancing over at her. 'I've planned some trips to the city, so you'll have plenty of time to go sightseeing.' She was relieved and though he didn't say anything, he surely knew it from her smile. 'I know how much you've always wanted to go to the Uffizi. I will take you on a tour. It's one of my favourite places in the world.'

'And the Ponte Vecchio. And the Duomo.'

'Yes,' he said laughing. 'All of those too. Are you ready to meet Sofia?' he asked, raising his eyebrows a little.

'Of course!' she replied with so much fake enthusiasm she surprised herself. 'So excited.' She plastered on a wide grin, which Nico seemed to buy, and as he relaxed behind the wheel, she felt like a guilty fraud. Fake it till you make it. That's what purple-haired Ava always said when she had a meeting or presentation that was making her nervous. She'd have to do the same thing. Showing her true feelings wasn't going to help anyone or make for a nice holiday so she didn't really have any other option.

Nico grinned, his eyes hidden behind his shades, though she saw the corners crinkling attractively behind the dark lenses. With the sun shining brightly overhead, Olivia found hers and put them on. 'She's going to love you, Olive. And you're going to love her – I just know it.'

'I'm sure I will. And all I ask, as your best friend, is that she makes you happy.'

'She does. It was love at first sight.'

She didn't believe in love at first sight. Never had and never would. You couldn't know someone enough to love them and to say so seemed foolhardy. She'd thought she'd love Jack from the moment she saw him all those years ago in the student bar, but it couldn't have been love, could it? Because she didn't know the ins and outs of him, the good habits and the bad. To her, to love someone was to know all their faults inside and out and want and need them regardless. That was love. Love at first sight was just another word for lust, in her opinion. Not that she was about to share any of this with Nico.

With the busy streets of the city left behind, the beautiful countryside of Florence opened up before her. The swelling and surging hills criss-crossed with green fields she'd seen from the plane window were studded with the tall thin spikes of cypress trees. In some places, where the green grass was turning yellow from the heat, sat small squat olive trees. All the shades of green she could ever have imagined were painted in the world around her and she could feel the history of this beautiful country, carrying on the air.

Olivia lowered her window and took a breath of the warm summer air. Unlike England, where the breeze would smell of roses and honeysuckle tinged with earth from a recent rainfall, the Tuscan air was dryer and smelt of herbs and lemon. She didn't know where exactly it was coming from, but the sun was lifting it from the world around them. They passed olive groves, vineyards, and fields of rosemary. She couldn't wait to eat her first meal, knowing that the flavours would be somehow sharper, clearer, more intense now she was here. Italian food in Italy had to be better than anywhere else in the world. The sun beat down on her face and she sat back in her seat, allowing the breeze to pass over her as they wound their way through the country roads and on to their destination.

'So,' Nico said. 'How is Jacob getting along? Is he working hard? Did that trouble with his so-called friend stop?'

Olivia laughed. 'We have three whole weeks to catch up on this, you know.'

'He's my godson! I want to know.'

'He's doing great. He's hormonal and stroppy and growing hair in places I rather he wasn't but he's working hard and growing into a respectable young man. I'm proud of him. He does all his homework and he's predicted good grades. That so-called friend soon got bored of trying to tempt him to drink and vape and disappeared off into another friend group. Life's pretty good.'

'But you miss him already?'

She nodded. 'Is that sad?'

'No. He's your son. It's why I appreciate you coming out so early. But I'm glad that friend has gone. I was worried about that. Sometimes the wrong people they . . . can lead us astray.'

A slight tension rippled through the air. Olivia knew that Nico blamed Jack for her ending up pregnant halfway through her first year at uni. Sleeping with him hadn't been her smartest move, and marrying him came a close second, but she'd made her own decisions whether for good or bad and here she was. She couldn't change it and had come to accept that life never took you on a straightforward journey. It always liked to throw as many obstacles in your way as it could. She just hoped one day she'd find her destination and it would all make sense.

'And how's Jack?'

'He's good, I think. He's looking forward to having a couple of weeks with Jacob. I think he feels he's in his element now, fatherhood-wise, now Jacob's a teenager who loves football.'

She thought about Jack's phone call and subsequent shiftiness but decided not to mention it. The less said about Jack the better really.

Nico shifted his hands on the wheel. 'I'm glad he's okay.' He didn't look at her and she decided to change the subject.

'Jacob really can't wait to come out and see you. He was surprised you were getting married though,' she added, glancing over at him to see his reaction. He didn't take his eyes off the road.

'I'm not surprised. I do know it seems too quick to everyone else. But he hasn't met Sofia yet. He only knows we've been dating a few months. I told him I wouldn't want him to do something so important so quickly.'

Olivia's head shot up. Jacob hadn't mentioned this,

51

and she was surprised to hear Nico say it. 'So why are you?'

'Because I'm in love!' He laughed like getting married after six months' dating was the most natural thing in the world. 'And like you have always said, life is too short. Better to live it and have regrets than regret not living.'

The way his eyes gleamed as he talked about her, Olivia could see he was in love and she silenced the voice in her head, placing her hand over Nico's where it rested on the gear stick.

'He's pleased for you. We both are. It was just a little unexpected that's all. You're so happy, it's – it's wonderful to see. You deserve to be happy.' She turned her attention to the scenery, pushing down the pain tying her stomach in knots. 'Getting married here is going to be spectacular.'

'Wait till you see the wedding venue. Sofia has been so excited about it. A castello not far from the house. It is *belissimo* – beautiful. Expensive,' he added a second later. 'But beautiful.'

After half an hour in which Nico had asked her about work, her love life (awkward to say the least) and about Jacob and his plans for the future (which she didn't really know anything about as his career aspirations changed from week to week), they pulled off the road and up a long winding track that meandered towards the top of a hill. The car made light work of it and as the road evened out,

52

she saw the house. If you could call it a house. It certainly was a step up from her small two-bedroom terrace in one of the cheapest suburbs of London.

Behind a swell of deep green cypress trees and a well-trimmed laurel hedge that protected beds of brightly coloured flowers, the track opened into a wide, sweeping drive. The large building loomed in front of her, its appearance softened by the rustic walls made of sand-coloured, rough-cut stone and the terracotta, barrel-tiled roof a shade or two darker than the walls. The windows were a mishmash of shapes with some small and square, while others were decorative and arched, and the doors were like something from a medieval castle, with their double width, heavy oak and black ironwork. A central door in the middle stood open and through it Olivia spotted pale marble floors and wooden beams.

'*Belissimo*, isn't it?' Nico said, coming up behind her with her luggage.

'This is where I'm staying?'

Nico laughed at her incredulity. 'Do you like it? Sofia and her parents have owned it for generations. They're very proud of it.'

'I can see why. How many rooms is it?'

'Seven,' he replied casually. As if seven-bedroom houses were perfectly normal and everyone in Italy had them. Voices sounded from inside and Olivia turned towards the open front door. 'Sofia's parents are here,'

Nico said. 'They're looking forward to meeting you later. They've heard all about you.'

Suddenly intimidated by the grandeur of it all, Sofia's evident wealth and her own feeling of shabbiness, she hesitated. 'Nico, maybe I should stay in a hotel. This is too . . . it's too much. Too generous.'

Plus, three weeks was a long time to watch the man you've always secretly loved prepare to marry someone else.

'No, no, no! You have to stay here. You're family. Besides, the nearest hotel is half an hour away and you'd need a car. I insist.' She glanced at him knowing apprehension showed in her eyes. He placed an arm around her shoulders. 'Don't be nervous. And don't forget, I know you better than anyone else. You don't need to feel awkward with all Sofia's family around because you're not staying in there.'

'I'm not?' She didn't know whether to be relieved or not. 'You'll be staying here.'

He signalled to a small single-storey building of the same design to their right. The outside was lined with trimmed rosemary bushes, the scent drifting towards her and reminding her how hungry she was. Through the windows she could see into an open-plan living and dining room, a high-end modern kitchen lined the walls at one end and a comfortable-looking sofa stood on the other.

'I know how you've always liked your space and I thought when Jacob and Jack get here, you'd prefer to be together. As a family.' She looked up at the hint of something in his tone. Something she couldn't quite put her finger on. 'I don't want Jacob feeling awkward with so many new people and being in the house is going to be . . .'

'Intense?' she finished for him.

'Indeed. Let me go and get the key and we can store your case before—'

Sofia appeared on a wave of perfume so strong it made Olivia sneeze before she had even reached them.

'*Salute*,' Nico said as Olivia wiggled her nose.

'Thanks.'

Sofia's long legs were encased in wide-leg trousers ending in platform sandals. A thin-strapped white vest showed off her smooth burnished skin and the long-line white gauzy jacket made her look like elegance personified. Enormous sunglasses, which reminded Olivia of an owl or a fly, took up half of her face.

'*Ciao, cara*,' she declared walking up to Nico, placing a hand either side of his face and pulling him in, planting a long, lingering kiss on his lips.

Olivia smiled at first, partly to convince herself she wasn't jealous and partly because it felt like the polite thing to do, but as the kiss went on, and on, and on, she eventually had to look away, studying a particularly interesting stone in the gravel drive. She tipped it about with the toe of her scruffy, well-worn trainers and waited, dying inside.

Eventually, Nico un-suctioned himself from Sofia's face and Olivia was aware of the rather smug smile and proprietorial hand that slipped into the crook of his elbow.

'Sofia, this is my best friend Olive—'

'Olivia,' she corrected quickly, thrusting a hand out so she didn't seem rude. She didn't want anyone but Nico calling her that. 'It's lovely to meet you.'

Sofia slowly took her hand, staring at Olivia's with her short, practical nails as if she were about to touch a live snake. For the first few years of motherhood her hands had been pulling things out of Jacob's mouth with monotonous regularity. At one point she'd been convinced he was the only toddler in the world who did that sort of thing and the relief to find out he wasn't had been palpable. As he was now a teenager, she probably could have had manicures but there'd always been something more important to spend the money on: school uniform to replace or birthday and Christmas presents to save up for. But as she saw her hand in Sofia's smooth, perfectly manicured one, she decided it was time to start looking after herself a bit more.

'It's lovely to meet you,' she said to Sofia.

'*Sí*,' she said slowly. Her eyes ran over Olivia's body, clearly unhappy at what they saw. She probably did look a little dishevelled in her everyday jeans and T-shirt, but then, she normally looked dishevelled. That was the problem with wild curly hair that seemed to do whatever it liked no matter how much cream, mousse and wax she put on it. Olivia had the distinct impression she'd been assessed and found wanting. A tense silence began to grow and when Nico's gaze shifted from Olivia to her, Sofia added rather begrudgingly, 'You're not what I was expecting.'

'Am I not?' Olivia gave a surprised laugh to hide her embarrassment. What sort of comment was that to make?

She'd been doing her best to reserve judgement on Sofia but the way this conversation was going, not to mention Sofia's body language and general demeanour, she was more certain than ever that not only was Sofia a bad match for Nico, but she now worried she wasn't a very nice person either. She could totally understand her being threatened by her close relationship with Nico. Both of them had dealt with boyfriends and girlfriends who found it hard to understand that they really were just friends. Obviously she hadn't told her boyfriends about her lifelong, unrequited love, but that wasn't the point. So far no one had been openly hostile.

'What were you expecting?' she asked, gripping hold of her self-esteem as a shield.

'The way Nico described you I thought—' She cast her hand up and down Olivia's body.

'You thought what?'

57

'I don't know.' Before Olivia, who was feeling decidedly attacked, could answer, Sofia broke into a wide grin. 'It's lovely to meet you.'

A slightly awkward silence descended, and Olivia felt the need to speak, wondering if she was the only person feeling it. Had she misread Sofia's slightly prickly attitude towards her? Were her own insecurities making her see things that weren't there? Perhaps she'd misunderstood the encounter.

'You too. The house is gorgeous,' she said to move the conversation along.

'*Grazie*. The Allegretti family have lived here for generations.' She cast her hand out to show off the villa, then turned back to Olivia expecting something in reply.

She had no idea what to say. 'How wonderful.'

Another silence began to form. One in which the two women sized each other up. Olivia refused to be cowed by Sofia's hard eyes and slightly pursed mouth, even though inside she was begging for the moment to stop.

Before it grew too intense, Nico said, 'I was just about to show Olivia to the guest house.'

'Yes, do. I'm busy so . . .' Sofia turned to Olivia shrugging. 'Wedding preparations are incessant. There's so much to do. You understand?'

'Of course. I work in events so I know—'

'It is not quite the same,' she said, cutting her off. 'Everything must be perfect. My wedding must be perfect.

I'm an influencer, you see. People expect much from me.'

'I think it's quite similar,' Olivia bit back, unable to stop herself. 'I want my events to be perfect too.' As Sofia scowled at her, Olivia smiled. 'But I'm happy to settle in and then have a bit of a walk by myself. The scenery around here is breath-taking.'

'I can give you a tour,' Nico said, earning a glare from Sofia. 'You'll want to know where the swimming pool is, I'm sure.'

'But we don't save sun loungers here,' Sofia added. 'This isn't Benidorm.'

Was that a joke? Should she laugh? Olivia's concerns suddenly solidified into a rock-hard ball that lay in the pit of her stomach. Where was the legendary Italian hospitality she'd seen in every television show and film? Sofia was being decidedly prickly towards her. All she could hope was that it wasn't personal, and she was like this with everyone. But she couldn't deny that on first impressions at least it was a giant warning sign that her best friend and his choice of wife weren't suited.

'She's joking,' Nico said, leaning in to Olivia and laughing.

'Right.' She gave the best approximation of a chuckle she could manage but could tell from Sofia's narrowed gaze and crossed arms it was a warning.

'Darling—' Sofia grabbed hold of Nico again and gave him another kiss that made Olivia feel decidedly uncomfortable. 'Will you come and make a video with me? My followers are dying to meet you. Please.'

Nico shifted uncomfortably. 'Sofia, you know that's not my thing.'

'Just one little video so they can meet my husband-to-be? Please?'

'Maybe later,' he conceded and she pushed herself away from him, her face clouding, and she swept back towards the house.

'*Arrivederci*, Olivia.'

'*Arrivederci*,' she replied, even though her pronunciation was decidedly clunky and very, very English, without any of the flair and beauty of the Italian accent. Sofia snorted and Olivia was sure she muttered something rude. Her face began to flame and she dropped her eyes.

'Hey, that wasn't so bad,' Nico reassured her, nudging her arm. 'You've said far worse over the years.'

'Ha ha.'

All Olivia's apprehension galloped into her stomach and tightened into a heavy ball. She'd been worried Sofia and Nico weren't suited but had hoped to be proved wrong by someone who was as kind and happy as Nico was. But Sofia Allegretti was none of those things. She seemed spoiled, prickly and snobbish. Olivia was going to have to do everything in her power to hide how much she disliked her. What the hell was Nico doing? The man she knew would never have gone for someone like Sofia. She couldn't imagine Sofia stomping through the hills as Nico liked to – or exploring the beautiful architecture and history of a place.

'I'll get the key,' Nico said, totally oblivious to what had just passed between his best friend and wife-to-be. 'You can settle in for a few hours and call me when you want a walk. I'll show you around, but you need to be back and ready by six o'clock.'

'Why? What happens at six o'clock?'

'There's a family dinner tonight.'

'Family dinner?' she repeated dumbly.

'I know!' he replied excitedly. 'It's going to be fun, just be yourself and everyone will love you.'

Fun? Dinner with Sofia's family? All she could hope was that they had some of the renowned Italian hospitality Sofia was missing.

Olivia glanced around once more at the path to the swimming pool, the beautiful house in front of her and the gorgeous scenery spreading out all around her. Right now, despite the luxury and beauty, she was starting to think coming out this early had been a decidedly bad idea and, worst of all, there was absolutely nothing she could do about it.

Chapter 4

The apartment was cool with pale white marble floors and a modern, white, shiny kitchen with dark quartz countertops. In the living room, the sumptuous sofas sat in front of the most enormous TV. Jacob was definitely going to like that. She had even taken a picture and sent it to him, to which he'd replied with the single word: *Awesome*. She'd craved more – a conversation or as close an approximation as she normally got to one – but that had been it. She tried to be glad. At least it meant he and Jack were having fun together.

Seeing how Sofia had dressed earlier, Olivia decided to wear a dress to the family dinner. She and Nico had taken a short walk, but Sofia's calls to him had been incessant and, after a while, Olivia had feigned the need for a nap and returned to the apartment knowing they wouldn't get a chance to catch up as she'd hoped. After she'd kicked off her shoes, she'd taken advantage of the quiet and though she'd only meant to lie on the bed for a minute, she'd actually fallen asleep, taking a short nap on the soft four-poster bed, snuggling into the luxurious pillows and sheets.

Now, as she stood in front of the mirror studying her appearance, she didn't look half bad. When she'd awoken, she'd got to work, knowing that if she was going to look even half presentable next to Sofia's gorgeousness, she had to sort out her frizzy red hair and tone down any redness in her skin. It was already reacting to the sudden change in temperature with a pinprick red rash. She'd applied a cold, damp towel and it had helped somewhat but the remnants of it were still visible.

The maxi dress she'd chosen, a baby blue, the same colour as the cloudless sky outside her window, slipped over her slightly rounded stomach and hung elegantly from her shoulders. She was wearing gladiator-style sandals and had painted her toenails the same colour as her dress. Her red hair, the waves tamed (for now) gently brushed her shoulders. She'd left her make-up understated. Too much always made her look older than she was and she liked her freckles. Her pale skin seemed to suit something gentle but she'd added an extra coat of mascara, so her green eyes stood out. With a swipe of pale pink lip gloss, just enough to give her lips a kissable shine, she stepped out the door to head towards the path.

A clamour of voices sounded immediately through the front door, which stood open as it had when she'd arrived. They were deep and male, jockeying for attention, the volume rising with every step she took. Olivia turned right into the house but was unable to see further than the rear of the bulk of a man in front of her. He spun, his eyes lighting up, and she recognised him instantly.

'Livvy!' Nico's dad declared, throwing his arms around her and squeezing her so tightly she could barely breathe. His thick dark beard, peppered here and there with grey, tickled her cheek, but she'd always loved the feel of it. This was the Italian hospitality she had grown used to. Even though Nico's family had moved to England when he was young, they had never lost their ability to make you instantly part of the family. From the first time they'd had an after-school playdate, she had been treated like a daughter.

From over Giovanni's shoulder she saw Nico smile fondly while Sofia, stood at the back of the room with whom Olivia presumed to be her parents, wasn't smiling at all. In fact, all three of them were sneering as if they could smell a fart.

Giovanni held her at arm's length for a second, assessing her, then tugged her back in for another bear hug. 'It has been too long, Livvy! Where have you been? Why haven't we seen you and Jacob? The last time was . . .' He finally let go. 'How long ago was it?'

'I think it must be three years now. I'm so sorry, I—'

'No!' he declared, wiggling his finger in front of her. 'I am sorry. We haven't invited you and we should have. We are in the wrong, not you.'

'I think it's probably both our faults. We're all so busy, it's easy to forget how much time has actually passed. It doesn't matter now though. How are you? You look so well.'

He smiled and took a slow turn on the spot, running his fingertips down the arms of his well-cut suit. 'You cannot beat an Italian suit. Slimming, yes?' Though his large belly wasn't exactly concealed the suit hid a multitude of sins as did his larger-than-life personality. Standing at almost six foot five he was a giant of a man, but she'd never met anyone as kind and genial.

'You look fabulous.'

'As do you! Nico, doesn't she look as beautiful as ever? More so, I would say.'

'She does,' he replied, his dark eyes flashing with something she had once thought might be attraction but had clearly been wrong. Yet, his gaze lingered on her for longer than was necessary. Was he worried she'd embarrass him? Maybe the dress didn't look as nice as she'd thought. 'You remember my brothers, don't you?'

Three men, nearly as handsome as Nico, stepped forwards. They'd been chatting and jibing all the time she'd been talking to Giovanni, and they lined up to give her hugs. For a long time, they had been like brothers to her too, even though she had one of her own now living in Australia. Aldo, Davide and Dante stepped forwards, enfolding her in turn, paying her compliments that made her blush. From the corner of her eye, she watched as Sofia glared at her mother who shared a disdainful look. Olivia ignored them, relieved the family dinner was to include the second family she had grown up with. Seeing Sofia's parents, if it had been just her, Nico and them, it would have been far more difficult.

They were just edging further into the house, Olivia searching for something to say to Sofia and her parents, when Giovanni's voice boomed over the din.

'I always thought it would be you he married, Livvy. We all did.'

Olivia froze in absolute mortification, a chill running down the length of her spine and bouncing back up again like one of those test-your-strength things at a funfair. Sofia's head spun towards them, her glare hard and piercing. And though she hadn't been the one to say it, Olivia felt instantly guilty. No matter how rude Sofia had

66

been to her at their first meeting, that couldn't have been nice to hear, though she pressed down the part of her that wanted to agree with him.

'We've been friends for too long for that, Giovanni,' she replied, laughing it off. She cast a glance at Nico who looked just as mortified and dropped his eyes.

Sofia suddenly appeared at Nico's side, and he opened his arm out to her. The gesture was clearly designed to reassure her and, though Olivia hated seeing his arms around her, she loved that he was trying to make her feel better.

'Shall we move into the room?' Sofia asked, gesturing towards the living room area. As with the apartment, the living and dining areas were open plan, separated by decorative arches, edged in the same rough-cut stone as the outside of the house. 'The housekeeper has set out drinks in the corner and some antipasti on the table.'

Housekeeper? They had a housekeeper? Olivia quashed the feeling of being royally out of her depth as Sofia led Nico away. She followed, Giovanni talking at a million miles an hour about his work and his brood of boys and the trouble they were getting themselves into.

As she passed through the stone archway into the main living room, the space opened up before her, going on forever. Light flooded the room through three long arched windows and a heavy, medieval-looking door that had been cast open. The furnishings were all white, from the thin, light curtains, to the sofas and even a piano that stood in the corner of the room and on which Sofia's dad was leaning. He was long and lean with a Roman nose and blond hair turning grey at the temples. His skin was deep, tanned bronze, the same as his wife's, though Olivia had the distinct impression they were both topped up by sunbeds from the dark, almost mahogany hue they were giving off.

'Olivia?'

She turned to see who had called her name, the voice unfamiliar. But as the woman walked towards her, realisation dawned and a wide, happy smile grew on Olivia's face.

'Maria?'

'Hey!' The two women embraced as Olivia rewound the years both in her mind, and from Maria's face.

They'd met in Singapore while she and Nico were travelling, and they'd hit it off instantly. For a while, the three had been inseparable as they visited the same locations, danced on the beach till the sun came up and lived as if there were no tomorrow, but then Maria's travels had taken her off somewhere different, and Nico and Olivia had come home. Unsurprisingly, they'd lost touch over the years, but Olivia had always remembered her vivacity, her total and utter coolness, and most of all, her infectious laugh.

'What are you doing here?' she asked, throwing her

arms wide for a hug as if the time they'd been apart didn't mean anything at all.

'Didn't Nico tell you?'

'Not a word.'

The man himself appeared at her shoulder. 'I wanted it to be a surprise.'

'When did you – how?' Olivia threw her hands in the air, too many questions to verbalise.

'You'll never believe it, but I was here on a mini-break a few weeks ago and spotted Nico. We got talking and he told me he was getting married and said I should come along, so I've extended my stay. I'm on a sabbatical. Turns out the travelling bug never really left me.'

'That's amazing! What do you do now? I mean, how are you? How's life? Are you married? Kids?' Olivia pressed a hand to her head. 'Sorry, so many questions!'

'It's fine. I've got just as many for you, though Nico filled me in on a few bits.' Olivia glanced at him, wondering what he'd said about her choices. He'd never openly criticise her, but sometimes she felt the regret coming off him that her life had panned out the way it had. 'We've still got lots of catching up to do though and, thanks to this wedding, time to do it.'

'Are you staying here too?'

'Just for dinner. I'm staying nearby at an *agriturismo*.'

The equivalent of a bed and breakfast. After Giovanni's comment, Olivia thought she'd quite like to join her there.

She wasn't sure the apartment was far enough from Sofia's attitude. 'You really haven't changed a bit,' she said, meeting Maria's bright blue eyes.

Back then, Maria had been tall and slim with a naturally athletic frame. She'd been happy to climb up mountains, waterski, do whatever activity she felt like, and age had only added to her beauty. Her features had softened a little but life and vivacity still radiated from them. Her hair was still a vibrant blonde and her skin smooth and line-free.

From the corner of her eye, Olivia spied Aldo talking to Sofia's parents. The conversation didn't seem to be going very well as he spoke animatedly at their unmoving faces. A moment later, after an awkward lull, he muttered something and strode away. Though she didn't want to, she was staying on their property, and Olivia knew she had to go and introduce herself. It was the grown-up thing to do, though she wasn't sure what response she'd get. Aldo was naturally funny, not to mention charming, but even hadn't been able to raise a smile. Perhaps Sofia's mother was incapable of smiling. There were definitely more than a few fillers in her face. Olivia excused herself from Maria and approached slowly, taking a glass of prosecco from the table for support. She clutched it tightly. More than one might be required to get through this evening.

As she passed Aldo, now chatting to his father, he paused his conversation and said, 'Good luck over there.

It's like talking to a wardrobe.'

She hid her chuckle and headed off. If she could handle awkward clients, and her beast of a boss, Portia, she could handle this. 'Hi,' she said brightly, holding out her hand. 'I'm Olivia.'

'*Sí*,' Sofia's mum responded, her top lip moving as much as the suspected Botox would allow. '*Benvenuto*. I am Adele and this is my husband, Salvatore.'

Oh dear. She was going to struggle pronouncing that without sounding like she was taking the mickey. He nodded.

'It's lovely to meet you both and so kind of you to let me stay in the apartment.'

'Nico suggested it,' Adele said.

'Right. Well, it's really kind of you. Thank you. Sofia said the Allegretti family had owned this house for generations.'

'*Sí*.'

Salvatore wandered off to the antipasti, the back of his cream linen jacket wafting behind him as he began to delve into a bowl of black olives and prosciutto-wrapped asparagus.

Adele suddenly continued. 'We own much of the land around here.'

Unsure what sort of response was required, Olivia nodded. 'I see.'

No more conversation was forthcoming, though Adele

71

seemed perfectly happy to stand and stare in silence at Olivia. Occasionally her eyes would drift over her shoulder at the crowd gathered in her living room, but mostly they stayed on her, raking over her dress, her shoes, her red hair. At least that's what it felt like. Struggling, she took a drink of her prosecco and the bubbles tingled her nose, almost making her sneeze. She managed to hold it in, just like she did in meetings, but must have pulled the same, slightly insane face that often made Ava laugh as Adele visibly flinched.

'Sorry!' Olivia said once her face had relaxed. 'I was about to sneeze.'

'*Salute*,' Adele replied nervously, clearly unsure whether to say it or not given that no sound had actually come out of Olivia's mouth and instead she'd just gurned like a maniac. 'So you and Nico are friends? Unusual, is it not, to have a male best friend and him a female?'

'Oh, I don't know. It's just the way things turned out. We kind of just hung out at primary school and never really stopped. Well, until he moved here, I guess.' She remembered the pain of that first parting, knowing their friendship would change forever.

'But Italy is the best place in the world. Of course he would want to come here and connect with his roots.'

'Yes, Tuscany really is wonderful,' she added, worried she'd offended her terrifying host. 'Very beautiful.' She took another sip of prosecco, careful not to let the bubbles force her into any more ungainly expressions. Salvatore had now rejoined them and she was desperately searching for something to say to him, preferably without having to say his name, when a matronly woman in a large floral dress suddenly appeared at the archway to the dining room.

She shouted, 'Dinner is served,' at a volume previously unknown to mankind and the strident tones made Olivia jump, a tiny bit of prosecco hitting the skirt of her dress. Adele looked at her as though she was unhinged and clearly shouldn't be allowed out in public.

Well done, Olivia, you're clearly winning this one, she thought and, with a small smile, she followed Giovanni and the boys through to the dining room, grateful for the comfort of their noisy conversation. She looked out for Maria, hoping for more of a chat with her but she'd been swept away by Davide, Nico's middle brother.

Dinner continued to be an absolutely hideous affair of stilted conversation and unhelpful comments made worse by Olivia at one point accidentally knocking over her glass of prosecco, to which Adele said: 'Is she drunk?' to Salvatore in perfect English.

'No, no!' Olivia exclaimed, feeling her cheeks burn with embarrassment. 'Just clumsy. Sorry.'

The one saving grace of the whole affair was that the food was delicious and there was a lot of it, which Olivia could absolutely get behind. She had hoped to be near

Maria but found herself down the other end of the table with Sofia's parents. Aldo had been right – speaking to them was like talking to a wardrobe, and a particularly sneery one at that.

Nico and Sofia were in the middle, opposite each other, sharing puppy-eyed glances that made Olivia drink more prosecco than was actually good for her. Down the other end, Nico's family seemed to be saying stupid things on purpose. They clearly hadn't warmed to Sofia or her frozen family, but it was like they had bets on to see who could say the most embarrassing thing about Nico or her and, so far, Aldo was winning. Somewhere between the starter (roasted fennel, burrata and crispy Parma ham bruschetta – delicious!) and the main course (grilled fish with artichoke caponata – eaten so quickly she earned another glare from Adele), he had pronounced that: 'This is so weird. You two were endgame, weren't you?' He pointed his knife at Nico then Olivia in a vaguely threatening manner. 'We always thought so. Livvy must have got wise to you before it was too late, Nic.'

Olivia's heart had leapt into her throat and her sympathy had been completely with Sofia who must have been hating it as much as she was. She replied with: 'Don't be stupid Aldo. This is why you're still single.' Which earnt a guffaw from the rest of his family but a cold stare that could have iced a car windscreen from a hundred paces from Sofia. Olivia was too scared to look at the rest of her family and instead toyed with the stem of her empty glass turning it around and around in tiny circles on the pristine white tablecloth. The matronly housekeeper suddenly leapt over her shoulder and filled it up for her, making her jump again so she knocked her cutlery against her plate. Olivia drank half of it in one go. When she did venture to look up, Maria caught her eye, giving her a compassionate glance.

'When I met them, they were best friends, that's all,' she said, backing Olivia up. 'Definitely nothing more. Maybe Olivia's right, Aldo, and it's your singledom throwing your senses off.'

Olivia could have kissed her. Nico, his cheeks pink with embarrassment, deftly turned the conversation to Salvatore's business.

Hours later, the ordeal was finally over and Olivia slipped away from the crowd and out into the gardens at the back of the house. It was clear the Allegrettis had a gardener or, more likely, several gardeners on their list of staff, as the exquisite gardens spread out in front of her. It gave the impression of being wild and natural, but she had a feeling it had taken a lot of work to make it that way. Lavender bushes were in full bloom, their heady scent infusing the air. Cypress trees lined a meandering path down through the garden towards the hills, and brightly coloured flowers – buzzing with bees and insects – broke up the plethora of green.

Down the bottom was a small stone bench and she headed towards it, deliberately sitting with her back to the house so she could look out over the fields and hills around her. A small ginger cat strolled out from the shrubbery and wound its way through her legs. She stroked it, listening to its purr.

'Well that was . . . interesting,' she said to it. The cat ignored her, continuing to purr instead.

When it moved a little further away, Olivia pulled out her phone and texted Jacob a picture, hoping he'd had a good day with his dad. It felt like days since she'd seen him last rather than a few hours – so much had happened in such a short space of time. So many emotions, from the thrill of seeing Nico again to that difficult first meeting with Sofia and now this awful, torturous dinner.

'So—' Maria sat down beside her. 'That was pretty awful.'

'And you had the good end of the table. Giovanni and the band of brothers are lovely. Well – usually. Talking to Sofia's parents was like picking the top off a scab. Actually, it was less satisfying than picking a scab. I got the clear impression they hate me.' Maria faked a cough and Olivia hid her head in her hands. 'Please don't tell me they're behind me.'

'Nah, I was only joking.'

Olivia batted her arm.

'To be fair, I think they hate everyone. When I

told them I was taking a sabbatical after working for years in a veterinary hospital, they looked at me like I was single-handedly murdering puppies. His brothers certainly thought you and Nico were destined to be, didn't they?'

'Maybe once,' she replied wistfully. 'But that was a long time ago.'

'Poor Sofia. I mean, she's pretty standoffish and bit snooty but she didn't deserve that. That must have been awful for her.'

'No. I did try and – I don't know – play it down.'

'You did good. What's going on there though?'

Olivia spun on the bench to see what Maria was referring to. Up on the terrace at the back of the house, Nico and Sofia, heads close together, were talking in animated whispers. It was difficult to tell if it was an argument or whether Nico was just waving his arms around as he normally did.

'Oh, hang on,' Maria said as they both spun back around. 'They're coming this way.'

'Do you think they saw us watching?'

'We'll find out in a minute.'

Within seconds, Nico and Sofia were with them. He was smiling widely and though Sofia was trying to, there was a tension to her lips and jaw and no light behind her eyes. Whatever was about to happen, she wasn't particularly thrilled about it.

'Maria,' Nico said. 'Do you mind if we have a word with Olive in private?'

Oh no! Olivia nearly reached out and grabbed hold of Maria's arm, begging her to stay.

Maria glanced at her from the corner of her eye, clearly wishing she could stay. 'Yeah, sure. No worries.' She got up. 'See you later, yeah?'

Maria left and Nico offered the seat to Sofia. She sat facing Olivia, her gaze powerful. It didn't waver from her face and Olivia felt her stomach fall. All the prosecco she'd drunk at dinner began sloshing around and she felt a tiny bit queasy.

'There's something Sofia wants to ask you,' Nico urged.

Olivia swallowed. Was it whether the comments from Giovanni and the stupid boys were true or had once been? What would she say in reply? She couldn't admit to still having feelings for Nico, but she was also a terrible, terrible liar. Nico would read any untruths on her face in an instant.

For a second, a hint of nerves fluttered across Sofia's eyes and she glanced at Nico for reassurance. He nodded and she prepared herself to speak. The tension mounted as the seconds (which seemed to last a lifetime) ticked by. She could feel it pressing down on her chest, hot and heavy, making her sweat.

'I would like you to be my bridesmaid,' Sofia said

matter-of-factly.

Olivia, for some reason she would undoubtedly spend the rest of her life questioning, let the air out of her lungs in a shocked huff that rippled her vocal cords and made a honking sound like a goose. She pressed a hand to her mouth, her cheeks flaming.

'Sorry. Sorry. I've never actually made that sound before in my life.'

Nico giggled, then arranged his features. 'So?' His cheeks lifted attractively as he smiled. 'Will you?'

Bridesmaid? What the heck? What was she supposed to say to that? The actual answer was, *'No, thank you. I'd rather not because I'm still in love with the man you're about to marry and to walk down the aisle towards him as your bridesmaid will kill me. And if that doesn't, watching you sail down the aisle and exchange vows with him definitely will.'* But of course she couldn't say any of these things. She suddenly realised her teeth were clenching and chomping down on the inside of her cheek. She released her jaw.

'Umm . . . yes, of course, but – don't you have someone else you'd rather, Sofia? A best friend or something? If you do, I really don't mind.'

Sofia's jaw was set. 'Nico would like you to be part of the wedding. As his . . . best friend.'

She said the words disdainfully as if they'd left a nasty taste in her mouth. Olivia was beginning to think the response she'd kept internal would have been the better one.

'It's not just that,' Nico added quickly. 'I mean, I do want you to be part of my wedding, of course I do, but well . . .' He glanced at Sofia, clearly unsure whether to say what he was about to. 'Most of Sofia's friends are online as she's an influencer, but they're not invited to the wedding. We – and Sofia's parents—' that bit was definitely added on with a tone of forced cheer '—wanted it to be a family affair.'

'Right.' Olivia didn't quite know what to make of that. Nico's emphasis on the parents part made it clear who'd laid the law down. Once again, she felt a pang of sympathy for Sofia but when she glanced at her to see her virtually snarling some of the sympathy faded.

'So there's no one else you'd rather ask?' she asked Sofia.

She gave a quick shake of the head but nothing more.

'Please, Olive? It would mean a lot to me,' Nico added and the way he looked at her melted her heart in a giant puddle.

How could she not, considering how long they'd been friends? With everything he'd done for Jacob? She had to put her feelings aside and his happiness before her own. Still, it wasn't quite enough to remove the horrid taste in her mouth. Not only was she going to watch the man she loved marry someone else, she was going to be a bridesmaid while doing it. Could this whole thing get any worse? At least it would help her get over him. Nothing said 'I've moved on' like holding the train and the bride's bouquet while she said 'I do' to the man you've always wanted.

'Well,' she replied brightly, 'I'd love to. It'd be my honour.'

Nico beamed. 'See,' he told Sofia. 'I told you she would.'

Sofia's cold demeanour was back, and she nodded, unsmiling. 'Thank you.'

Was that it? Sofia didn't seem the hugging type but still. She was icier than Mont Blanc on a particularly cold day. And yet Nico was, and always had been, warm and friendly. She just didn't get it. Olivia stuck on her widest grin and slugged back the last of her prosecco, studying the empty glass. 'I think I'll get another one of these.'

'Tomorrow, I will show you the castello where we are getting married,' Sofia replied, ignoring her remark, her tone hard. 'And tell you what I need you to do.'

'Brill!' The slightly manic edge to her voice rang around the garden. Tell her what she needed her to do? If it could have, the sinking feeling pulling her down would have sent her into the ground. 'Fabulous! Can't wait to see it.'

And she charged off up the garden at a speed normally kept for gazelles being chased by lions, though with far less grace as her sandals slapped angrily against her feet.

As she left, she heard the words: 'Your friend . . . she is very strange. She better not ruin my wedding.'

'Chance would be a fine thing,' she muttered to herself. But as much as she didn't want this wedding to take place, she'd never do that. She couldn't deny though that the thought had crossed her mind.

Chapter 5

Olivia awoke to the sounds of a thousand birds singing right outside her window. Bees were buzzing through the rosemary bushes and she lay for a moment rubbing her eyes and appreciating their cheerful chirruping. She had no idea how long she'd slept but it was long enough to have avoided a prosecco hangover.

Sofia's request had sent her into a bit of a tailspin, and she'd consumed another few glasses before loudly declaring she needed sleep and waddling off to the apartment. Adele hadn't looked amused. In fact, after they'd all come in from the garden, Sofia and her mother had ensconced themselves in a corner. The exact moment the news had been shared had been clear to her, as Adele's head had snapped round and her icy eyes pinned Olivia to the spot.

After a few more ill-advised glasses, she'd thought she'd wake up groggy and sluggish, but for the first time in ages she felt rested. Clearly waking up naturally instead of when her alarm clock angrily summoned her to was good for the soul.

A smile spread across her face, rapidly falling away as a shrill, angry voice outside grew louder, its pitch higher than that of the birds. Actually, the pitch was bordering on something only dogs could hear and the words were indistinct but becoming clearer as whoever it was moved about. Olivia pulled back the covers, quickly changing into a pair of shorts and a T-shirt before heading to the window and peering out. The voices sharpened into ones she recognised and anxiety began to mount.

Nico and Sofia were edging their way outside, Sofia shouting at the top of her lungs down her phone. For a moment, Olivia had worried she was shouting at Nico and was very much prepared to march outside and give her what for, the protective urge still strong, but it was clear Nico wasn't the subject of her ire. Sofia spoke in Italian with such speed Olivia wondered how anyone could keep up. Her arms were flailing madly as she gesticulated and jabbed at the air, and her cheeks were growing redder. For the first time since she'd met Sofia, she seemed actually human and less like a statue, as a small circle of sweat appeared under her armpit, darkening the sand-coloured vest top. Whatever was wrong had really riled her up, and what a temper she seemed to have. Olivia hoped she'd never be on the receiving end of it, especially with regards to bridesmaid duties.

Urgh, bridesmaid duties. Whyever had she agreed to that? Because she was an idiot, that's why. She should have been able to come up with some excuse. Jacob maybe? She wanted to spend time with him as soon as he was out here. They'd never really had a proper family holiday before. She should have used that as an excuse. Or maybe she could have said that she was allergic to something. Organza? Silk? No, that was ridiculous. But it didn't matter because she'd opened her stupid mouth and agreed, all because Nico had smiled at her. Urgh, she was an idiot.

Sofia's tone grew even more hysterical as she shouted something down the phone. Nico circled around her making calming gestures. She turned her back on him. A second later, she screeched like someone had just stamped on her foot, then looked at her phone while thrusting a hand into her hair (which looked immaculate, as usual).

'He hung up on me! On me!' She pointed at herself, thrusting a thumb into her chest so hard it left a mark near her collarbone.

'You did call him a—'

'The wedding is off!' she shouted in Nico's face. He stepped back like he'd been pushed.

Olivia, who wasn't normally such a horrible person, wanted to walk out there and push Sofia right back, but she also felt guilty at the surge of happiness those words brought. She stepped away from the window for a second, leaning against the wall, wishing it didn't make her feel so elated, so relieved. Did she mean it? Sofia had certainly looked as if she did. But as Olivia returned to the window, watching as Sofia stormed off and Nico chased after her before she said something else in Italian and he stopped dead in his tracks, she wished that whole incident hadn't happened. He looked heartbroken.

A second later, a car screeched down the drive, Sofia at the wheel.

Olivia watched Nico as Sofia sped off leaving nothing but car fumes and dust from the gravel drive in her wake. Nico dropped his head before crumpling onto the ground, sitting down. Olivia's relief faded as he looked like he was going to cry. She waited a second, wondering who would be the first to come out of the house. There was no way Giovanni or Sofia's parents couldn't have heard that conversation. Sofia's voice must have been heard all the way back in Florence. But no one came and she wanted nothing more than to put her arms around him.

Slipping on her shoes, Olivia made her way outside to be greeted by the lazy cat she'd seen the night before.

86

Unable to stop to pet it this time, she ignored it and made her way to Nico, the morning sun already hot on her skin. His knees were drawn up, elbows resting on them, and he toyed with a flower he'd taken from a nearby plant.

'Hey, you,' she said gently, placing a hand on his shoulder. 'What's up?' She sat down next to him, lazy cat toddling over and joining them too.

Nico lifted his head, his dark hair flopping forward a little over his forehead. Her heart somersaulted, but the sadness in his eyes was unbearable. 'You must have heard, Olive, the wedding's off.' He looked away from her and she knew it was because tears were close to the surface.

'Sofia was just angry – I'm sure she didn't mean it. What's happened? Who was she talking to on the phone?'

'The castello. It's fallen through. They can't take the wedding now.'

'Why not?' Her voice was so high, the cat looked up from cleaning her paw. 'That's outrageous given you're only weeks away.'

'A footballer who plays for Fiorentina wants his wedding there on the same day so of course, they have gone with him and cancelled us.'

'But that's – that's—'

Nico looked up, a tiny light in his eyes. 'Outrageous, I know.'

'They can't just cancel a contract with you. What are you supposed to do?'

87

'I wish I knew. But they'll make more money and get more coverage with a footballer. They don't care about us. They'd said they'll refund everything we've paid, but because they were providing everything – the entertainment, the catering, the photographer – we're left with nothing. Sofia's right, the best thing to do is to call it off.'

'Just because the venue's fallen through doesn't mean you two shouldn't still be getting married.' She couldn't believe she was saying this and, unable to meet his eye, fussed the cat instead. 'You just need to find another venue, that's all. What about here?'

He shook his head. 'Her parents would never allow it. They're quite . . . inflexible. And they're not best pleased about the wedding either.'

'Why not? You're the best.'

'They think it's too soon.'

Olivia wondered what to say, but unable to do anything other than agree with them, which wasn't something she'd thought she'd be doing last night, she kept her mouth shut.

'I know Sofia doesn't mean it. Not really. She's just upset. But what else can we do?'

'Let's go for a walk.' She stood up, dusting off her bum. 'A good walk always helps me clear my head.' Nico rested a hand on her shoulder and rubbed the top of her arm. His touch sent a jolt through her body. It must have shown on her face as he met her eye before dropping his hand away and pointing instead.

'You'll need some sunscreen. Your skin is hot already.'

'I'll be fine for a bit. Come on. We need to figure out what you're going to do.'

'You're always so calm, Olive. How do you do it?'

'Oh, I don't know. Life's thrown me a few twists and turns. Maybe I've just learned to roll with the punches.'

'This certainly feels like a punch.'

'It doesn't have to knock you down though. Come on.'

Without thinking she threaded her arm through his and they headed away from the house, the cat following, walking towards a dirt track cut into the lush green fields. From a distance they looked smooth and even, but up close the fields were covered in shrubs and tufts of grass or olive trees. Yellowing wheat fields were just visible on the horizon and here and there farmers marched across the land. Her skin began to tingle under the cloudless sky. Perhaps she should have applied some sunscreen after all.

'You have a friend,' Nico said, nodding down to the slinking ginger feline.

'I hope she won't get lost.'

'She won't. This is her home. All of it. She knows these fields like the back of her hand. Her name's Hera, queen of the gods.'

'A big name for such a small cat.'

'She has a big personality.'

It had been such a long time since they'd walked together, talking like this. All she wanted to do was slip her hand into his and entwine his fingers with her own. She'd wanted to do that many a time, but it had never happened. If only it had.

'So,' Olivia said, resisting the temptation to reach for him. 'What are you going to do?'

'I don't know. Wait till Sofia calms down and convince her to find another venue.'

'I'm afraid all the high-end ones will be booked up by now. You're only three weeks away from getting married.'

'She won't settle for anything less.'

She might have to, Olivia thought, if marrying Nico was the important thing and not what it looked like on social media. She chided herself for being mean. 'There must be somewhere nearby that's just as beautiful. Maybe a bit smaller and simpler, but somewhere you can hold it, then you can arrange caterers and a photographer separately.'

'And for entertainment my brothers can take turns singing. Do you know what I had to do to stop them last night?' For the first time that day he smiled, and light flickered again in his eyes.

'I can do a turn. Remember when we did karaoke in that bar in Thailand?'

Nico pressed his temples. 'No, don't remind me. I can still feel that hangover.'

'You were a bit rough the next day.'

'I've never felt so ill in my life, and you weren't exactly okay. You were sick in a pint glass.'

'Urgh, I'd forgotten about that.' She caught his eye, reflecting on a moment of shared history between them. That had been a couple of days before they'd sat on the beach and he'd told her he was moving to Italy. Pain flashed across her heart at the reminder, the memory of their near kiss floating just behind it. 'Anyway, we can decorate somehow ourselves. All is not lost just yet.'

Nico seemed to look at her with fresh eyes. 'When did you get so positive and resilient?'

'Having a baby at eighteen, having to drop out of uni, not being able to get any job you want because you need to work flexible hours . . . those things tend to make you a solutions person. There's always an answer, we just have to find it, and it might require a bit more work – that's all.'

'Do you know, I sometimes forget how amazing you are.'

The complement lit her like a Roman candle. 'All the event work I've been doing has been going really well. I've learned a lot and I finally feel like I've found something I'm good at. I have a mentor. Her name's Margot and she runs an events company in Paris. We met on an online training course she was teaching and hit it off straight away. She gave me her number and she's been amazing. Anyway, this is the most important day of your life, yes?'

He nodded. 'Then I want to help make it happen. Look—'

Olivia took out her phone and began typing. Within seconds a number of possible venues popped up on her screen. One in particular caught her eye. The building was about half the size of Sofia's home. The house was made of the same rough-hewn stone but most of the walls were softened by deep green ivy reaching across them. The gardens were full of mature olive trees and looked out over acres of fields in a patchwork of green. She could just imagine an arch of flowers under which she and Nico – Wait! What? – Nico and Sofia, she corrected herself, would get married. She shook the thought away. It was a Freudian slip – that's all.

'What about this one?' she asked, showing him her phone.

Nico shook his head. 'It's called Castello Chateau.'

'So?'

'That means Castle Castle. It makes no sense.'

She gave him the side-eye and pulled up more details. 'Look at it though! It's so pretty. And look at the grounds! We can hang lanterns from the trees and it'll be magical with a long table full of candles. I'd love to get married somewhere like that.' The words were out before she could stop them and she felt her cheeks colouring. Quickly, she moved the conversation on. 'See here, it's called Castello Chateau because the architect was a Frenchman who fell in love with Italy. His Tuscan wife refused to live in a completely French-style castle – that's chateau in French—'

'Thank you for that.'

'So they compromised with Castello Chateau and it has elements of both French and Italian architecture. Isn't that lovely and a good metaphor for what marriage is like? It's all about compromise, so I'm told.'

'It is . . .' She waited with bated breath for his response. 'It is interesting, I suppose, but I don't think Sofia will go for it.'

'Okay, well there are loads more. I'll ring round this afternoon and find out if any are free for your date.'

Suddenly downcast, his enthusiasm fading, Nico said, 'We only have three weeks, Olive. Do you really think we can do this in time?'

Whether it was the blazing sun that was making her so positive or heatstroke, she wasn't sure, but as she became aware of the cloudless sky above, of the beautiful scenery all around her, she smiled.

'I might need to rope in some of your brothers – maybe all of your brothers – and your dad, but we can definitely have somewhere wedding-ready. I'm sure of it.'

'I'm putting all my faith in you.'

'I know. And I won't let you down. So, tomorrow shall we go and have a look around some of these?'

'All right.'

'Yay! I'll get on it straight away.'

At least she'd be able to add this to her résumé of events and it would give her some good answers when she went to job interviews. Not many people could pull a wedding together in three weeks. It was going to be tough. More than tough. But she could do it. She knew she could.

'Don't get too carried away, Olive. We still need to tell Sofia and I have no idea how she'll take the news.'

Maybe that was the problem when you tried to marry someone you'd only known for six months: you didn't know them well enough to foresee their reactions. She shook her head, admonishing herself once more for being mean. But Nico was right. Would Sofia go for something like this, and would she even agree to put in charge someone she clearly couldn't stand? Olivia scooped up Hera and cuddled her to her chest. The cat rubbed her head under her chin.

Why was she putting herself through all this? Why did she keep throwing herself in deeper and deeper? The only answer she could come up with was that loving Nico meant doing everything she could to make him happy, no matter how painful or how much hard work that was going to be. And if she failed? A chill ran down her spine. That result was too scary to contemplate.

Chapter 6

They returned to the house to find Sofia no longer angry but crying into a live feed to her followers. Olivia thought it highly distasteful, but Nico didn't seem to mind as he leaned in and said: 'She does this all the time. She won't be long.' As they waited patiently, Sofia speaking in both Italian and English, Nico spotted the housekeeper. 'Mathilde, can you make some coffee, please?'

'Did you have breakfast?' she asked slightly accusingly, as if missing it was a personal insult. A few strands of her grey-brown hair had fallen from her bun, framing her face.

'We had an emergency to deal with.'

'*Sí*. I heard. You need food!' She bustled off to the kitchen and returned a moment later with a tray full of coffee things as well as several small plates of biscuits. As Mathilde carried the tray to the coffee table, Olivia's gaze followed the food, her stomach grumbling loudly at having been denied breakfast.

While Sofia finished her broadcast, thanking her loyal followers for their kind comments and yes, it was absolutely ridiculous to cancel her big day in favour of some pathetic footballer, Olivia picked the order in which she would eat the biscuits. There were three different plates, all with different treats on them. The first was biscotti – she knew that because they sold those in Starbucks. The others though were unknown to her.

'These,' Nico said, 'are *Baci al Cacao* – hazelnut and chocolate.'

'Ooo, yummy! And these—'

'*Cantucci*. They're delicious almond biscuits and Mathilde is the best at making them.'

She took one of each, not bothering with a plate as they wouldn't be in her hand that long, and began munching. Sofia joined them, staring at Olivia as if she were a pig at a trough. Her opinion clearly didn't improve when Olivia wiped her hands on her shorts as Nico began to explain about their possible solution to her wedding woes.

'We've got a number of options,' Olivia said, showing Sofia her phone. She knew it would help to make a shortlist of possible venues. Sofia's interests leaned heavily towards venues that had giant ballrooms, vineyards attached, and chandeliers Buckingham Palace would be proud of. Things came to a crashing halt when she showed her pictures of Castello Chateau.

'You want me to get married there?' She couldn't have looked more shocked if Olivia had suggested she get married at a landfill site.

'Don't you think it's sweet?' She'd thought the strangely named castle was beautiful. Stunning even, in a simple way, but Sofia's lip had curled, and she was categorically not impressed.

'It's a ruin.'

'It's not a ruin!' Olivia couldn't help laughing at the overly dramatic description, earning her a glare that said: *You're here under sufferance – don't push your luck.* She cleared her throat. The building – with its series of small, square windows – wasn't much to look at, though Olivia thought it looked rather magical all covered in ivy, but the gardens were the winner and as they were in Italy and it was a gazillion degrees, there was no reason they couldn't hold the whole thing outside.

'I was thinking,' Olivia began after snaffling another biscuit for moral support, 'that we could put tables in this sort of area and have a beautiful flower arch somewhere like—' She pulled up a different photograph. 'Here. It'll be lovely and romantic. And we can have candles and white tablecloths and flowers everywhere.'

'It's not the beautiful fresco-painted room we were going to get married in,' Sofia replied sulkily, flopping down onto the seat and holding out her hand for Nico to take. Honestly, what did he see in this woman? She must have had some good qualities to attract him in the first place, but she was doing a great job of hiding them from Olivia.

'No, it's not, but Sofia, that place has gone.' She sat down in front of her in full parenting mode. Good mum, this time, not bad mum: sympathetic and understanding rather than shouting and telling her to suck it up, buttercup, life wasn't fair sometimes. 'I know you're disappointed and when you feel like this, it's easy to see every other option as less than, but while your wedding won't be what you originally intended, it can still be absolutely beautiful. Everyone's here to see you and Nico get married because you love each other.' Her throat closed over and she pushed down the pain, reminding herself to put Nico's happiness above her own. 'That's what is important, isn't it?'

Sofia thought for a moment and then said, 'I suppose you're right.'

Suppose? That wasn't exactly reassuring. She wondered if Nico had noticed Sofia hadn't actually answered the question with anything particularly reassuring.

'Wherever we choose will need to be beautiful. We

will need a lot of pictures. My followers want to see everything. They were so impressed with the castello it'll need to be just as good.'

'How many followers do you have?'

She shrugged. 'About 450,000.'

'Right.' No pressure then.

'When will you see these places?'

'Tomorrow. We'll see as many as we can.'

'Including this place with the stupid name?'

'It's not a stupid name! It's sweet.'

'It is stupid,' Sofia declared. 'I will have to call it something else.' Sofia stood, tapping gently underneath her eyes, though her make-up hadn't moved even with all the crying. 'You and Nico will have to sort it. I have too much to do, but he knows what I like, don't you, darling?'

'It'll be perfect,' he said, cupping Sofia's face. 'I promise.'

Olivia repressed the biscuit trying to work its way back up her throat at the vomit-inducing sight before her. When they'd finished, Sofia turned to Olivia.

'You must start wearing sunscreen. Your nose is red. And your cheeks. And here—' She helpfully demonstrated, waving her hand in front of her entire face and upper body.

Unable to stop herself, Olivia touched her nose and, embarrassed, made her excuses, grabbing a handful of biscuits before she left.

She was just opening the door to her little apartment when Maria arrived, carrying several shopping bags.

'Been into Florence?' Olivia asked.

'Nope. I brought lunch. We've got a lot of catching up to do.' She held up the bags, grinning.

'Is there alcohol in one of those?'

'A whole bottle of limoncello. Why?'

'Come inside and I'll tell you about my morning.'

Chapter 7

Olivia showed Maria in and checked her appearance in one of the large ornate mirrors decorating the living room. She turned her head this way and that. All right she was a little pink but it wasn't that bad. She'd been much, much worse.

'Do I look sunburnt to you?'

Maria shook her head. 'No. You're a tiny bit pink, that's all. Get some after-sun on and that'll have faded in an hour. Wow, this is a lot nicer than my *agriturismo*.'

'I would invite you to share but my ex-husband and son are coming out soon.'

Maria laughed, shaking her head. 'You really better start at the beginning.'

'You first,' Olivia prompted.

As she put out plates of olives, sundried tomatoes and coppa, ham and salami, Maria cut the focaccia and found glasses for the limoncello while updating Olivia on her life to date.

'Nothing that interesting really. I'm not married. I just got out of a serious relationship though. That's partly why I started travelling again. I'm a vet – which I love – but when my boyfriend left – ex-boyfriend – I just kind of got to a point where I thought, what am I doing? I'm working so hard – my job was pretty emotionally demanding – and I thought, I need a break from everything. And I mean everything.'

'I can imagine,' Olivia replied.

'I just thought, that's it. I'm taking some time off. I need to travel again. So here I am. I didn't see much of Europe when I was travelling at eighteen. It wasn't exotic enough for me, so I'm doing it now.'

'That sounds amazing. And your job is waiting for you when you get back?'

'Yep. They didn't want me to go but knew I was determined, so they offered me a sabbatical rather than me quitting. I think after another six months, when my year's up, I'll be ready to dive back in and give it my all, because I'll have recharged myself, you know?'

Olivia knew exactly what she meant. Though her break had been enforced because Jacob was young and no one would employ her, by the time he'd started school and she was fit for work again, she'd been raring to go.

Hera, the cat, came wandering in through the still-open door, her nose twitching at the smell of meat.

'You can have a little bit if you're good,' Olivia said as Hera jumped up onto the window ledge and watched them.

'So?' Maria prodded, popping food into her mouth. 'What about you?'

'Well—' Olivia began with the last time they'd seen each other and everything that had happened since: Nico moving to Florence, her falling pregnant, her failed marriage and the years of struggling as a single mum.

'Whatever made you marry Jack?' Maria asked.

She shrugged, the limoncello relaxing her after the crazy morning she'd had. 'I was bearing his child. It seemed like a good idea at the time. And I did love him back then. We thought we'd make it, you know? Sometimes you don't see how unsuitable someone is at the time.'

'Ain't that the truth.' Maria hesitated before knocking back her limoncello. 'Tell me if I'm way out of line here, but . . . am I the only one who thinks Sofia and Nico are like chalk and cheese? He's so kind and friendly. Like, when I saw him again last month, it was

103

like we'd always been friends. I mean, he even invited me to stay for his wedding for heaven's sake. But she's . . . well she's—'

'Not like that at all?' Olivia gave a wry smile.

'Exactly. The first time I met her she looked at me like I was wearing a clown mask and flippers.'

'Yeah, I don't quite get it. She's not who I'd imagine him being with. And she quite clearly hates me. In fact, I think she hates pretty much everyone.'

'Everyone except her followers. I know that sounds mean,' she said, seeing Olivia's eyes widen. 'But she's like a totally different person online and I don't know if that's the real her and she's acting with everyone else, or if she's acting online and the real her is the ice queen we've met so far. Have you watched any of her videos?'

'A few.'

'Well I've watched loads and she seems really sweet and friendly on there. Down to earth. She tries to tempt Nico in quite a lot but he never does it.'

'He's never really been into social media, especially that whole influencer thing. It's another reason they seem so incompatible.'

Maria sat back in her chair. 'I always thought you two would get together, you know.'

Olivia paused, a slice of salami halfway to her mouth. 'But at dinner last night you said—'

'I was lying! Trying to save your bacon.'

'Well, I appreciate it, but no, we never . . . It just didn't happen and then he moved away and our lives seemed to run sort of parallel to each other but never intertwining the way they had when we were younger.' The way she'd thought they always would.

'And now you're planning their wedding.' She chuckled. 'You really need to learn to say no.'

Olivia felt Maria's gaze lingering on her, but she wasn't about to admit she was only doing it because she was still in love with Nico. Not only did she not want to make Maria uncomfortable, she was supposed to be doing everything she could to get over him.

'I don't mind. I've been doing events stuff in my job and I love it.'

'Yeah, but that must be hard for you. I can see that you—'

'I'm happy for him. I really am.' She had to cut her off. Hearing someone else say the words would make them too real. She was going to get over him. She had to. 'I wish I could understand what he sees in her, that's all. He's normally a really good judge of character so there must be something for him to have fallen in love with her. He's never been shallow or obsessed with looks. I just need to find out what it is.'

'Well with being her bridesmaid and now their wedding planner, you're going to get plenty of opportunity to find out.' Maria topped up their glasses of limoncello.

'This is all a really, really bad idea, isn't it?'

'I really think it is.' Maria grimaced from ear to ear.

Olivia sunk down, hiding her head in her hands. She couldn't help but agree.

Chapter 8

Sat in Nico's baby blue sports car, they wound their way through country roads, curving through dells and over hills towards the first of their proposed venues. Olivia checked her nose and cheeks in the side mirror and was happy to see the redness had faded a little since yesterday. This morning she'd lathered herself in sunscreen and even brought the bottle with her. She could well imagine Sofia pointing out any further redness and quite frankly she didn't need it. It wasn't the daunting task that was dampening her spirits though.

'You're missing Jacob, aren't you?' Nico asked, glancing at her.

'How did you know?'

'You've been quiet this morning. Quieter than you usually are. Is he okay?'

'He's fine. He's happy. Having a great time with Jack.'

'So?'

'So he's just busy and not really talking.' She kept her eyes forward on the road. 'We had a quick chat this morning and then he went out with his mates. I know it's me, not him. He should be going out with his mates. I think it's just being so far away, that's all.'

'You're doing great.' He moved his hand from the gear stick and took hold of hers where it had been resting in her lap. As the warmth of his skin permeated her own as he squeezed her fingers, she wished that somehow he could feel it too. Would things be different if he knew how she felt? He'd nearly kissed her all those years ago then stopped, and it hadn't happened for them since, so that was her answer. He didn't feel the same way she did about him, and she had to move on.

'So where's first?' Nico asked, trying to chivvy her along.

They were already following the satnav, but Olivia described the luxurious-looking Borgo Lucca. As they pulled up, the gorgeous stone building and manicured lawns gave her a sense of dread that was only heightened by the glossy woman who met them as she saw them round the sumptuous interior. There was no way this place wasn't booked up for their requested date.

'And you're definitely free in three weeks' time?' Olivia asked.

'Three weeks?' the woman asked, her eyes wide. 'We cannot possibly organise a wedding in three weeks. You should have said when you booked your appointment. I wouldn't have wasted your time.'

'I did,' Olivia replied. 'I said in my email that we were working to a tight schedule.'

'Damn that girl,' the woman said vehemently. 'I'm sorry. The girl in the office. She never reads things properly.' She shook her head again. 'I'm sorry. We have a few weekends for next year but that is all. I'm sorry.'

'That's okay,' Nico replied. 'We understand. We knew it would be difficult. Our venue was cancelled at short notice.'

'I'm sorry to hear it, but I doubt there will be many places available now.'

They left, Nico frowning and downcast.

'Don't worry,' Olivia said. 'We've still got a few more to see.'

They went to the next venue that was a real fixer-upper, the complete other end of the spectrum. When they arrived it was to discover that the pictures they'd seen had been specially curated as they didn't show the pigs and chickens running around or the general tattiness of the house. When they were shown to the 'venue' by a man dressed like a farmer – to be fair to him, he probably was a farmer – it was to a barn that was virtually falling down and, at that very moment, was full of hay.

'I'll clear all that out,' he confirmed in Italian to Nico and Nico translated to her.

Olivia typed into her translation app and then said, '*See da squelchy altra party?*' The man looked at her in total and utter confusion and Nico burst out laughing, hiding his mirth behind a cough.

'Do you mean—' And he repeated: 'Is there anywhere else?' in perfect Italian.

'Yes, that's exactly what I mean.'

He giggled again as the farmer looked at Olivia like she was an idiot before replying with a definite no. The same answer greeted them at the other three venues they tried.

'It seems Castello Chateau is our last chance,' Olivia said as they drove towards it.

The beautiful landscape didn't fail to take Olivia's breath away. They passed vineyards with trees loaded down with fattening grapes and fields of crops. Dirt tracks cut across the lush green pastures decorated with clusters of bushy trees. They passed through a little town, Olivia craning her head out of the open window as she studied the higgledy-piggledy houses, all crushed together, painted in pale blue, pink, orange and yellow. It was utterly stunning with its watchtower and cobblestone roads, and she couldn't wait to go back there for a better look.

Soon they were at their destination and as Olivia went from desolation and mounting dread to excitement and elation, she jumped out of the car giddy with excitement.

'Oh, Nico, it's gorgeous! Even prettier than I thought it'd be.' She ran around the front of the car, Nico grinning at her childlike enthusiasm. 'The pictures don't do it justice at all, do they?'

'It is very charming,' he said, scanning the house over, examining it with his architect's eye.

The main building appeared similar to Sofia's house except for its size and the creeping ivy covering the walls. The shutters were a matching dark green and Olivia wondered if the colours matched that of the surrounding farmlands on purpose. There wasn't a grand drive, as Sofia's house had, but the small area would be more than big enough for the few cars that would be arriving.

At the end of the building, on the right-hand side, stood a French-style turret. The type you'd normally see on chateaus in the Loire Valley.

Nico was staring at it.

'What?'

'There's a French turret stuck onto the building.'

'I know. And you can go in it, right to the top. Imagine the views from up there. Sofia could throw her bouquet from the window. Do you guys do that in Italy?'

He made a non-committal grunting sound as a man ran out of the house to greet them.

'*Buongiorno! Buongiorno!*' His arms were outstretched and welcoming, softening his bear-like appearance. His wild dark hair spilled out around his face and he had a heavy, lustrous beard. His wife, smaller than him and thinner with long dark hair that flowed down her back, had a kind face and rolled her eyes at her husband as if he were a naughty, overenthusiastic dog. 'Welcome to Castello Chateau,' he barked. 'The only chateau in Italy!'

That was quite a claim to fame as far as Olivia was concerned and only added to its charms.

'My name is Angelo and this is my wonderful wife Francesca.'

'It's a pleasure to meet you,' Olivia replied, holding out her hand. Angelo shook it wildly. She could just feel her teeth beginning to rattle when his wife stepped forward.

'Let her go, Angelo, or you'll hurt her. You don't know your own strength half the time.'

'I am *very* strong,' he added mischievously. Olivia decided she liked them both immensely.

'It's very nice to meet you. So, you are looking at getting married here? What a beautiful couple you make. Just look at them together, Angelo, aren't they gorgeous?'

'*Sí. Sí*—'

'No, no!' Nico cried, leaping forwards and waving his

112

hands in the air. A reaction that was a little over the top in Olivia's opinion. The idea of marrying her couldn't be that hideous to contemplate, surely? 'No, I am marrying someone else. Olivia is here as our wedding planner.'

And best friend. And bridesmaid, she added mentally, ensuring her lips were pressed together so the words couldn't sneak out.

'I see,' Francesca replied. She stared for a second in confusion before clapping her hands together. 'Well, let us show you around Castello Chateau. It is a little unusual but we're very proud of it.'

She began to explain about its history. How it was built in the fifteenth century, but they believe some type of house had stood on the site since the Etruscans. Olivia wasn't sure when that was, history having never been her strong point, but it sounded ancient and romantic and she soaked up Francesca's words, ready to recite them back to Sofia.

'The outside of the house is very much a traditional Italian castello except for the turret on the end. The architect of the turret was a man called Louis Beaumanoir who was travelling through Italy and fell in love with, and married, a woman called Gia De Stefano so he settled here, close to her family, whom she didn't want to leave. But, missing his home, he decided to add on some French design elements and that is why we have a French-style turret here and a small pavilion further down the gardens.

Come inside though – that is where you'll see more of the French influence.'

Nico, who had been hanging off Francesca's every word, followed, still studying the building.

'You're warming to the place,' Olivia whispered.

'Maybe,' he replied with a smile that lit her heart on fire. She stamped down the flame before it could take hold.

'See. He was a weirdo architect, you're a weirdo architect; it's like it was meant to be.'

The doors opened into a rustic living room and kitchen. It wasn't fancy like Sofia's house was, but as they were planning to have the wedding outside, it didn't matter. Here, Olivia began to understand a little of what Francesca had said about the design as Nico began pointing out details you would normally only find in a French chateau. Rather than the decorated ceilings and frescoes of an Italian villa, the house had fancy cornicing, and rather than the deep, rich tones Olivia normally associated with renaissance Italy, the colours were paler and softer, definitely more Louis XIV than Medici.

'What happened to them?' asked Olivia.

'Louis Beaumanoir and Gia De Stefano?' Francesca asked. 'They were ridiculed a little for their French tastes, but they didn't care. They loved their home and each other and lived here all their lives, producing thirteen children.'

'Thirteen?' Olivia couldn't even begin to understand how someone could have that many children. Well, she understood the mechanics well enough, but the idea made her flinch. One had been more than enough for her.

'They were very happy here, which is why we want to host weddings. We think they'll bring the couples good luck.'

'That's lovely. Isn't it, Nico?'

'So will we be your first wedding?'

Francesca's smile was a little fixed and Angelo's eyes darted to his wife's. '*Sí*. I hope that won't be a problem.'

Her hands were clasped together in front of her, and Olivia could see it was because she was nervous.

'It's not a problem at all!' Olivia replied enthusiastically and their hosts visibly relaxed. 'Is it Nico? I think it makes it even more exciting.'

Nico was still busy examining the walls and the design of the house, his eyes roving over every detail while Angelo watched him quizzically. 'Yes,' he agreed abstractedly. 'It is a very interesting house and a wonderful story. This property is so unusual to find here in Tuscany. I can't believe I didn't know of it before.'

'As my wife says,' Angelo began. 'We are at the start of our journey into offering weddings. There is much work to do to get the house and the bedrooms ready for guests.'

'Don't worry about that,' Olivia cut in, quick to reassure him. 'The guests are already staying locally so there won't be a need for bedrooms. And we're hoping to hold pretty much everything in the gardens.'

'Then I will show you those.' He beamed.

They moved out of the house through a heavy, dark wooden door and onto a small, terraced area full of giant flower pots holding bushy little orange trees. The citrus scent hit Olivia's nostrils immediately and she craved a glass of sweet orange juice, freshly pressed, sitting in the sun and definitely not the stuff she normally drank straight from the bottle, standing up in the kitchen.

Angelo led them down a set of central steps and the gardens opened up before them. A small farm building with a roof but no front stood to the side and the roof of the pavilion Francesca had mentioned was just visible in the next field.

'That'll be perfect for storing wine and everything we need for the wedding,' she said to Nico, pointing at the outbuilding. His hand brushed hers as they walked close together and he glanced at her, his expression unreadable. 'And look,' she continued quickly, worried he was thinking it was as bad as the hay place. 'We can have a really long table with candles all down the middle for when it gets dark.'

'The sun will set over there,' Nico said, pointing to the sky over a vista of fields. 'We'll be able to watch it go down.'

Olivia could just picture it, the wedding breakfast

underway, people laughing, cheering, dancing, bathed in the elegant colours of a Tuscan sunset: deep oranges, rich pinks, warm yellows all slipping down under a blanket of velvety blue. It would be the most gorgeous way to end a wedding day. Excitement bubbled in Olivia's stomach.

'The wedding arch can be here, can't it?' She ran over to the furthest end of the garden. 'With chairs set out here. The tables for dinner will be here—' She jogged a little further along. 'What more do you need?'

'Nothing,' Nico replied, smiling widely, relief visible on his face as he stood beside her. 'It'll be perfect.'

'Really? So you're happy? We can go ahead?'

He gazed around him, taking in the fields, the view, and the house once more. 'Yes.'

'Yes?'

'Yes!' He shook his head as he walked towards her. 'You're *fantastica*, Olive. *Grazie!*' Elated, he picked her up and swung her around. Olivia squealed as his strong arms wrapped around her and the world spun. Francesca and Angelo watched on, frowning slightly. This wasn't normally how a groom and wedding planner acted. Nico dropped her on the ground, and she stepped back, pulling down her T-shirt and clearing her throat.

'Perfect. And that fact it's such short notice isn't a problem?'

Angelo shook his head. 'Not at all. We love a challenge, don't we, Francesca?'

'Anything is possible and there is always a solution,' she agreed.

'Well, we better head back and tell Sofia.'

'Yes, yes,' Nico said, a little unsure of himself. Had he made himself dizzy? He seemed slightly discombobulated. 'Yes, we should go and tell her, then get started on the preparation. There isn't any time to lose.'

There really wasn't but the daunting nature of the task excited her, and worryingly, the feel of Nico's hands on her waist was doing exactly the same thing.

Chapter 9

Olivia walked into the villa for breakfast the next morning, excited to get started on wedding planning.

The day before, she and Nico had returned from Castello Chateau and broken the news that this was where the wedding was to be held. Olivia had taken a number of photographs before she'd left and showed them to Sofia to prove that it wasn't a ruin and even if the building was, if everything was held outside, it didn't even matter. She'd had to enter full mum mode to explain that there simply weren't any other choices.

Olivia didn't feel that Castello Chateau was a particularly bad choice either. In fact, she loved it but when Nico had explained about the unusual architecture, his eyes shining with excitement and interest, even this hadn't swayed Sofia who only worried about the pictures being 'Insta-worthy'.

Olivia had left at this point, afraid that if she stayed, she'd open her mouth and say something she regretted. She simply couldn't understand what Nico saw in Sofia. Later, Nico had stopped by to say Sofia was happy and excited for the new venue, which Olivia suspected was a giant lie but nodded anyway.

Today, though, was a new day and whether Sofia liked it or not, this was the wedding venue she had ended up with and Olivia would do everything she could to give them the wedding of their dreams. She had just loaded her plate with delicious meats and pastries laid out by Mathilde and sat down at the table next to Giovanni when Nico appeared.

'So what do we do first, Olive?' he asked, sitting beside her with an equally laden plate. She glanced again at his abs, the flat of his stomach hugged by a bright white T-shirt, and she felt her body come alive.

'Yes,' Giovanni said, dabbing his mouth with his napkin. 'Nico said you are saving the day. You're a wonderful person, Livvy. Where would we be without you?'

'It's my pleasure,' she replied, dampening the fizzing with thoughts of a giant to-do list and the most pressure she'd ever had in her career. 'I think the first thing we need to do is make a list.'

'Shall I get a pen and paper?' Nico asked and Olivia shook her head.

'I work better when I'm not actively thinking about something. Especially at this stage. I was going to go for a walk or maybe visit Florence and do some sightseeing. By the time I come back here I'll know exactly what I need to do and by when.'

'I have a great idea.' Nico turned to face her, bouncing in his seat. 'There's a wonderful antiques market in the next village. Let's go there and wander around. You always used to love the local markets when we were travelling. Is that a good plan?'

'That's an excellent plan. I bet by the time we finish we'll have a list of everything we need to do and possible businesses to approach. Can I finish my breakfast first though? This is absolutely delicious.' Over the other side of the table, Sofia was pushing a nibbled-at pastry around her plate. 'Is it okay if I borrow Nico for the day, Sofia? I don't want to get in the way of any of your plans.'

She'd thought she better ask so she didn't seem like she was stealing Nico away from her. Goodness knows Sofia already had a low enough opinion of her.

Sofia waved a hand. 'It's fine. I have some videos to record and a meeting for some paid advertising. They're impressed with the way I'm handling the cancellation of the wedding and want me to endorse a range of herbal remedies to deal with stress and insomnia.'

'Oh, that sounds fabulous.'

If you asked her, Sofia wasn't handling the cancellation of the wedding all that well. Although if she were, Olivia wouldn't have this opportunity to do something amazing for her own portfolio so she supposed she should be grateful, and if it gave Sofia more exposure and more opportunities for her own career then good for her.

'Isn't she amazing?' Nico said, flashing his puppy-dog eyes at Sofia. Sofia gave a small smile, which didn't match the intensity of Nico's, and once more Olivia wondered at the odd pairing, wishing she could simply ask him what he saw in her and point out all the ways they weren't suited. She stuffed another piece of pastry into her mouth and chomped down on it in frustration.

Once breakfast had been eaten, they climbed into Nico's car and made their way to the village. Lying in the dell of a valley, it couldn't be more different to the hilltop villages she had seen on the drive yesterday. The place seemed to fit into the dip in the land as if the deep green fields were holding it in the palm of its velvety-gloved hand. The streets were cobbled, the houses made of the same rough stone, the windows and doors higgledy-piggledy in size. But everywhere, the green of the surrounding landscape infused the town, from the ivy and climbing plants growing over walls to the pots that lined the fronts of the houses.

Nico parked in a small, narrow street and they climbed out.

'Is this going to be safe here?' she asked pointing at the car.

'I think so. This is a quiet street. It's where I always park when I visit the market and it's never been damaged yet.' As he pressed the button to lock the car, the wing mirrors automatically folded in, and she followed him through the streets.

Noise and the clamouring of voices grew louder, and as they exited the narrow alley, she and Nico were soon engulfed in the swell of people, the shouting of the traders and the air of excitement. Lines of glass-topped cases filled with all manner of things were mixed with tables overflowing with bric-a-brac. Some of the stalls had large white parasols shielding them from the sun, while others were bare, the traders used to a lifetime of work in the heat, their skin dark as mahogany, wrinkles creasing as they smiled and chatted. Everywhere, the gorgeous Italian language surrounded her, and Olivia wished she had more skill at learning it. French might have been the official language of love, but for her it really was Italian.

'Where shall we start?' Nico asked and Olivia simply stared at him in wonder. He smiled. 'Shall we just wander around?'

They began to explore the different stalls and as they reached the first one laden with old-fashioned radios from the 1950s, she pulled out her phone. 'Music. We need to decide about music. DJ or band and if a band, who'll be available at such short notice? DJ might be best, but it depends what Sofia wants. Does she want people up and dancing or does she want something more sedate and elegant?'

'We had a band organised for the reception at the castello and she'd given them a very specific playlist. They weren't very happy about it, but she told them it was her wedding and she wanted what she wanted.'

'Okay.' That was both terrifying and brilliant all in one go. Olivia couldn't help but admire her strength. Sofia knew what she wanted for her wedding and was prepared to fight for it, but what did that mean for Olivia? What if she got something wrong? The frightening thought was pushed to the side as someone walked past her eating something delicious that smelled of bacon. 'Food. We need to find a caterer as soon as possible. That has to be a priority.'

'You're very good at this,' Nico said, placing both hands on her shoulders and guiding her forwards as she walked head down, typing on her phone. 'I can see what you mean about not actually thinking about things. It lets the mind be free. I might have to try that the next time I have a sticky architectural problem.'

She finally looked, enjoying the feel of his strong, large hands on her shoulders. 'Do you get sticky architectural problems?'

'You'd be surprised.'

She was about to make a dirty joke then decided better of it. The skin-on-skin contact was already threatening to override her senses. Her attention was taken by shiny glass objects in an old-fashioned museum-type case. She went over, studying the beautiful jewellery laid out on a black velvet cloth. The age of the gold was evident in its burnished, bronzed look, the gems shining in all the colours of the rainbow.

'These are gorgeous,' she said, before moving on.

'No sudden flash of inspiration for the list? It hasn't reminded you we need . . . I don't know . . . sweets for the children or bunting in a particular shade of blue?'

She giggled. 'No, they were just really pretty and I wanted to look at them.'

He shook his head in disbelief then laughed. 'Come on, I want to look at this stall. It has things for the garden, and I'd like to get Dad something.'

'Don't forget it'll need to be something he can take home in his suitcase.'

'I'll get it sent to him, don't worry. I'd already thought of that.'

As they perused the stall full of ceramic and wooden pots, tiny wheelbarrows for planting things in and older, more expensive statues and bird baths, she began typing again.

Nico stood from examining a storm lantern. 'What is it now?'

'Storm lanterns would look lovely in the evening, lit with giant candles as the sun goes down. We can have them all around the garden, lining the path from the front of the house, and maybe a few smaller ones on the table. I'll source a supplier.'

'We could just buy these?'

She shook her head. 'That'll be waste of money as they'll only get one use. I'll see what I can do first, but get his card so we have a back-up plan.'

'Seriously. When did you get so good at this?'

They began walking towards a café, both naturally drawn to its beauty and the delicious smell of coffee emanating from it. They were so in tune, neither needed to ask the other if they wanted a break or something to drink. They just knew and it reminded Olivia how close they'd once been and why Giovanni – and she – had always thought they'd end up together. They sat down, ordering espressos.

'I know this sounds stupid but organising kids' parties is a great way to develop event-management skills. It's not an example I could give in an interview, I'm hoping organising a wedding in three weeks, from a standing start, will do that, but people don't appreciate what goes into being a mum.'

'By people you mean corporate bosses? Mostly male corporate bosses?'

'Yes, unfortunately. *Grazia*,' she said to the waiter as he deposited her coffee.

'I think that's a magazine,' Nico whispered.

'Oh.' Olivia clamped a hand over her mouth and giggled. 'Maybe I should stop trying altogether.'

'Definitely not. You may not always get it right, but we Italians appreciate anyone who attempts to speak our language. It shows you're not just a rude tourist. Not all British people try.'

'You're British too,' she reminded him.

'Half British. The grumpy half is British and the happy, suave and sophisticated half is Italian.' He sipped his coffee and a tiny drip fell from his cup, staining his pristine white T-shirt. He stared at the expanding brown mark.

'Very sophisticated,' she commented, as a huge laugh emerged. When they'd both calmed down, she began again. 'The amount of life admin involved in kids is hugely underrated. Fitting work in around your children's needs, managing when they're sick, playdates, school plays, uniforms, fancy dress, presents for parties, all while making sure the house is clean, there's food in the fridge and the little person you're looking after doesn't die. It's a lot of juggling and time management, which is very similar to events and communications.'

'Even harder when you're on your own,' Nico commented and she glanced at him from over the edge of her cup.

'I know you think Jack should have done more after we separated but it was hard for us both. We were both still so young and at least he's now found a job he loves.' She hoped. The memory of that slightly dodgy-sounding phone call the day she left flashed up but she pushed it aside. 'Try not to be so hard on him. Please? If we made mistakes – and we both did – it was a long time ago and Jacob's a good boy. For all our faults, I think we've done a pretty good job and I include you in that as his godfather.'

'Thank you. You know how I love you both.' He paused then suddenly cleared his throat. 'I'm glad I've been able to be there for you and him.'

'I couldn't have asked for more. I probably don't tell you how much I appreciate it either.'

'It's hard being apart as much as we have been.'

'It has.' Silence fell and she checked her phone for any new messages knowing full well there weren't any. 'I'm looking forward to seeing Jacob. And Jack's very excited to be invited. It was nice of you.'

'I took a leaf out of your book. You've always been a generous person, Olive. Perhaps too generous. Too nice.'

Perhaps that was why she'd ended up firmly in the friend zone. She simply hadn't been sexy or cool enough to be considered girlfriend material. As she placed her cup down, her mind lingering on the depressing thought, she suddenly pulled out her phone again and started typing.

'What now?' he asked, smiling.

'If we're doing everything from scratch, we're going to need cups and saucers, plates, knives . . . all the crockery and cutlery for a full sit-down meal.'

Nico leaned forward, resting his head on his hand.

'What is it?'

'There's so much to do. How can it all be done in such a short space of time?' he asked.

Without thinking, she reached out and took his other hand, holding it tightly. 'We'll find a way. I promise.'

He tightened his fingers around hers and the noise of the market seemed to die away. He caught her eye, his gaze unwavering, and if she hadn't known better, she'd have thought herself catapulted from the friend zone faster than a rocket headed into space. She tried to meet his eye as his best friend but couldn't. Somehow she knew that her love for him – romantic love – would show on her face even though he'd never felt that way about her.

'Shall we get back to the villa and start making a list of possible vendors?' she asked, breaking the moment before it became too much for her.

Her question seemed to startle him awake and he pulled his hand away. 'Yes. The sooner we get started on all of this the better. Just make sure you tell me, Dad and my brothers exactly what you want us to do. You know what they're like. You'll ask them to book a DJ and they'll think it's hilarious to book a clown who plays the ocarina or something equally ludicrous.'

'I will, don't worry. I don't think Sofia would see the funny side of that, would she?'

'No. She does have a sense of humour though. Really. I think she's just finding all the family together a bit overwhelming.'

'Of course.' She hated that Nico had felt the need to say that and smiled to reassure him. Olivia hoped that was the reason and it wasn't simply that Sofia was a cold fish who didn't deserve her kind, wonderful, Nico.

Though he wasn't hers, she reminded herself. And he never had been.

Chapter 10

Olivia's plans to dive straight in to source suppliers for everything, from flowers and table settings to chairs and cutlery, were put on hold the next morning when Sofia summoned her as soon as she'd finished her breakfast. In fact, she hadn't summoned her. Mathilde, the housekeeper, was the one sent to fetch her.

She knocked on the door with three loud, rapid bangs made by hands used to pummelling dough and as soon as Olivia opened the door, she briskly said, '*Signora* Sofia needs to see you.'

'Now?' Olivia asked, tying her hair into a ponytail.

'*Sí*. It's urgent. Come, come! Quickly!' She hustled

Olivia out of the apartment and across into the main house.

Olivia's nerves were mounting. Had she changed her mind about the venue? Was the wedding off again? Had something happened to Nico? She tried to calm her racing thoughts and hurried into the house to find Sofia sat with her parents at the dining table, casually sipping coffee and all staring at her like she'd just announced her presence with a megaphone and party poppers.

'Olivia,' Sofia said. 'You didn't have to come straight away. You could have changed out of your pyjamas first.'

'I have changed out of my pyjamas,' she replied a little crossly. She'd thought the playsuit looked cute. The shop assistant had certainly told her it was 'in' and suited her body shape, even complimenting her legs. Now she worried she'd been lied to in order to secure a sale. She crossed her arms over her chest self-consciously, then dropped them, refusing to be cowed by Sofia and her jibes. 'Mathilde said there was an emergency.'

'Not an emergency, but we do need to leave soon.'

'For what? I need to go and start sourcing suppliers for—'

'I have a dress fitting.'

'A – you – right. And I'm needed because . . .'

'You're my bridesmaid.' She placed her cup down carefully and went to pick up another pastry, pausing as Adele cleared her throat. Sofia withdrew her hand and placed it in her lap.

'You don't need another *cornetto*, Sofia, or that dress will never fit.'

Olivia bit her lip. She hated when women did that to other women, commenting on their shape or size. How could her mother say something like that to her?

'Would you like one, Olivia?' Adele asked, moving the plate away from Sofia as if to remove the temptation. 'You don't seem to mind what size you are, do you?'

Olivia could feel the pressure mounting on her chest and clamped the inside of her cheek between her teeth to stop the words coming out. She normally only felt this angry when someone was rude to her son – that primal, maternal need to fight and protect. But she couldn't start a row now. Not when Nico's wedding was only just back on again, and seeing the venue and their shopping trip yesterday had made him so happy. She stopped herself from saying anything and instead remembered his hands around her waist as he'd spun her around at Castello Chateau, the happiness she'd felt in his arms and the way she'd held his hand the day before.

Taking a deep breath to chase the thought away, she decided to play Adele at her own game and marched forwards, taking the *cornetto* and stuffing half of it into her mouth in one go. Sofia stared at her wide-eyed as if she'd gone mad, then she dipped her head and for a second, Olivia was sure a smile played on her lips. Adele, on the

133

other hand, looked absolutely furious.

'So when are we leaving?' Olivia asked when she'd finally managed to swallow the too-large mouthful. It had taken longer than she'd anticipated and chewing while being watched by onlookers made her feel like a cow in a field or an animal in a zoo.

'In twenty minutes,' Sofia replied. 'Now the wedding is back on, I need to make sure the gown still fits.'

'Okay. Are you driving?'

'Mother is.' There was a slight pause. 'She's coming with us.'

Adele looked up, her eyes steely, her Botox brow unmoving. There was a definite challenge to her eyes, daring Olivia to say something she didn't like.

'Lovely,' Olivia replied, wondering if she had time to nip back to her apartment and grab the remains of the limoncello Maria had brought. She had a feeling she was going to need it.

***

The bridal shop was in Florence and though Olivia didn't get to see much of the city, they did walk past the Cathedral of Santa Maria del Fiore with its famous dome – known as the Duomo. Olivia had wanted to see it for years and couldn't help stopping to look at it in the mid-morning sunshine.

'Olivia, keep up!' shouted Adele and she ran to catch

up with them as they turned down small alleyways away from the tourist-filled restaurants already overflowing with customers.

Adele pushed open the door of the dress shop and waltzed in, greeting the owner with air kisses on each cheek. They spoke in rapid Italian and at one point Olivia was sure she'd been talked about as Adele tilted her head towards her and the owner glanced in her direction then gave Adele sympathetic looks. Sofia had pulled out her phone and was live-streaming something. Olivia hoped she wasn't caught on camera in her 'pyjamas', which she'd resolutely refused to change out of. She sat on one of the plush velvet sofas texting Jacob. He probably wouldn't reply, but it made her feel closer to him to send him something.

Sofia joined her a moment later, making no effort to start a conversation. Unable to endure the awkward silence, she said, 'I take it your mum and this lady know each other?' The two women were still talking and as yet, no one had said a word to Sofia or made a move towards the wedding dresses.

'They've been friends for years. Since childhood.'

'It's a lovely shop.'

'Boutique,' Sofia corrected. 'Signora Panzeri will throw you out if you call it a shop.' Olivia was just about to respond with something sullen and childish when Sofia continued. 'I did it once when I was little, and mother

135

made me wait outside until they were finished talking. They were an hour and a half.'

There'd been plenty of times Olivia had wanted to do the same with Jacob when he was small and wouldn't stop touching things or hiding in the middle of clothes racks so she'd panicked that he'd been snatched up and taken away by a stranger, but she hadn't and never would have sent him outside while she chatted away. She could just picture a young, pretty Sofia standing outside looking in. Adele had clearly been a strict disciplinarian from an early age. No wonder Sofia never argued with her and did as she was told, just as she had done this morning when she'd wanted something else to eat but hadn't been allowed.

'Are you excited?' Olivia asked.

'I am not four years old,' she replied coldly and again the moment of empathy faded. No one could say she wasn't trying to like Sofia. It wasn't her fault Sofia was doing everything she could to be unlikeable. 'Excitement is for children at Christmas. I am not a baby.'

No, Olivia thought. *But you are about to try on your wedding dress.* If she were trying on a wedding dress, one she'd picked out and was going to wear to marry the man she was in love with, she'd be ecstatic. Every fitting would be a moment to celebrate, joyous.

Biting her tongue, she stood and wandered over to the dresses, aware of Signora Panzeri and Adele watching her from the corners of their eyes. She made sure not to touch anything, certain they'd tell her off if she tried. But she couldn't help looking at some of the dresses. The long, 1920s-style ones were her favourites: the simple lines, the beads and fringing. Elegant. There was one in a dusky pink with silver beads criss-crossing the front. She imagined walking down the aisle in it. Nico waiting at the end. And then shook the thought away. She'd already been married once. Done all this shebang. Did she even want to do it again? Yet the image of Nico in a well-cut morning suit, smiling, eyes a little misty with tears had imprinted itself in her brain and wouldn't shift no matter how much she blinked or tried to think of something else – puppies, kittens, Aidan Turner – nothing helped. She ambled back to her seat, wondering what Sofia's gown was like and imagined something close-fitting with spaghetti straps and little decoration. Something a little cold, like her.

After about twenty minutes of talking, Signora Panzeri flapped her hands at an assistant who disappeared for a moment then came out with glasses of prosecco. Sofia was shepherded into the large changing room, about the same size as Olivia's living room in London. While she waited, she pulled out her phone to see Jacob had texted. He'd been playing on the games console Jack had recently bought and later they were watching the football on television. A sudden need to hold her son gripped her tightly and she counted how many days it would be until he was there with her. They could have a swim together, some fun in the pool. Go for walks. She just wanted to hold him, though he'd shake her off.

Signora Panzeri signalled to the assistant to pull back the curtain, which she did as dramatically as an opera star on the stage, to reveal Sofia looking stunning in a romantic champagne-coloured gown. The bronzed skin of her shoulders looked beautiful against the pale fabric in an off-the-shoulder design. The peasant-style sleeves softened the look of the boned corset and the flowing tulle, decorated with a pale silver abstract design, flowed around her legs. There didn't seem to be a train, which Olivia found surprising given Sofia's need for everything to be absolutely extra, but the dress was going to look beautiful in the gardens of Castello Chateau amongst the sunset and candlelight.

There were tears in Sofia's eyes and for a moment, Olivia thought she was about to warm to her, but then the tears dried as she looked at her mother, unsmiling and cold, and fury took over. Sofia's cheeks coloured as Adele set her lips into a small, nasty line. Signora Panzeri stood behind her, holding something at the back of the dress. Olivia imagined the train was about to be unveiled magnificently, but then she noticed the signora was also scowling.

She said something in Italian, but Olivia recognised the world '*problema*'. Signora Panzeri spun Sofia around to show a gap between the two sides of the dress. It wasn't large, less than an inch or so, but clearly it was enough.

Adele marched forwards her voice rising angrily. 'I told you! I told you not to keep eating all those treats! I will tell Mathilde to stop making them, even for the guests. You cannot be trusted to control yourself.'

Nico's dad and brothers weren't going to like that.

'You have me on the strictest diet in the world!' Sofia wailed. 'I'm hungry all the time. I only had a few to stop feeling faint.'

A little dramatic, Olivia thought, then reminded of the story Sofia had told earlier and seeing Adele's mutinous expression, as though Sofia had deliberately sabotaged her own dress fitting, she could believe Adele would be that strict with her daughter. Maybe that was why Sofia seemed so miserable. Olivia had always been miserable whenever she was hungry.

'I have you on a diet so your dress will fit. You decided to order it three sizes smaller than you actually are when one would have been enough.' Olivia couldn't believe this was the response Sofia was getting. 'Stupid girl,' Adele continued.

Tears began to fall from Sofia's cheeks. 'Why do you always have to do this sort of thing? You're the stupid one. I—'

Before any more insults could be thrown, Olivia

stepped in, hoping to calm the waters. 'Can the dress be let out?'

There was an audible gasp from every single person in the room.

'What?' she asked, genuinely perplexed. 'Can't the dress just be let out a little bit if she ordered it three sizes too small?' They were looking at her like she'd committed a cardinal sin, like saying Italian food was fine but, you know, a bit meh.

'Of course we cannot do that,' Sofia cried. 'I'm not looking like a whale on my wedding day. You might not mind, but I do.'

Ignoring the barb, Olivia plunged on. 'You won't look like a whale; you have a gorgeous figure. The thing that makes a bride beautiful is her happiness. That's all that matters.'

'I cannot believe after the venue and everything else, now this.'

'On that we can agree,' Adele said. 'You must have been stress eating,' she added unhelpfully to Sofia. 'A biscotti here, a grissini there.'

Olivia wasn't sure a couple of biscuits or breadsticks were going to make that much difference. To her, it was clear that Sofia had set an unrealistic and, to be perfectly honest, unhealthy target for herself.

'Okay,' she said, still trying to find a solution. 'So perhaps a couple of weeks of good Mediterranean food and exercise and you'll be fine. If you're determined.'

'You can join me,' Sofia replied, nodding. 'It will be good for you.'

After watching her for a second, Signora Panzeri said, 'I can let the dress out a little if needed. A few centimetres – an inch – if absolutely necessary. It won't spoil the lines.'

Despite her comments, she could see the pain under Sofia's features. It was just like when Jacob would say something hurtful but only because he was hurting and didn't know what to do about it. 'You look beautiful,' Olivia said to Sofia as she turned in the mirror to look at the gap. 'Forget that and just look at the front.' Sofia did as she was told and her jaw began to soften. She ran her fingers down the fabric. 'It doesn't matter what size something is. It's how you look in it and how it makes you feel. Happiness and confidence, remember?'

'Do you think so?'

'Definitely. If you feel beautiful, you'll look beautiful.'

Adele took a sip of her prosecco and crossed her arms over her chest. Olivia couldn't believe she didn't have even a few words of comfort for her daughter.

After a few minutes of tinkering, Sofia was able to look at herself properly. They spoke of veils and make-up, hairdos and jewellery, and the atmosphere softened.

'Now,' said Signora Panzeri, snapping her fingers at the assistant who scuttled off into the back of the shop. 'Are you ready to see your bridesmaid dress?'

Realising the question was directed at her, Olivia startled. She should have known she'd be expected to try on her dress. Why hadn't she thought of it? She cringed. She'd thrown on her comfiest knickers and favourite bra that was no longer white but had turned a sort of dove grey from the number of times it had been washed. She never could be bothered to sort her loads into whites, colours and darks as her mum had always suggested. Now she was going to have to display her manky pants in front of the assistant.

Realising they were all waiting for her to respond, Olivia shouted, 'Yes!' a little too enthusiastically. Her voice rang around the shop, bouncing off the windows and coming back at her, about three decibels higher than normal. She cleared her throat and tried again. 'Yes, I'd love to.'

Sofia's dress was so beautiful and spoke to her good taste so she was excited to see what had been chosen for her. Perhaps it would be something simple and elegant. Something to complement her pale skin and red hair. The assistant came back carrying a bright orange sack and Olivia hoped it was just some kind of covering for the dress.

It wasn't.

The assistant let the rest of the dress fall from her arm and held the hanger up high so Olivia could see it in all its glory. And glorious, it most certainly was not.

Oh sweet Jesus.

Neon orange is not a colour for redheads. It makes them look like carrots or Solero ice lollies. And she'd had more than enough of being called carrot top at school. But it wasn't just the colour that was awful, it was the style. High-necked with long-sleeves and no visible waistline – she was going to look like a small, squat orange. A tangerine or clementine. A little orange ball waddling down the aisle before Sofia arrived in all her gorgeousness – there for comedic effect.

Why would Sofia have chosen something like this for her? She cared about visuals and the impression she gave. She was all about image and for once she didn't have her phone out documenting this for her followers. Olivia could only imagine that Sofia didn't plan to have her in any of the pictures, or if she was, she wouldn't be in any that were shared online with her followers. This was clearly a calculated decision. A decision made deliberately to make her look as awful as possible on Sofia's big day. She'd be the ugly sister to her Cinderella.

A slight smile was doing its best to fight the fillers on Adele's top lip and push the corners of her mouth up. She looked like the cat that had got the cream – or the cat that could sniff the cream but wasn't able to move her mouth enough to actually lick it. And Olivia knew this had partly, if not totally, been her idea.

'Can you come with me, please?' the assistant asked,

and Olivia followed as if walking to her doom.

In the changing room, the assistant helped her into the dress, tutting at her comfortable, un-sexy underwear. Clearly, she'd been in training with Signora Panzeri for a while as her lip curled. The woman was clearly unable to hide her disgust, judgement clear on her face. A moment later, not waiting to look at herself in the mirror, Olivia left the changing room and stood on the little block for everyone to examine her orangeness.

A smattering of something passed over Sofia's face but Olivia couldn't tell if it was pity or glee. When she glanced at her mother to read Adele's reaction, Olivia was sure it was amusement, and anger began to fire in the pit of her belly.

'I think it needs a belt,' Signora Panzeri said, rummaging around at a stack of ribbons and pulling a wide, cream satiny one from the pile.

Oh yes! A belt will make all the difference. Let's add a belt.

She took it over and pulled it tightly around Olivia's waist. 'What do you think? *Sì?*'

The effect was unanimously awful. Not only did it emphasise her stomach, she now looked like a traffic cone. Was that a step up or down from a tangerine? She couldn't quite decide. Olivia's cheeks began to turn pink with the embarrassment.

'She will need make-up to stop that,' Adele said

to Sofia. 'She cannot have red cheeks, or she'll look ridiculous.'

Yes, because that was what was going to make her look ridiculous: her blushing. Nothing to do with the hideous dress or the general humiliation she was being put through. Olivia bit the inside of her lip and tried to smile. 'I'm fine. It's just a bit hot in here.'

Sofia must have taken some pity on her as she said, 'No, I don't like that colour ribbon. I think it should be the same colour as the dress.'

That was something at least. Be grateful for small mercies. That's what she told Jacob sometimes when you had to just suck something up and make the best of it. With a matching ribbon tied in a bow she looked very much like a Seventies boho queen. A bright orange one still, but perhaps if she wore her hair down and wavy she might get away with it. She looked at herself again in the mirror. No, she definitely wouldn't get away with it and the thought of Nico seeing her in this made her toes curl. Jack would have a field day and probably get a hernia from laughing. At least she could rely on Jacob to make a non-committal grunting sound, which she could decipher any way she wished and pretend was a compliment.

'So what do you think?' Adele asked.

Olivia smiled, refusing to let Adele enjoy this moment. 'I love it! It's very Seventies hippy. Were you a hippy in the Seventies, Adele? Is that where the inspiration came from?'

Sofia stifled a laugh and turned away. Adele pursed her lips either upset at the accusation she had ever been anything other than elegant and sophisticated or acknowledging that she was old enough to be around in the Seventies. Olivia suspected it was both.

'And the colour?' Adele asked maliciously.

'Gorgeous. I'd never normally go for something like this but it's good to step out of your comfort zone, isn't it? I feel like a ray of sunshine.'

Okay, that might have been a bit much.

Adele had no answer and instead held out her glass for a top-up of prosecco. The assistant all but ran to the counter to pick up the bottle and back to Adele to top it up as quickly as possible.

'Do you mind if I take a selfie? Just to send to my son?' Adele and Sofia shared a worried expression and Sofia nodded. After snapping the picture, Olivia asked, 'Are we done then? Because I'd quite like to start sourcing things for this wedding of yours, Sofia. As we've only got three weeks and I'm basically planning it from scratch.'

This little reminder that they were reliant on her went some way to making her feel a bit better about the dress situation, but not much. Having Adele as a mother-in-law seemed like a recipe for disaster. She just hoped Nico knew what he was doing.

Chapter 11

A couple of days after the dress fitting, Nico and Olivia visited the small town they'd passed when he'd been driving them to Sofia's house the day she arrived. As he drove them in his ridiculous sports car, the sky a matching baby blue with wispy white clouds dotted here and there, she replayed the moment she'd seen the terrible bridesmaid's dress in her head.

After they'd left the shop – sorry, boutique – she'd been subjected to more snide remarks from both of them on the drive back to the villa. Comments about food predominated but there'd also been cracks about her job and how they hoped she was going to be able to pull it all off. She'd told them about her mentor Margot and Adele had wondered if she was available. Olivia had made clear she wasn't. She spent the summers in Provence with her partner, her daughter, her ex-husband and his wife.

After, Sofia had recorded a video in the car, where she'd focused heavily on the fact that she was getting help from an event planner from an exclusive firm in Paris, rather than Olivia. Honestly, you'd have thought the woman could show some gratitude. How could Nico be marrying this woman?

She glanced at him from the corner of her eye. The light caught in his dark hair, turning the strands a chocolatey brown. A smattering of stubble lined his jaw and she wanted to run her fingers over it. She pressed her hands together on her lap and turned to look out of the window. She hadn't mentioned anything to him about how awful the fitting had been. Instead, Olivia had played along that it had been fun and that she was more than happy with the dress and being a bridesmaid.

I will get over him, she told herself repeatedly.

With every lie tumbling from her mouth, she reminded herself she was putting his happiness above her own and that's what friends did. He couldn't have any idea what Sofia and Adele were up to, or he'd have intervened. Again, though, it didn't bode well to Olivia that he and his future wife weren't on the same page.

'So,' Nico said, 'are you ready to explore?'

She beamed back at him. 'So ready. I'm glad you'll be there to translate though. You know how bad I am at languages.'

He giggled, thinking back on some of the mistakes she'd made. 'Yes, it's probably a good thing. We don't need you asking for a penis when what you need is a pencil.'

'Ha ha. I'm so glad you remembered *that* episode.' His quiet chuckling grew into a laugh. 'It wasn't that funny!'

'Oh, it was. Your face was scarlet. Penis!' He started laughing again.

'All right, all right. Don't run us off the road in your amusement.'

Soon the endless fields of the countryside gave way to the town. Built on a hill, it grew out of the horizon naturally, as if it was perfectly right it should be there. Not like London, which loomed and exploded in a mass of concrete and glass. The terracotta roofs reflected the bright sunshine and the remains of a city wall could be seen encircling and protecting the small houses all piled on top of one another.

Nico parked the car, and they began to stroll along the narrow streets. The houses had dark, thick wooden doors and matching shutters but nearly all had terracotta pots and window boxes overflowing with plants outside them, softening their appearance. Others were covered in ivy or framed by bay and olive trees.

Everywhere was alive with the sounds of Italy. People spoke rapid, quick-fire Italian and Vespas and cars could be heard honking their horns in greetings, goodbyes and get-out-of-the-ways. Underneath it all, the melodious sounds of bees buzzing and birds singing mingled with televisions and radios playing from open windows. Olivia revelled in the feeling of life here: a strange mix of relaxation and urgency, of chaos and tranquillity.

'Where shall we start?' asked Nico. 'With coffee?'

'That sounds like a plan.'

Like old times, Olivia thought. On their travels they'd always started each day with a coffee. Mainly to cure a hangover but it was a habit that had lasted. Whenever they saw each other, they'd go out for coffee each morning and talk. She'd missed their conversations, not just about the past but about the future too. They'd always been entirely open with one another. Until now, that was.

Nico led them to a café away from the central shopping area of the town. The noise carried towards them, but the street was peaceful. Outside a large building cut of pale rugged stone, they settled at a table covered with gold and red cloths, a white awning overhead and the Italian flag flying high over the door.

Nico ordered an espresso and Olivia joined him. She'd always loved strong coffee, and no one seemed to make it like the Italians. The owner treated them like old friends and when Nico explained Olivia only spoke English, he immediately reverted to that language so she could join in. How she wished she could do the same. She hated the way so many British people were so bad at learning other languages whereas almost everyone in other countries spoke more than one. It just seemed a bit arrogant to her, but she'd never been any good no matter how hard she tried.

'We need to organise basics first: tables and chairs. That sort of thing. Then it's crockery and cutlery. Glasses. Food and drink. Flowers and decorations. I need to get the flower arch sorted too as that'll take a while to make and I want to sign off any designs before they get started.'

Now she knew she was going to be wearing a hideous orange dress, she'd have to make sure she didn't clash with the flowers.

'You're really good at this, aren't you?'

'Stop sounding so surprised.' After the barrage from Sofia and Adele she was feeling defensive.

'No, no. I'm not. It's just . . . you didn't know what you wanted to do for such a long time and now you look like you've found it.'

'It wasn't so much I didn't know what I wanted to do. I liked organising events and things, even at uni. I organised all our travelling, didn't I?'

He nodded.

'It was just that after having Jacob, things were

151

different. I wanted to be at home with him when he was tiny because it felt right and then when I started trying to get jobs it was really difficult. There wasn't much I could apply for because I didn't want to be out all hours of the day and night and not see him, but I also didn't have the qualifications for anything.' She took another sip of her coffee, preparing herself to admit this next part to him for the first time. She hadn't mentioned it before as it made her feel so ashamed, and she worried that part of it was actually true. 'And I'm sure a lot of interviewers thought I was a flake. That I'd screwed up my life by having a baby at eighteen and wouldn't be worth a shot because I'd probably leave after two minutes or get sacked for being incompetent.'

His brow furrowed. 'You've never said anything like that to me before, Olive.'

She shrugged.

'Why didn't you tell me?'

'I don't know,' she replied honestly with a sigh, but it was good to have said it to him now.

'If anyone treated you like that, Olive, it was because they had the problem, not you. If they'd known you—'

'Yeah, but they didn't, did they? It was their job to make a snap decision about me and my past—'

'Is the past, Olivia. It's done with now.' He smiled and she felt a warmth grow inside her. He'd always known just what to say and she hoped that perhaps he too had come to accept her life choices. 'I'm very impressed with your plans for the wedding and I trust you completely to have it all in hand.'

'You do?'

'Absolutely. And so does Sofia.'

Was that strictly true? Once again, he seemed to have no idea of the real Sofia. Or perhaps he saw the real Sofia and Olivia only saw a demon version. Regardless, it was time to get started.

'In that case—' Olivia rose. 'We better get going.' Nico stood too and they moved away from the table. '*Grazie*,' she called over her shoulder to the owner who waved them off.

'That's not bad,' Nico said with a grin. 'Not bad at all. Better than shouting the name of a magazine at random people.'

'Thank you,' she replied, ignoring his teasing. 'See, I'm trying, even if some other Brits don't.'

'You've always been too stubborn to give up.' He wrapped an arm around her shoulder as they walked, and the feel of his skin against hers sent her body tingling. There was no sign that he'd felt it too and she didn't know whether to be relieved or miserable, then he started giggling and muttering 'penis' under his breath and both emotions were overtaken by embarrassment as she pushed him away and then began laughing too.

The narrow alley opened up into the main shopping

area of the town and despite her plans to do things in an orderly fashion, Olivia was drawn to the beautiful flower stall taking up a whole corner. The busy square was surrounded on all sides by a mixture of squished-in houses and larger, grander buildings. Their flat walls of sand-coloured stone were topped with crenelations, arched windows reflecting the sun. One even had a clock tower reaching up into the sky. Groups of people mingled here and there, chatting on doorsteps. An older woman swept hers with a thick brush while gesticulating to a neighbour as she spoke. Once again, she was distracted by the bright blooms of the flowers that stood out against the muted colour of the stone. She'd never seen anything quite like it and didn't know if it was the bright sunshine making the flowers more vibrant or if everything was just bolder and more beautiful in Italy.

'Nico!' she gasped, pointing. 'We have to go over there first.'

Matching her smile with one as wide as his own, Nico gestured for her to lead the way.

'*Ciao*! *Buongiorno*!' the owner called out as they walked towards the vast array of blossoms and greenery. She was a young lady with tumbling dark hair and dark eyebrows that framed her smiling eyes.

'How do I say everything looks beautiful in Italian?'

Nico told her and she repeated the phrase as best she could.

'*Grazie*. Thank you.'

'Oh dear, was my accent so bad you could tell I'm British?'

'No! Not at all. You said it very beautifully.'

Olivia smiled widely in response, beaming with pride.

'Can I help you with something? Are you looking for a particular flower?'

'I don't know, to be honest,' Olivia admitted, nervously playing with her lip. She glanced at Nico for his opinion and was surprised to see him watching her. He turned away to study one of the flowers as soon as their eyes met. He looked embarrassed. Had she done something wrong? Was it rude to play with her lip in public in Italy? She knew that different countries found different things offensive, but the stallholder didn't seem annoyed. 'What flowers had Sofia ordered from the other venue? I didn't ask her before we came out as it wasn't on my list to sort today.'

'She doesn't care. She just told them she wanted everything white or cream and big.'

'Right.' She supposed it was a good thing as she could choose whatever she liked. She surveyed the array in front of her. 'Do you do wedding flowers?'

'Of course, when is the wedding? Is it for you two?'

This time she was the one to wave her hands around and refute the accusation, her cheeks burning. 'No, not us. I'm his friend, that's all. No, he's getting married to someone else.' He was back looking at her and, unable to stand his gaze and the unnerving look in his eye, she bent down to sniff the bright red flower in front of her. Eventually, when her nose was tingling so much she might sneeze, she stood back up. 'The wedding's in just over two weeks' time. I know it's short notice, but could you do something?'

'Hmm.' The stallholder called to another woman of a similar age and they spoke in their native tongue. After a slightly frenzied-sounding conversation, they both nodded. 'Yes, I think so. What exactly do you want?'

As Olivia outlined her ideas for the table flowers, the flower arch and some other arrangements in the garden of Castello Chateau, the woman took notes on her phone. 'And the types of flowers? I can show you what we've done before. Here—' She turned her phone and brought up an Instagram account, flicking through different pictures. Olivia stopped as one particular display caught her eye. It was perfect for the tables. Small and compact and not too large that people wouldn't be able to see each other.

'This is beautiful,' she exclaimed. 'Elegant but so pretty.'

'Thank you. We often find table decorations can be so large they disrupt people's enjoyment of the evening. They are . . . how you say . . .'

She said something in Italian and Nico translated. 'Blockers.'

Olivia nodded enthusiastically. 'Yes! But these will be perfect. Have you heard of Castello Chateau?'

'The strange French and Italian place? I didn't know they were doing weddings.'

'They're just starting. I think we're their first. I mean – Nico and Sofia will be their first.' Embarrassment at her slip burnt her cheeks and from the corner of her eye she caught Nico visibly swallowing.

'I will have to go up and introduce myself.'

'I'll make sure to tell them all about you, too.' Olivia smiled.

Olivia also preliminarily booked some bouquets but said she'd have to check with Sofia first. After they'd exchanged details, Olivia went away smiling.

When they were far enough away from the stall, Olivia said, 'Sorry about that. The whole sounding like it was our wedding. I didn't mean to. I just meant—'

'I know what you meant,' Nico replied with a smile, though it was only skin-deep. Inwardly, she cursed. She had to be more careful with what she said.

'Well that's one thing we can tick off the list,' she said with extra brightness, hoping to move the conversation on. 'And it isn't even half past ten yet.'

'Not a bad start to the morning.'

'Not bad at all.'

They shared a genuine smile, the awkwardness forgotten, and as they walked away, she had to resist the urge to slip her hand into his. It was there, right beside her, their fingers almost touching, and the pull felt so natural. Fighting it was like fighting the urge to sneeze or cough. Her body craved it. But she reminded herself firmly those feelings were very one-sided. Still, her brain muttered to itself: *if only he felt it too.*

'So what's next?' he asked, tucking his hands into his jeans pockets.

'I think we need to sort out a caterer, but I've struggled to find one that isn't already booked up. I'm hoping we can get a local restaurant to do something.'

'Actually,' Nico said, stopping and turning towards her. 'I might be able to help with that. Follow me.'

This time, he did take her hand and the thrill it sent into her body ricocheted around until she thought she might explode. He led her down some more side streets to a restaurant called Trattoria Mario. It was smaller than the café they'd sat at earlier and her hopes weren't high that they'd be able to deal with something as big as a wedding. Sofia had already confirmed the menu from the original place and Olivia was hoping to match it or at least do something similar. Would somewhere this small have the capacity for that?

They were greeted as enthusiastically as they had been by Giada, the flower stall owner, but this time by a young man in a crisp shirt. He embraced Nico like a long-lost brother.

'Where have you been? We haven't seen you for months.'

Nico blushed slightly. 'Oh, just around. You know what life is like.'

Olivia's nerves tightened. Nico was lying. She could always tell. Well, nearly always as that night in Bali had proved. But something was definitely up.

'Well, my friend, it is good to see you. Come in and sit. Sit!'

Inside, the trattoria was a little dark but the smells emanating from the kitchen were utterly delicious. Fresh garlic, herbs and onions filled the air and even though it wasn't quite lunchtime, Olivia's mouth began to water. Nico began to introduce the young man, who was eyeing her with interest when another man bustled out of the kitchen. He was tall and slim in bright white chefs' whites with slicked-back blond hair.

'Nico! *Mio amico*, it's good to see you – and who is this?'

'This is my friend Olivia. She's visiting from England.'

'Olivia?' The chef said looking between her and Nico. '*The* Olivia?'

The Olivia? What did that mean? Had Nico told them about her having had a child so young or was it more that they were such old friends?

'Yes,' Nico replied quickly. 'Now say hello.'

The two men stepped forwards ready to embrace her.

159

'I am Peppe,' said the one in the suit, 'and this is Mario.'

'So your name's over the door?' Olivia asked.

'*Sí. Sí*,' Mario replied. 'It's good to meet you at last. We've heard a lot about you.'

'Have you?'

'Of course. The one that—'

'Confused pencil for penis,' Nico said quickly, cutting him off. Mario looked slightly confused then shrugged as Peppe pulled him back.

'Into the kitchen with you. You cannot be trusted around people.' His tone was teasing but Mario did as he was told, smiling all the while. 'Now, what can I get you two to drink?'

'Just a coffee please.'

He stuck his lip out. 'Really? Are you sure?'

'Absolutely,' Nico said. 'And you can join us. We need to talk to you.'

Peppe began to prepare the coffees, telling them to take a seat.

The day was so warm and bright they moved to one of the only tables outside. As she manoeuvred into her seat, she brushed the small orange tree marking the end of their part of the building and the scent rose into the air. It was totally different to oranges in England. Somehow more vibrant and intense.

'This place is nice. Why haven't you been here in a while?' asked Olivia as she watched Nico do the same thing.

'You noticed that, huh?'

'You started blushing.'

He scratched his cheek as if checking if the blush was still there. Then he leaned forwards, glancing inside, checking no one was coming. 'I haven't been here since Sofia and I got together,' he whispered.

'Why not? It seems lovely.'

'She never liked it. We were going to eat here once, got as far as the door but then she saw inside, said it was small and stuffy and wanted to go somewhere else. Luckily I got away before Peppe or Mario saw me. They'd never forgive me if they knew. I've been coming here since I moved to Florence. Peppe and I were at university together though he left to take this place over from his parents. And now he runs it with his husband.'

'So she didn't even taste the food?'

'No. And it's some of the best I've ever had in this region. In fact, maybe we should stay here for lunch. It's already eleven thirty. We could have an early lunch and then carry on with all the wedding stuff.'

'Sounds good to me. The minute I walked in my stomach started rumbling.'

'I'll ask Peppe to recommend something special.'

The alarm that had been sounding ever since she'd met Sofia began to ring again. Nico had excused her behaviour when they'd met as wedding nerves but if this was before they'd got engaged it showed she

161

wasn't just suffering from the stress of the wedding. How could he not see that she wasn't who he thought she was? Or the type of woman he should be with? She toyed with her fingers wishing she could say something.

'So you think these guys could do the wedding?'

'I hope so. Mario is an amazing chef. I just feel bad asking for a favour when it's been such a long time since I saw them.'

'I'm sure they won't mind. Maybe just say that you've been busy though.' *And brief Sofia to be nice when they meet her.*

'Good idea.'

'Coffee's here,' Peppe declared coming to join them. 'Now, what did you want to talk to me about?'

Nico looked to Olivia and she began to explain that Nico was getting married.

'Oh Nico!' Peppe exclaimed, jumping up and gripping Nico so tightly around the shoulders and neck he almost had him in a choke hold. 'I am so happy for you! And for you Olivia. We know all about—'

'Not to me—' she shouted at exactly the same time Nico said: 'Not to Olive! To Sofia Allegretti.'

'Oh.' Peppe sat down, his eyes searching Nico's face, his brow furrowing in confusion. 'Oh.'

Why did everyone keep doing this? It was beyond embarrassing.

'So you two . . . ?'

'I'm their wedding planner,' Olivia replied as Nico dropped his eyes under Peppe's confused stare. 'The original venue has fallen through and we were hoping Trattoria Mario would do the food for the new wedding. She showed him the menu from the other place. 'It doesn't have to be exactly the same. This is just what Sofia – the bride – had originally chosen but—'

'This menu is so old-fashioned,' he declared before taking a giant gulp of coffee that cleared his cup in one go. 'We could do something so much better. A mix of traditional and modern. You know how Mario likes to play with his food. In a good way,' he added touching Olivia's arm in a friendly, conspiratorial gesture. Despite the confusion earlier, she was warming to Peppe immediately. She also loved his 'can-do' attitude. She wasn't in the business of negativity, especially working to such a tight timescale.

'What changes would you suggest?'

'Now, let's see . . .' He perused the menu, then called into the trattoria. 'Mario? Mario, come here.'

A moment later, he appeared, wiping his hands on a cloth that he then tucked into the belt of his apron. 'One minute you send me away the next you call me back again. Make up your mind!'

'Sit. We have weddings to discuss.'

'Nico and Olive?' The sheer joy on his face made Olivia dip her head. 'How wonder—'

'No! Nico and a lady called Sofia.'

'Sofia?'

'Who I'm sure is wonderful.'

He was wrong, Olivia added internally then told herself off.

'Anyway, what can we do about the food? This is what they were originally having. Don't ask questions, I'll tell you all about it later.'

'We are catering?' Mario asked. Peppe nodded slightly solemnly, in Olivia's opinion. 'Then I would swap bruschetta for starters and change to a wild mushroom raviolini with truffle oil. So intense you only need a little of it and so elegant.'

'And then?' Peppe prompted, smiling with pride at his husband.

'Not everyone likes fish. Are you sure you want that for your main course? Is there an alternative?'

'I don't think so,' Nico replied.

Clearly Sofia had wanted fish so that's what people were going to have. She couldn't help but wonder if Adele had had a hand in that decision, not wanting her daughter to eat anything too fattening.

'Hmm . . .' Mario thought for a moment. 'Okay, so maybe have fish and something like beef. And for the *contorno*—'

164

'Side dishes,' explained Nico to Olivia.

'*Sí*. Side dishes—' He smiled at Olivia. 'We can keep the sweet baby carrots but maybe add chargrilled aubergines too? And maybe a sauce that will work with both fish and beef. A red wine sauce? Made with local chianti.'

'It's making me hungry already,' she replied, her mouth watering. The wedding itself was going to be painful and heart-breaking but at least she'd be able to comfort herself afterwards with this delicious feast. 'And for dessert? Desserts are my favourite I can't lie.'

'A woman after my own heart,' he said with a grin. 'We must have a *millefoglie*. It's tradition. I cannot believe it isn't on here.' Olivia cast a glance at Nico, but he didn't make any objection. He didn't seem to know why it wasn't on there either. 'What we can do is have small, individual desserts – some panna cotta, some tiramisu, some *millefoglie*. We won't plate them, we'll put trays and trays of different ones on the tables and people can help themselves. That way it is more modern and relaxed. Yes, Nico?'

'It sounds wonderful.'

'Absolutely wonderful,' Olivia added. 'We can even decorate the table with some food too. Pomegranates, huge bunches of grapes and strawberries.'

'Yes, yes! Wonderful idea. I like her,' Mario said to Nico and Peppe. 'I knew I would.'

She looked at Nico for an explanation, but he offered none. She could only think she'd been mentioned over the years when Nico had told them anecdotes of his youth and the things they'd gotten up to.

'And you're sure you can do it?' Nico asked. 'It isn't too late notice?'

'Of course. You are our friend! Both of you. We feel we know you already, Olivia. We'll be proud to. Now, what would you like for lunch?'

'Can you surprise us?' Nico turned to Olivia for approval and she nodded in agreement.

The two men disappeared inside, and Olivia settled back into her seat, grateful a huge item could be ticked off her list. After all Mario had said, she was more certain than ever this wedding was going to be a success. An Insta-worthy one at that. She'd email Margot later and update her on progress. The only thing she wished was that people would stop thinking it was her marrying Nico. Every time they did it was like a giant knife being stabbed in her heart.

'Are you okay?' Nico asked, eyes crinkling in concern.

'Of course,' she replied, sipping the dregs of her coffee. 'Are you?'

'Yes, yes.' But as he glanced back inside the trattoria, she had a feeling he was lying.

'Don't feel guilty about not seeing them for a while.

Life is like that. They'll understand. That is what you were thinking about wasn't it?'

'Yes, yes!' he replied, dropping his eyes and running his hand down his top. 'Yes. It was.'

Another lie? She couldn't really tell anymore.

Chapter 12

Maria wiped the tears from her eyes as she rolled back onto the sun lounger. Her wet hair was plastered to her face and the towel underneath her rucked up as she squirmed and rolled about.

'It's really not that funny,' Olivia replied, unable to stop her own laughter bubbling beneath the surface.

'You look like . . . you look like . . . a . . . a . . . I don't even know!' She fell into fits of giggles again. 'A giant orange crayon? A . . . a – wait, who was that tall Muppet with the orange hair?'

'Beaker?'

'Yes!' she cried hysterically, jabbing her finger towards

her. 'Beaker! You look like Beaker.'

Olivia slid her phone back into her bag and lay back on the sun lounger, adjusting her sunglasses, feeling her smile lift her mouth. 'Whoa! Beaker's a bit harsh. My hair isn't anywhere near as crazy as his.'

'No, your hair's gorgeous – and your complexion. I've always thought so, but that dress? It's next level.'

'Terrible, isn't it?'

'Really terrible. I once had to wear a hideous bridesmaid's dress, but it wasn't anywhere near as bad as that. I can't believe Sofia chose it. I thought she'd have you in something classy like a column dress or something. You'd have thought she'd want you perfect for her numerous social media posts.'

'I don't think I'm going to be in any, which is absolutely fine with me. I don't need a record of that dress online.'

'Are you really going to wear it.'

'I don't really have much choice, do I?' She dried the last of the moisture from her legs and applied some sunscreen. 'It's what Sofia wants, which means it's what Nico wants, which means I have to because I'm his best friend.'

'Wow. There's a lot to unpack there.'

'There is, but not today, okay?'

'Fair enough.' She sipped a cool glass of wine and soaked up the late afternoon warmth.

The temperature was sizzling and Olivia alternated a

169

dip in the pool with a stint reading on her sun lounger. The sky overhead was a bright azure-blue, clouds lazily floating across it and a slight hint of a breeze that did nothing to fight the warmth of the day. The long rectangular pool with water shimmering in the light was surrounded by pale white flagstones. They sat the opposite side to the view so they could see out over the small, ornate wall, complete with overflowing stone urns full of flowers, to the green vista around them.

Though the organisation for the wedding had been all guns blazing, Nico had insisted that Olivia take the afternoon to relax and unwind. Since they'd been to the restaurant, they'd organised a supplier of tables and chairs, and all the crockery, cutlery and glasses they were going to need, as well as table linen and napkins. Apart from a few minor wrong turns and a lot of ringing people and trying to use her terrible Italian, things were going well, even if she did say so herself.

The only major problem so far was that while Sofia had been sort of happy with the new dessert menu, she was insisting on a large cake to cut with Nico. Apparently, it was to be a seminal moment for the wedding photographer to capture. A photographer Olivia was yet to find, but she was working on it. After some searching online, Olivia had arranged for Nico and Sofia to go cake testing the next day at a local bakery so with that out of the way, tomorrow would be spent organising a photographer.

'My stomach hurts,' Maria said, rubbing her stomach.

'It's probably all the laughing you've just done. I'm surprised you didn't pull a muscle.'

'It's not that. It's my food baby.'

'Me too.' Olivia cradled her own rounded tummy. 'I can't believe we ate three hours ago.'

There'd been another enormous family lunch with Nico's dad and brothers, and Sofia and her parents, plus Maria and Olivia as guests of honour. It hadn't been exactly pleasant though the food had, as usual, been delicious. Mathilde really was an amazing cook.

She laid her head back feeling the sun warm her skin and the tensions from lunch receding. While Aldo hadn't made any more cracks about her and Nico being endgame, there'd been a few barbed comments about Sofia's lack of friendliness. More than one member of Nico's family had commented to her that the Allegretti family were not typical Italians with their lack of fun and inability to laugh. A little harsh, Olivia thought, but she couldn't deny they were yet to see if the Allegretti family knew how to let their hair down and have a good time.

Nico hadn't seemed to notice how his family were feeling towards his soon-to-be in-laws. Giovanni had hidden his feelings well and been his usual cheerful self, talking endlessly when the conversation lulled, which it often did if anyone tried to include Adele or Salvatore in it.

171

'So how long have you got left of your sabbatical?' Olivia asked Maria.

'About two months. I'm leaving straight after the wedding and travelling around the rest of Europe. I want to spend some time in Germany and Austria particularly. I've heard Vienna is one of the most beautiful cities in the world.'

'It sounds amazing. We'll have to make sure we keep in touch this time so you can send me lots of pictures.'

She flicked down her sunglasses. 'Why don't you have a sabbatical? Do the same thing?'

Olivia shook her head. 'I did all my sabbaticalling when I had Jacob. Now I'm getting some freedom back with him being older, it's time to focus on my career. This wedding could be a big starting point for me. If it goes well.' She'd hidden these flashes of insecurity from Nico, not wanting to give him something else to worry about, but with Maria she felt that she could be more truthful about her worries and self-doubts. While she was keen to take her chances and grab the opportunities that now came her way, she was still, like everyone, plagued by worries that things would go wrong. Things she didn't have the skills and experience to put right.

'You said it's all going well.'

'It is. And I love working with my friends at the agency I'm at now. It's just my boss is a bit of a harridan and I'd quite like to do my own thing, you know? Be my own boss. Manage my own time. Work from home when Jacob's sick without having to report in to anyone. Starting my own events business would give me all that but it's a big leap financially and career-wise.' She'd thought about this often over the last year but she had a mortgage to pay and Jacob to look after. In the middle of the night when she woke and the thought came tumbling into her head she couldn't shift it, but it seemed like a faraway dream. Something she'd achieve one day, but not any day soon. 'It all sounds mad, doesn't it?'

'Not at all! It's good to have ambition. So what's holding you back?'

'I haven't been doing it for very long and I just don't think people will see me as qualified. I've only been working in events for a couple of years. Most people who go freelance or start their own companies have decades of experience and clients to take with them.'

'I think you have a natural talent for it and that's worth any amount of experience.'

'Really?'

'Definitely. And if it'll actually make your life easier, being your own boss, then it sounds like a great idea.'

Perhaps she could chat to Margot about it later. They were due to catch up soon. Olivia felt her shoulders relax at this affirmation. She also felt them burning and added some more sunscreen as Sofia wafted down in a bikini and kaftan, her hair tied into a topknot. She elegantly draped herself onto a sun lounger next to Olivia.

'Ah, Olivia, there you are. I thought you'd be busy with the wedding.'

'Nico suggested I have the afternoon off to relax.'

'Really?' She shifted, kicking off her shoes and pulling her long legs onto the lounger. 'I'm not sure that's a good idea when there are only two weeks to go.'

'I am technically here on holiday,' she replied. Nico had said all of this at the family lunch. 'And Nico kind of insisted. Didn't you hear him?' She had. Olivia knew she had because she distinctly remembered Adele leaning into Sofia and whispering something. Olivia hadn't caught what it was, but was sure it wasn't very complimentary. Nothing that came out of Adele's mouth was.

Sofia, however, showed no visible signs of a reaction and simply looked around.

Maria waved at her. 'Hello! Are you joining us for the afternoon? I was just going to dive back in for a swim. It's so hot this afternoon, isn't it?'

'No. Chlorine is bad for the hair.' Sofia pushed her fingers into her long, velvety-smooth, honey-blonde hair.

'Oh. Okay. Well you're welcome to.'

'I know I am. This is my house.'

Wow, Olivia thought. *That was cold.*

'Was there something you needed then?' Olivia asked before Maria could say something on the wrong side of polite.

Sofia's phone pinged with some sort of notification and without even looking at Olivia, she pulled it out of her kaftan pocket and began typing furiously. Olivia knew from her own investigations that Sofia had just posted a video of her doing some kind of a 'Get ready with me' video and was now, undoubtedly, responding to the millions of comments. When she'd finished, she said, 'I need to speak to you about tomorrow. The cake tasting. You will have to do it.'

'Me? But it's your wedding. Your wedding cake. You're the one who needs to like it not me.'

She shook her head. 'I won't be eating any.'

Maria started and sat forward. 'But it's your wedding day. You have to eat some of *your* wedding cake on *your* wedding day. That's the law.'

'I won't be,' she barked back.

'But—'

She held up a solitary finger, pausing Maria while she turned her attention back to her phone and replied again to messages. Maria stared open-mouthed in response, her eyes darting to Olivia's behind the dark lenses of her sunglasses.

Eventually, she turned back to them. 'And I can't afford to eat any now anyway. Not when there is so little time left.' Her tone was harsh and cold but having seen her reaction at the dress fitting, Olivia felt it was coming more from fear and embarrassment than from anger. Had

Adele told her she wasn't to eat anything nice? Olivia could well believe she might and that she'd be watching her like a hawk too. She felt another flash of sympathy for her.

'It's only a tasting,' Olivia replied gently, touching her arm. 'You won't be eating lots of cake, just a few little mouthfuls to see what you like and what you don't. It could be fun for you and Nico.'

Sofia stared at her hand as if unable to understand why it was there. Though Olivia didn't have millions of friends, she had a few good ones who were there for her when she needed them, giving hugs and letting her cry on their shoulders. It seemed Sofia didn't have anyone like that. Just her controlling mother and a troupe of social media followers who couldn't actually be around when she needed support.

'A couple of mouthfuls of cake won't make a difference, and you and Nico haven't spent much time together since we all arrived.'

This observation had suddenly occurred to her last night. She'd spent more time with Nico looking at suppliers than Sofia had recently. It made her feel awkward, though neither of them seemed bothered by it. Still, she didn't want it to become a problem or be accused of being one herself.

Sofia suddenly shifted, moving her arm away so Olivia's hand slipped down onto the plastic armrest of the sun lounger. 'Nico and I are fine. Not that it's any of your business. I just don't want to go and eat cake when I have a million other things to do. You might be sorting out the venue but there are other wedding things to take care of. Make-up, hair, an outfit to go on honeymoon in. You're not the only one organising things, Olivia. I just don't need to waste my time tasting cake I won't even eat. Now can you do this for me or not?'

'If it's really what you want,' Olivia replied calmly. Luckily she'd dealt with clients similar to Sofia before, but none so far had been quite as taxing.

'Good. *Grazie*.' She stood up and strode away leaving Olivia to fall back into her chair. She turned to Maria who shrugged in response.

'I take it back, she's not only not suited to Nico, she's also a complete self-centred, rude—'

Olivia coughed, her eyes widening and Maria's face froze in panic.

'Is Adele behind me?'

'No, I was just getting my own back for earlier.'

'What?' Maria laughed and threw her damp towel at her. 'I still can't see it. I know they say men are from Mars and women are from Venus, but honestly, I think she's from one of the circles of hell and Nico's from . . . I don't know where.'

'South London.'

They giggled again but the relaxing atmosphere

177

that had existed before Sofia arrived had completely disappeared. Olivia took a long slug of her wine, trying to push down the guilt building inside. The more time she spent with Sofia the less she liked her and the worse her fears became. Yet she couldn't say anything. Nico clearly wanted to be with Sofia – everyone could see it – and they were getting married! She couldn't ruin someone's wedding.

Still, the thought of spending another day with Nico sent tingles through her body. Was it wrong she was happy that she and Nico were going to get some more time together? She wanted to make the most of every second of this holiday because a dull, niggling pain had begun to develop deep inside that everything would change after this holiday.

Chapter 13

When people said death by cake, Olivia had always thought it'd be the best way to die. Now, as yet another piece of light and fluffy sponge was put in front of her, she was having second thoughts. Perhaps Sofia had been right in her decision not to come after all. Olivia had severely misjudged the number of options that would be available to them and the size of the tasting samples. She'd imagined dainty little squares, but the wedges in front of her were more than generous. Her stomach was full to bursting and the wonderfully exuberant and enthusiastic hostess wasn't taking no for an answer when it came to trying even more flavours.

'I'm going to text Jacob. This might be the last message I ever send to him. I'll tell him I've left him all my worldly belongings and the mortgage. He'll be pleased about that. Is that enough to count for a last will and testament?'

'A text message?' he asked, leaning back in his chair trying to give his flat stomach some room. 'I don't think so. Here, you better write something on this napkin.'

They both laughed as she sent her son another picture of cake. This time he was responding more quickly, clearly jealous of the food she was eating. She also took some pictures for Sofia. She'd been instructed this morning to take lots of beautiful photos for her to share on her channels. It had riled her at the time, but she was quite enjoying sharing them with Jacob too.

Nico widened his eyes in alarm as another sample tray was brought out. Renata spoke little English so Nico was translating as she enthusiastically pointed at the delicious-looking baked goods and listed the ingredients.

'This is pistachio and rose,' Nico repeated in English. 'And that one's apparently champagne.'

'Champagne? You can make a cake taste like champagne? Isn't that illegal in Italy or something? I thought you guys were all about the prosecco.'

'Believe me, we are. I don't think Sofia would like that one.'

'Fine with me.'

She adjusted the waistband of her denim shorts.

180

Perhaps she should have worn a more stretchy fabric. Her playsuit that Sofia thought looked like pyjamas, maybe? She might have got a look of disgust from Bridezilla but right now it would have been worth it. Her current clothes were leaving war wounds.

They'd already tried the traditional flavours of chocolate and vanilla, and something with strawberries that was delicious but Olivia worried would be a little too squishy. Then there'd been chocolate and hazelnut, lemon and orange and something that had tasted like potpourri. She hadn't been a fan of that one.

'This one tastes like Pimm's,' she said, closing her eyes to enjoy the unusual flavour. It was a bit strange in cake form and while Olivia was totally on board with it, she wasn't quite sure anyone else would be. 'How do you say Pimm's in Italian?'

'Pimm's,' Nico replied, deadpan. 'It's a brand name.'

'Oh.' She giggled. 'What do you think of that one?'

Nico pulled a face, then glanced at Renata in terror, relieved to see her cheerfully serving another customer.

'Don't worry, she didn't notice.'

'Good. She might murder me in cake batter. So what do you think to that one?' asked Nico, taking a bite of the pistachio-flavoured one.

'I think I'll need a walk when we've finished here. My digestion's going to need all the help it can get.'

Nico grinned, looking particularly handsome today in

a deep red shirt, the topmost button undone so a little tuft of dark chest hair kissed the top. *Kissing*. She shouldn't think about kissing. Especially not with regards to Nico.

'And for the wedding cake?' he asked.

'I mean, I love chocolate so I'd probably go for that but what does Sofia like? This is really hard without her here. I don't want her to be disappointed.'

'She's not really a dessert person so I don't think she'll care.' His tone was full of sadness. 'But you're right. She should be here to do this. I know she's still disappointed the original venue fell through, but I can't undo that.'

'Don't be too annoyed with her,' Olivia replied. 'I think . . . I don't want to speak out of turn, but I think Adele puts lots of pressure on her. She's got her on quite a strict diet – which is totally unnecessary – and I'm sure that's why she didn't come today. Not because she doesn't care about you or the wedding.'

She couldn't believe she was sticking up for Sofia and congratulated herself on adulting and being a good person. Goodness knows she'd found it hard enough being with Nico, her feelings for him pushing up and into her body at every available opportunity.

'I know. I've told her she is beautiful, and I don't care about her weight or dress size or any of that stuff. I just want to marry her.'

Olivia felt a distinctive squeezing in her heart. It was painful and pitiful at the same time. Why couldn't she just meet another gorgeous Italian man and get over him once and for all? Her life would be so much easier if she could.

'I wish she didn't have as much influence over Sofia as she does.'

'Have you tried talking to her about it?'

'Sometimes, but she just shuts down. She won't hear a word said against either of her parents. Family is everything here.'

Though his mother's death was the reason he'd moved here, they'd never really had the chance to talk about it in detail. Their visits to each other were never quite long enough and with Jacob around, there was always something else to talk about. Olivia decided to take her chance now.

'Are you glad you moved here, Nico? You say family is everything, but you had to leave some of your family in England to connect with your mother's side here. Was it everything you hoped it would be?'

'Yes and no. Of course I missed my dad and brothers – and you – but I loved living the life my mother lived before she moved to England. I was devastated when her mum and dad passed away, but I'm glad I got to spend time with them before that happened. They were so happy when I came here to study.' He lifted his eyes, checking her reaction, knowing how hard it had been for them both that first year.

The closeness they'd always had had fallen away a little

as they navigated a new, long-distance friendship. The first couple of months had been rocky, their conversations short and less intimate but with time they'd found the rhythm of their friendship again.

'The Italian way of life is beautiful,' he continued. 'It's what I'd like for my children, when I have them.'

This was the first time he'd ever mentioned having children and the idea of him and Sofia starting a family almost forced Olivia to open her mouth and lay out her concerns that Sofia wasn't the woman for him. She was getting ever closer to feeling she should, as his friend, but each time she worried about the damage she would do – not just to him or his wedding, but also to their friendship. It could be irretrievably broken. Unfixable. And she wasn't prepared to take that risk. Instead, she picked up a fork and shoved another piece of cake into her mouth. She had to do something to stop herself speaking.

'I thought you were full?'

She mumbled some unintelligible words and Nico chuckled.

'You always knew how to make me laugh, Olive.'

She swallowed before repeating. 'I just wanted to triple-check that was my favourite.'

'And is it?'

'I think so.'

'I do miss England,' he said gently, catching her eye. There was something in his expression she couldn't read.

Something she would have once hoped was a hint at some deeper meaning, that their friendship was more than just platonic, but that couldn't be the case now. Not when she was there to watch him marry someone else. Not when it was clear their one chance had passed them by. 'I miss everyone there.'

Ah, so it wasn't just her. He was referring to everyone: his dad, his brothers, Jacob. Sadness threatened to ruin her mood, but she locked her feelings away. It wasn't anything she didn't already know. Her love for him had always been decidedly one-sided.

'Shall we make a decision and go for a walk?' he asked. 'If I eat any more I might actually die.'

'Yes. What do you think? I mean I like chocolate but if Sofia isn't a chocolate person, then we should probably go for plain vanilla or something.'

'Okay, let's go for vanilla.' He tapped his fingers on the table. 'You can't really go wrong with that, and we have all the other smaller desserts – this is really just for show anyway, isn't it?'

'Decision made then, yes?'

He nodded, wiped his mouth on the napkin and stood up, confirming everything to Renata. Another thing Olivia could tick off her list at least. She couldn't have been more pleased with how things were going.

They left the bakery and Olivia allowed Nico to lead the way. He knew this town, this area, better than she did and he promised a walk that wouldn't make her feel sick while also helping them to work off some of what they'd eaten.

They strolled through the narrow, cobbled streets, the houses barricading them against the midday sun. The muscles in her legs began to burn as the hill grew steeper. Before she knew it, they were reaching the top, a light sweat on her upper lip and prickling her hairline. The houses had thinned out as they reached the remnants of city wall and the view was utterly breathtaking.

Above the terracotta roofs and the tops of the streetlamps the blue horizon lay utterly cloudless before them. A haziness emanated from the ground, disappearing into the warm, unmoving air. Beyond the village, to one side, was a forest, the trees bushy and lush with green leaves and after that, the hills and patchwork of fields she was growing used to in Tuscany flew away into the distance – some smooth, some bobbled here and there with bushes and shrubs.

'Wow. This is something special,' she said as Nico came to rest on the city wall beside her. She stopped looking at his tanned, toned forearms and returned her eyes to the view.

'Feeling better?' he asked, his body dangerously close to hers.

'A bit. I never quite got back into shape after Jacob was born, which is terrible when you think he's thirteen now.'

'He's a good boy. You gave up so much to have him.'

186

'What else could I do? I know there were other options, and I don't judge anyone else making that choice, but it wasn't for me. And marrying Jack didn't turn out great but—'

'He was never the one for you.'

'No, but he was there.' As soon as she said the words, she felt guilty. Nico had had his own life. There was no reason he should have put his career, his education on hold for her. They were friends – nothing more – and it wasn't as if he could have upped and moved back to England. 'And he stuck around,' she added lifting her tone. 'Which is more than some young fathers do. He's improved as he's got older too. And he does love Jacob; he always has. He has his faults but . . .'

An awkward silence descended, and she wished she could take the words back. She could feel Nico bristling but at what she didn't know.

After a moment's contemplative silence, Nico said, 'Will you have room for dinner tonight?' Panic filled her and must have been evident on her face as he laughed. 'Don't worry, I can tell them you need to work or that you want to speak to Jacob. It won't be a problem if you don't join us.'

'Thank you. I'm not sure I need to eat anything ever again. Although saying that I might be hungry later. You know what I'm like.'

'I do.'

There it was again. That little something she couldn't read and couldn't decipher. What did it mean? And his tone had changed. It was now laden with what she could only distinguish as regret, but regret about what exactly?

They stood in silence for a while, happy in each other's company. Happy to simply stare at the view, side by side. She didn't really know how long it was that neither of them spoke for, but by the time they did the sweat on her brow had dried and her breathing had returned to normal.

'I'm glad you're here, Olive,' Nico said, edging towards her so his shoulder gently touched hers. 'I've missed you.' He took her hand, wrapping his fingers over her own. Her heart beat hard against her ribs.

'I've missed you too.'

If only he knew how much.

Chapter 14

Castello Chateau looked even more beautiful than the last time they'd visited, and Olivia was more certain than ever it would make the most picture-perfect wedding venue. After a busy morning organising more things for the wedding, the afternoon was drawing into evening, and though the sun was still high and warm, the light was changing, carrying that burnished golden glow she had grown used to over the ten days she'd been there.

With a pen and piece of paper in hand, and Nico with a tape measure, they were planning out the tables and chairs. The wedding party was small but there would be more than enough guests to fill the space.

For a moment, she stood staring at the view, watching it as the sun began to sink lazily in the sky. She could imagine it as Nico had said, with the world bathed in orange, the night drawing in, and flickering candles on the tables. It would look absolutely perfect. Mario and Peppe had already visited that morning and approved the use of the kitchen, to Francesca and Angelo's delight. They would do as much prep as they could beforehand so the work at Castello Chateau was minimal. The two couples had warmed to each other immediately and Olivia prided herself on connecting the two businesses in a way she hoped would benefit them both as Castello Chateau took off as a wedding venue. She'd also praised Giada and her flowers so the list of vendors connecting through her was growing. Having got to know the delightful Francesca and Angelo a bit more, she was happy to do whatever she could to support them and their growing business.

'Olive?' Nico called. His voice sounded far away as she brought herself back to the task at hand. 'Olive? What do you want me to measure now?'

'I need to give Giada the measurements for the flower arch.'

'So?'

'So—' She walked towards him. 'Two of you stood together like this—' She turned so she and Nico were shoulder to shoulder, facing where the celebrant would be. They were so close the bare skin of her arms was touching his and when they turned to face each other, she could feel herself transported to a moment that could have been. Their eyes rose to each other's, and the world closed in around her. Her hands were clasped in front of her clutching her pen and paper as if she were clutching a bouquet and her stomach flipped, somersaulting over and over, wishing it were she and Nico getting married. The thought clogged her throat and as, under his unwavering gaze, it grew too strong, she turned to look forwards again.

'Umm—' She began trying to calm herself enough to think straight. 'I think we need it a bit wider so people can actually see you.'

'Yeah. Yeah of course.'

As he didn't move, she took a step away from him. 'About here maybe?' Her voice was tremulous, and she cleared her throat, pretending to cough. Nico released the tape measure and Olivia noted down the width and then the height they required.

'What's next?' Nico asked, his eyes focused on the tape measure as it wound back in.

In her mind's eye, she saw the chairs for the ceremony set out in a semicircle. For the purposes of planning, they were using a few old wooden chairs from the chateau and were counting along. 'Twenty on either side should be fine, shouldn't it?'

'Yes, people can sit where they like. We don't need to split into my side and Sofia's.'

There was a distinct weighting towards Nico's family.

'I'd have thought her family would have lots of friends around here,' Olivia said. 'Aren't they one of the most well-known families or something?'

'They've been here a long time, but Sofia's father isn't the most well-liked.'

'Why not?'

'He keeps to himself and he is known as a rather cut-throat businessman.'

'Salvatore?' Olivia asked incredulously, knowing her pronunciation of his name would send shivers down the poor man's spine. Half the time she forgot he was even there. To think he was a cut-throat businessman made her laugh out loud.

'I know he seems quite calm but when it comes to business, there's no stopping him. It's made him a lot of money, but not too many friends. Especially around here. Adele has more friends I think. Though they're mostly in Florence. She grew up there.'

'And Sofia?' She asked the question tentatively, unsure what response she'd get.

'She's made a lot of connections online but when she invited them, most of them couldn't come for one reason or another. She was devastated by it.'

'That's awful.' She felt genuinely sad for Sofia and

resolved to be a good bridesmaid for her, even if she did have to wear that hideous dress and put up with her rudeness. To be left friendless and with Adele as her mother, she'd clearly got the rough end of the stick in some regards.

'That's the trouble with living your life online, I suppose.' Nico shrugged, though she could tell from the sadness infusing his voice he wished he could make it different for Sofia.

'So when you said her parents wanted a small wedding – a family affair – that was a lie?'

'Only a little one,' he replied, shamefaced. 'It's true they didn't want lots of outsiders here, but I knew Sofia would be embarrassed when her family is so small compared to mine.'

'She doesn't have any brothers or sisters?'

'No and to be honest, I don't think Adele would have had her if she'd been given the choice. She clearly didn't want kids and has had as little to do with Sofia as possible. She's only become interested in this wedding as it's a chance for her to show off.'

'You don't like her, do you?'

'Not really, but what good would it do to say anything? Sofia craves her mother's love and I'm sure Adele's done her best.'

Olivia paused, making sure to catch his eye and show her support. 'That's very sweet of you.'

'I'm a very sweet guy.'

She was just about to internally agree when the door of the chateau suddenly burst open and Angelo, arms full of something, boomed towards them.

'Look what I have found. Lights! Lots and lots of lights!'

It was then Olivia noticed his arms were full of different strings of fairy lights and her smile widened. She glanced at Nico to see him grinning too.

'Where shall we hang them?' Angelo asked, catching up with them and slightly out of breath.

'How about around the trees there? That way, they'll frame this wonderful view.' She pointed to where the long table would be set out for the meal. Again, they were using an old, slightly rickety one from the open barn and had placed it in front of the gorgeous Tuscan vista that rolled into the distance. The lights, hung from tree to tree, would frame it beautifully, like the curtain of a stage. 'And it'll look gorgeous in the evening and on into the night.'

'When the party really starts,' Angelo added with a mischievous grin.

She could imagine Nico's family kicking back and relaxing. She and Maria would be up dancing too. Perhaps Sofia's parents would have a formal-looking slow dance but she couldn't imagine shoes being kicked off or Sofia dancing till the sun came up. Although, to be fair, it had been a long time since she'd done anything like that.

There was every possibility she might be in bed by eleven as the tension of planning a wedding in three weeks seeped from her body.

The three of them began hooking up the lights, laughing and joking as they did so. Angelo was great fun to be around, teaching her odd words in Italian, gently correcting her pronunciation. As he told her stories, she had the distinct impression he'd been rather a tearaway in his youth. He plugged the lights into a socket in the small, open barn to the side and they burst into life in a flash of twinkling glory. Though it wasn't completely dark yet, they still glimmered in the evening light.

'Oh, Angelo! It looks wonderful. Thank you!'

'It's no problem. They were just sitting there. I'm glad to see them go to good use.'

'We have guests,' Francesca called from the small terrace and the three of them turned to see Sofia and Adele. Sofia's usually hard face was softer, as though a smile was starting somewhere in her body, hoping to get out, but Adele's arms were folded in front of her.

Olivia's heart sank. She'd been having such a nice evening so far. Adele's lip had curled already and whatever had been happening with Sofia's expression had clearly stopped as it was now on its way to grumpy as they walked past the orange trees and down into the garden area.

'We thought we better come and see what is happening,' Adele said, eyeing Olivia suspiciously, as though she had really been just sitting on her bum all day and not running around like a lunatic trying to organise a wedding in the shortest timescale known to mankind.

'*Buonasera signora*,' Angelo said, shaking Adele's hand warmly. She didn't look impressed. Sofia smiled a little when he greeted her but was as cold and standoffish as usual.

Olivia found herself growing angry at their unexpected arrival. They'd given no indication they'd be coming by at breakfast that morning and she and Nico had been out all day. With everything everyone was doing for them, she had hoped they might show a little bit of appreciation but it seemed it was beyond them. As Francesca shared a worried glance with Angelo, Olivia stuck on a reassuring smile.

'Adele, Sofia, what do you think? Isn't it a gorgeous place?'

Adele didn't answer, but Sofia smiled a genuine smile. 'I'm impressed. It's going to be wonderful.'

'Do you think so?' Olivia couldn't believe the praise was actually coming from Bridezilla. As if to prove she meant it, Sofia took out her phone and began to snap some pictures, sending a thrill through Olivia. They'd soon end up online and be shared with her followers.

'Don't forget to tag Olivia,' Nico said, earning a scowl from Adele and a wave of the hand from Sofia as if she were batting away a fly. Olivia shot Nico an appreciative glance.

'Shall I talk you through everything?' she asked Sofia.

'*Sì. Grazie.*'

They began to move away, Adele ambling slowly behind them. She took them back to the front of the house and guided them along the route the guests would take from the front of the chateau, detailing how she planned to decorate the walkway with lanterns and candles. Then, in the garden she got Nico and Sofia to stand side by side, as he and she had done earlier, ignoring the pain in her heart as she described how it would look to everyone else and how beautiful a ceremony it would be. Finally, with the light more navy than gold, she showed them where the wedding breakfast would be as the fairy lights twinkled around them.

'Obviously the rickety table will be replaced with a long one, covered in a white tablecloth decorated with candles and flowers and Mario and Peppe, the new caterers, are helping me source some fruit too. Pomegranates and fat bunches of grapes. I saw it in a shot from another Tuscan villa and it looked wonderful.'

Sofia studied the imaginary table Olivia was gesturing to. 'It will be rustic,' she said, in a tone Olivia wasn't sure how to read. 'But it will be elegant. Simple. I can show my followers I don't need huge chandeliers and an enormous villa like boring footballers.' She began to walk away to a more well-lit spot. 'I'll record something quickly now. Just something quick.'

Without thought or embarrassment, Sofia stood in front of the view and recorded a video, praising the beautiful new location and hinting that the footballer's wedding at the big castello was trashy and just a little bit corny.

'One footballer's wedding is like any other footballer's wedding,' she said to camera. 'But this—' She spun on the spot. 'This will be beautiful, simple and elegant. Classically Italian, which is the only way to get married if you ask me.'

Francesca and Angelo were grinning from ear to ear and Olivia swelled with pride.

'Well,' Adele said, suddenly appearing at Olivia's side and frightening her.

'Argh! Sorry. Sorry—' She held her hand out. 'You made me jump.'

'You are a very strange girl,' she said without any hint of amusement.

'Yes,' Olivia agreed, nodding. 'It's been said before.' Behind Adele she could see Nico giggling.

'I wanted to say, this is—' Adele waved a hand and though Olivia knew she shouldn't really care what Adele thought, she wanted her to be happy all the same. 'It will look very good considering.'

Considering? Considering what? That she wasn't that experienced when it came to organising weddings in three weeks? That the new venue wasn't as luxurious as the old one? What did she mean?

'Umm, thanks.'

Adele nodded and walked away as Nico joined her. 'I think she likes you.'

'She's got a funny way of showing it.'

'Don't worry, she's exactly the same with me.'

Though Francesca and Angelo begged Adele and Sofia to join them for a drink and some canapés, unsurprisingly, they declined and headed back home. Sofia gave Nico a passionate kiss before she left. One that made everyone else say 'Aww' while inside Olivia was screaming 'no!' It went on for far longer than was decent in her opinion.

'I will ask Mathilde to prepare you something for when you get back,' Sofia confirmed and Nico nodded his agreement, giving her one last kiss before she left.

Angelo and Francesca saw them out and returned a moment later with a bottle of limoncello and four small-stemmed shot glasses.

'We must drink to celebrate,' Francesca said, visibly more relaxed now Sofia and Adele had gone, and gone away happy. 'A happy bride makes for a happy wedding.'

'Is that an Italian saying?' Olivia asked.

'It is my saying,' Francesca replied, cheekily. 'And it was true for us, and for our children. And a happy bride also makes for a happy life.'

'I'm sure that's true.' She held her glass out for

Francesca to pour in the pale, potent liquid.

They sat at the rickety table, Nico on the ground while the three of them used the old, not entirely dependable chairs they'd been shunting around the garden all afternoon.

'*Saluti*,' Angelo declared, and they all joined him. 'We are so excited for the wedding. This will do wonders for our new venture. We cannot thank you enough, Olivia. You are a wonder.'

Olivia beamed, happy to be helping them out. 'I wouldn't go that far.'

Nico threw back his head and drank his drink. 'I would.'

They smiled at one another, a magic spell she could feel in the air weaving itself through her. If only it would weave its way into Nico's heart as well. 'I'll make sure to share the pictures,' she said to Angelo. 'Then you can use them on your website too.'

'You are very kind,' Francesca said, standing and touching her shoulder. 'Now, we must go inside. We have much work to do.'

'Hmm?' Angelo looked up, clearly thinking it was time to continue drinking limoncello in the warm night air.

'Yes. Inside. Now.'

'Oh.' He shrugged, smiling and then, leaving the bottle and two of the glasses, Francesca ushered her husband inside as he urged them to finish the bottle.

Olivia felt suddenly exposed. The sky was dark, stars twinkling overhead and the fairy lights were casting a soft white glow over the table's surface.

'I like them,' she said, sipping her limoncello, enjoying the bitter lemon mixed with the sweetened alcohol.

'They're a lovely couple.'

'Hashtag couple goals.'

She turned to see Nico staring at her. She should have looked away but didn't and instead waited for him to do so. When he didn't either, something once again stirred inside her. They seemed to be drawn together, just like they had all those years ago, sat on a beach in Bali. Their eyes met, his sparkling in the light, and she saw her face reflected back in his dark irises, her own longing clear to her. She really wasn't doing a very good job of getting over Nico. In fact, if anything, spending so much time together was making her worse. She flicked her eyes to the smooth curves of his mouth and then, just as she was sure he was moving towards her, he turned away.

Embarrassment burned her skin. What was she thinking? It must have been a trick of the light, the movement of shadows. He was probably just grateful she was there, helping with the wedding, and she'd let her feelings for him override her good sense. Humiliated and tired from the work she'd been putting in for the wedding, she found herself saying, 'Why do you want to marry Sofia?'

Nico's eyes widened, shocked and hurt.

'I'm sorry,' she stammered, wishing now she'd kept her mouth shut. 'It's just . . . she's not what I thought she'd be. You know, the type of person I thought you'd end up with.' She tried to cover her tracks but couldn't find the words.

'Listen, I know you two haven't really hit it off. She took the venue cancellation pretty hard and all this pressure from her mum is making her act different from usual.'

'So what is usual? What do you love about her?' She was struggling to see it, but perhaps if Nico could articulate it, she'd suddenly see what was there between them.

'She can be really funny. Really cool.'

Cool was one thing Olivia was most definitely not. The majority of the time she felt like a frumpy, haggard mum, tired beyond measure. Cool was something she categorically couldn't compete with.

'And I love that I know where I stand with her. She always says what she thinks. Which a lot of people don't.'

Was that a dig at her? There was something in his tone that unsettled her. Over the years, he'd often said she should be more outspoken. That she should have told Jack to leave a long time before she did, but surely Nico understood she was simply trying to make her marriage work. Jack was the father of her child after all. She shook

202

it off, knowing she was probably reading too much into it.

'And she knows what she wants out of life. She wants to make this influencer thing work and she's doing everything she can to make that happen. Some people just coast along and never go after what they want.'

Okay, that was definitely a dig at her, she was sure. Nico had even glanced at her. Yes, there had been times she'd whined at him down the phone but that was when she'd been discovering what it was that made her want to go to work. He'd always wanted to be an architect and the route into that career was pretty clear, but for her, university dropout with babe-in-arms, she'd had to discover what options were open to her. It had taken a little longer; that was all.

'Like me, you mean?'

'I didn't mean that.'

'Didn't you?'

'No.' But his shoulders had tightened and his posture had stiffened as though he'd been caught out.

'I don't believe you.'

Now she was beginning to discover that events were what made her tick, she was thinking more clearly about where she wanted to go next, but with Jacob to consider, there was a lot she couldn't risk. And, in her opinion, it was selfish and narrow-minded of him not to appreciate that too. If he knew anything about her – anything at all – it was that her son was her whole life and he always came first, no matter what.

'Olive—'

'I couldn't go after what I wanted because I had a baby and you don't just give birth to them and it's all done. You have to raise them and that means they come first before the things you want, before the things you dream of. They are absolutely number one and everything else comes second.'

'Olive, I didn't mean you—'

'No?' She slugged back the shot of limoncello. 'Who else do you know who coasted along and didn't go after what they wanted?'

'I meant people in general. Not you personally.'

'Then why did you look over at me? Hmm?'

He didn't have an answer.

'Maria said you were thinking about starting your own business.'

'I am thinking about it.'

'But you didn't tell me? We used to tell each other everything. First. Always.'

'Things are different now though, aren't they? And though I'm thinking about it, there's a lot to weigh up. I was going to speak to you about it after I've spoken to Margot, my mentor. I wanted her advice. To know if she thinks it's a good idea. I'd have thought you'd be pleased I was doing my homework and not making rash decisions.' She shook her head. 'We should head back.' She stood and, finding her bag, shoved the piece of paper with her plan of the garden into it along with the tape measure.

'Olive—'

'I'm tired and I want to go to bed. I've been running around for the last week trying to sort out your wedding. You'll have to make my excuses to Sofia and Adele for not popping into the house. I just – I just can't tonight.'

He rose and the pain they both felt seemed to mix in the air between them as he scooped up his car keys. 'Olive, please, I didn't mean—' He made one last attempt to change how the night would end but it was no use.

Olivia tried to take comfort from it. In a way, it would at least make it a lot easier to get over him. Knowing now that that was what he really thought of her life and the choices she'd made, how could she remain in love with him?

From the corner of her eye she caught him glancing at her but she walked ahead across the garden and around to the front of the house without saying another word. What more was there left to say anyway?

Chapter 15

Nico pulled up in front of the villa and Olivia undid her seatbelt. The journey had been completed in silence with only the radio playing. Olivia noticed it was a playlist of Nico's favourite songs, some from their childhood. Ones that had marked significant moments in their lives and evoked special memories. Though she wanted to comment, make jokes and reminisce about old times, the words floating in her mouth, eager to be released, she clamped her jaw shut. A few songs weren't going to undo the hurt he'd caused her that evening and right now she wasn't ready to offer an olive branch. Feeling so judged, she wasn't sure she ever would be.

Was this Sofia's influence? The man she'd always known would never have said something like that to her. She'd always known there were choices he'd disagreed with (not keeping her baby. He'd always been one hundred per cent behind her on that score); marrying Jack though, had been one he had disagreed with.

'Olive—' he said as she climbed out.

Her reply was a closed door.

The evening had grown cooler and as the dark surrounded them, a pale moon shining overhead, she heard the chirping of crickets in the grass and the odd call of sleepless birds. Giovanni, Nico's dad, leaned against the wall, having a cigarette. He smiled as he saw her.

'Ah, it is the beautiful Livvy. How—'

'I'm sorry, Giovanni, but I'm not feeling so great. Goodnight.'

He frowned in confusion. She was aware of Nico saying something to him as she unlocked the door to her little holiday home, Hera the cat waiting patiently for her, but couldn't hear what and told herself she didn't care as she closed the door behind her. Let them all get on with their evening. Right now she wanted to call her son and find out what his day had been like. There were still four days until he came to join her and the thought of it sent her heart squeezing unpleasantly. From now on, all the love she had for Nico would be directed into Jacob whether he liked it or not, and he probably wouldn't as he already moaned she fussed over him far too much.

But solitude was not to be her friend tonight. Her phone began to ring and when she saw it was Margot, there was no way she could refuse the call. She put on her most cheerful tone.

'Hi, Margot, how's it going?'

'I am good, my friend.' Her strong French accent coloured her words beautifully but Margot had learned from experience not to bother saying anything in French to Olivia. There'd been some strange misunderstandings at the start of their relationship, which still made Olivia cringe. 'So, how are things with this crazy wedding?'

Crazy was right. Hera rubbed against her legs and she picked her up with one hand, cradling her to her body as she moved to the sofa. When she sat down, Hera turned in a circle before settling next to her. Olivia glided her hand over her and the rhythmic stroking calmed her somewhat. 'So far, so good,' she said cheerfully and began to reel off the things she'd done and the things she had left to do.

'You do not need me at all!' Margot declared happily and Olivia could hear the smile in her voice.

'Well, there is one thing I was thinking about.' Nico's words of earlier, his belief that she'd coasted through life riled her again and though she was nervous to raise the subject, her courage stiffened and she said, 'I was wondering about starting my own business. In events management. I know it would be hard but—'

'It would give you flexibility to be your own boss and look after Jacob, *oui*?'

'*Oui*.' That she could just about manage. 'I'm not saying I want to run some kind of events empire, organising parties for the rich and famous. I just want enough work to pay the bills. Do you think it's too soon?'

'Hmm.' The line went quiet and Olivia's stomach fell. 'No, I don't. You've done amazingly well since I've known you and to organise a wedding in three weeks – from nothing – that is no mean feat. You will just need to sit and plan your finances carefully. Make sure you save for when the business is quiet. Protect yourself. But you're not a stupid woman. In fact, you are one of the most determined, inspirational women I know.'

'I wouldn't go that far,' Olivia replied, pressing a hand to her chest. Tears were misting her vision but she wouldn't let them fall. Margot would immediately be able to tell.

'I would. We are similar, you and I, Olivia. You had your child young. I did too and that comes with sacrifices but you are grabbing hold of life now and if the business fails . . . pffft! Who cares. You go back to working for someone else. What have you got to lose?'

'Nothing, I guess, as long as I plan my finances properly.'

That was another underrated skill stay-at-home mums

gained that was often ignored by employers. When Jack had been out of work, she'd had to manage on a tight budget. Nico had helped sometimes for out-of-the-blue expenses but on a day-to-day basis she'd managed the household finances and got them through. She could do the same now.

'You will be wonderful. Just make sure you choose a good name for your business nothing . . . how you say . . . cheesy.'

'I promise I'll run the options past you first.'

'Good. Then goodnight, *chérie*. Keep me updated on the wedding.'

The glow Olivia felt as she rang off began to fade as the reality of the evening hit her again, the argument with Nico replaying in her head. A few minutes later, as she left Hera on the sofa and surveyed the remaining piece of stale bread and the few slices of cured ham that would have to be her dinner, there was a knock at the door. She closed her eyes, wishing whoever it was would go away, but a second loud whack that almost shattered the windows told her that wasn't going to happen. Olivia rested for a second against the counter, eyes closed, taking a deep breath. If it was Sofia, she'd have to save any moans and groans for tomorrow. Right now she just didn't have the strength. She pushed herself away and opened the door.

'Giovanni. I did say I wasn't feeling great.'

'I know but I didn't believe you. You looked like you needed some comfort.'

'Aren't you supposed to be inside having dinner?'

'I will get something later. Mathilde has promised me some leftovers. I told her I had an urgent call to make.' He smiled at her so warmly, she felt tears sting her eyes and quickly turned to blink them away but it was too late, Giovanni had already noticed. 'Now, now. What's all this?'

'Nothing. It doesn't matter. I'm just missing Jacob that's all.'

'Ah, I remember that feeling well. When Nico first moved to Italy I missed him more than I ever let him know. And he was eighteen at the time, nearly nineteen. You've never been away from Jacob for this long have you?' She shook her head. 'Don't worry, he will be here soon and it is good for him to miss you. He'll appreciate you more when he gets here.'

'I don't have much to offer you, I'm afraid,' Olivia replied wiping her eyes and changing the subject. 'It's basically tea or grappa that I found in the cupboard. No idea how long it's been there.'

'Grappa never goes off,' Giovanni replied, making himself comfortable on the sofa. 'Who is this?' Hera had moved next to him and was padding his leg as he stroked her back.

'That's Hera. Haven't you met her yet? She clearly likes you.'

'Everyone likes me.'

Olivia couldn't find a shot glass. She was pretty sure they were still in the dishwasher from when Maria had come round. So she grabbed two tumblers instead and brought them over, taking the seat opposite him. 'Still smoking then?' She raised one eyebrow in accusation.

'Don't look at me like that!' He buried his head in his hands dramatically. 'I am trying to give up, I promise. It's just so hard.'

'Well, keep trying. You're too important to everyone not to.'

'I promise I will. Once this wedding is out of the way I'll try again.' He raised his glass. '*Saluti*!'

Olivia raised hers and sipped. Considering she'd had more than one potent limoncello on an empty stomach at Castello Chateau, she wasn't sure grappa was such a good idea but she'd spent so many years not daring to drink too much as she had Jacob and couldn't cope with looking after him with a hangover, she might as well enjoy herself now. Plus, she wanted something strong to numb the pain still pulsing inside her.

Giovanni gave a long, satisfied sigh. 'That is good. Now, why are you and Nico arguing?'

Olivia tilted her head. 'Nico told you?'

'No. But I could tell as soon as you both got out of that car. So? This isn't like you two. You've been getting on too well. What's happened?'

212

She had no intention of lying. Giovanni had been the audience for so many of their silly teenage squabbles, he wouldn't judge her. Though this one seemed a lot less silly than many they'd had. 'He said something – it doesn't matter what – and—' Though anger still pulsed, the grappa was helping her relax a little. 'I'm sure he didn't mean to hurt my feelings but he did.'

'Have you told him?'

'Yes but—'

'Good, you must never go to bed on an argument.'

'Isn't that for couples?'

'And for friends too. But definitely for couples.' He suddenly tutted, concern crinkling his brow. He ran his hand over his beard and scratched his chin. Hera batted his hand, wanting it back stroking her. 'What did he say?'

She told him about their conversation, the implication he'd made and then denied.

'I can see why you'd be upset but Nico, he has always been proud of you. I think if he thought you were coasting through life, he would have told you by now. Has he?'

'No,' she admitted. 'Do you think I over-reacted?'

'I think you're missing your son, you're under a great deal of stress trying to organise a wedding in three weeks while you should be on holiday and—' He paused, running his hand over his beard. 'And I think you have the same worries I do.'

'Which are?' She couldn't bring herself to say them first.

He inhaled a deep breath and let it out in a loud sigh. 'I don't like Sofia, Olivia, and I don't think you do either.'

'Is it that obvious?'

'You're hiding it well but I know you. I can see when she is rude or inhospitable that you think the same as me. What am I going to do? I've tried to like her. You have too. We all have.' He cast his arm out, clearly referring to Nico's brothers. 'But she's so cold. So hard. And the mother—' The tut he gave Adele was even more powerful and accompanied by an eyeroll. 'She is awful. Just awful! What am I going to do? My son is kind and funny and full of life! These people they are . . . they're so awful.'

Olivia watched the clear, powerful liquid swirling in her glass, cradling it in both hands. 'There's nothing you can do, Giovanni. He loves her; he wants to marry her. All we can do is be supportive.'

'But it's a mistake!'

'Then he has to be allowed to make it.' She'd made enough of her own over the years and wouldn't have taken kindly to people warning her against things. In fact, in her youth, she would probably have done the opposite just to spite them. Thankfully, it was a trait she'd grown out of. 'He won't thank you – or me – for interfering.'

'But Oli—'

'No buts!' She wagged her finger at him and they both

smiled. 'I know you want to protect him. I know you want him to be happy, but you can't get involved in this.'

'He should be marrying you.' His words were so blunt they caught her off guard, even though she knew that's what everyone thought. They'd made it clear enough over the years and more recently at the family dinner, in the most tactless way possible. 'Why didn't it happen for you two?'

'I wish I knew.' Her confession resulted in a single bushy eyebrow being raised and she quickly moved the conversation on. It would only put Giovanni in an awkward position and she liked him too much for that. 'But it didn't and any chance we had was a long time ago. It's ancient history now.' She reached for the grappa bottle and topped up their glasses. 'This isn't bad, is it?'

Giovanni ignored her question, staring instead at his knees. 'He is so like his mother. Kind, caring. Funny. Do you remember how funny she was?' Olivia nodded as warm memories of being round Nico's house, eating with his family, his mum piling up her plate, making them all giggle as she teased and pretended to chide them filled her. 'Nico reminds me of her. She was the other half to my whole, but Sofia? I cannot see it. She doesn't suit him. They are two opposites, not two halves of the same whole.'

'Well, they say opposites attract.'

'Attract they might, but that doesn't mean they are

meant for each other. Attraction is fleeting. Look at me!'
He signalled to his face. 'I was handsome once, but age
makes us all the same. Elenora loved me and I loved her
no matter how life changed us. Sofia—'

'Nico said she isn't her usual self. She's under a lot
of pressure so maybe she's normally a happy-go-lucky
person.' Subconsciously, she gave herself a pat on the back
for being good and defending Sofia and, by extension,
Nico.

'She never smiles,' Giovanni said gloomily.

Olivia laughed. 'I'm sure she does.'

'No she doesn't. I've told her my best jokes and so
has Aldo and you know how funny he is.' Aldo was
definitely the funniest of Nico's brothers and could grab
the attention of a whole room with one of his stories. 'And
Adele and Salvatore . . . huh! They wouldn't know a joke
if it came up and grabbed their Botoxed cheeks.'

Olivia laughed and, momentarily distracted, asked,
'Does he have Botox too?'

'Of course! How am I to get along with Nico's in-laws
when I don't like them or his bride?'

She swirled the grappa in her glass. 'Bite your tongue
for the sake of your son, Giovanni. It's all any of us can
do.'

After a moment's silence, Giovanni slugged back his
drink and reached out for the bottle, topping up his own
and Olivia's. 'You were the other half to his whole. We

216

could all see that.' She shifted uncomfortably. 'That's why you've been such a big part of his life for such a long time. I just hope that doesn't change after this wedding.'

The horrible, niggling feeling she'd had in the back of her mind suddenly grew louder. The confirmation of her worst fears made it into a stabbing pain that pierced both her head and her heart simultaneously. This was her worst fear and to hear someone else say it only made it more real and more threatening. Because she had Jacob, and Nico was his godfather, she'd been hoping life would continue as normal. He'd call once a month, they'd talk and perhaps Sofia would join the call occasionally, though Olivia had assumed she'd stay away. It was their time. Nico's time with *her* family. But Sofia clearly didn't like her and there was every possibility that once Nico was her husband she wouldn't want him speaking to her.

What if, after the wedding, the calls became less and less frequent? What if they stopped altogether and this marriage meant they'd grow apart for good? Finally go their separate ways? She grew suddenly cold and rubbed her arm. Giovanni seemed to sense it too and reached out, taking her hand in his giant bear paw.

'You two will always be friends, Olivia. He wants you in his life. He always has. I'm sure that won't change. I'm probably just worrying over nothing. Too much ruminating and too much grappa.' She gave a small smile, knowing it wasn't anywhere near convincing enough for the man who had known her for most of her life. A man who knew Nico, and her, so well. But he didn't press. Instead, he said, 'Right. I must go and see what delights the wonderful Mathilde has kept for me. I'll see what she can rustle up for you too.'

'Does she have a soft spot for you, Giovanni?' Olivia raised her eyebrows.

'Of course! Who doesn't? But don't get any ideas.' He wagged his finger at her. 'There'll only be one wedding here in Italy. No one can replace my Elenora.'

Olivia knew that was true. It had been nearly twenty years since she'd passed and Giovanni had never even so much as looked at another woman. She supposed that was love. True love. What it meant to be two sides of the same coin. Her thoughts returned to Nico and she swallowed the lump in her throat. It was time to do what she always did when things got tough. She doubled down, worked even harder. Only this time she'd redouble her efforts to get over him. By the end of this holiday, by the day of this wedding, she'd be cheering him on, her heart empty of Nico and free to love someone else.

Chapter 16

After avoiding Nico all the next day, Olivia dressed and prepared herself to meet him and go hunting for something special for the wedding. The day before, Sofia had grabbed her as soon as she'd left her holiday home, hoping to go for a walk.

'Olivia. I need you to find something special for the cake to stand on.'

'Like a table?' Olivia had enquired, squinting in the sunshine. She'd forgotten her sunglasses and would have to go back in and get them.

'No!' Sofia threw her arms in the air as if Olivia were a complete imbecile. 'A simple cake stand on top of a table won't be good enough. I need something show-stopping and unique.'

'Like what? I'm sorry, Sofia but it's early, I didn't sleep very well and my brain's not functioning yet.'

'Clearly.'

She ignored the barb. 'So what do you want?'

'Something different! I don't know exactly what.'

'And you don't have any pictures or anything for inspiration?'

'No.'

Brilliant.

After this, Sofia had huffed off shouting, 'Just find something,' over her shoulder as she went back inside. Olivia had then stomped off on a long walk, hoping to rid her mind and body of the irritation, but as soon as she returned to the villa it had erupted again. Thankfully, a good night's sleep had followed and today she was in a better mood. Given that everything else had gone well so far, and Margot was supportive of her idea to start her own business, Sofia and her demands weren't going to ruin her mood. She'd dealt with every obstacle thrown at her so far and wasn't about to be beaten by this one. After searching for inspiration online, she had a couple of ideas up her sleeve.

However, it didn't stop the nerves beginning to jangle in her stomach at the thought of seeing Nico today. His words still hurt and her talk with Giovanni hadn't made it any better either. If anything, it had added to her stress over the situation, knowing he was as unhappy at Nico marrying Sofia as she was. She hadn't done very well at putting her love for him behind her but today was a new day. A day, she decided, she'd make headway with that whole thing.

With a final touch of mascara and some lip balm, she went to meet him at the house to continue with wedding preparations.

'Morning, Sofia,' she trilled as she walked into the living room of the Allegretti villa. Sofia looked radiant in a long white column maxi dress that hugged her curves. Adele sat opposite her, watching while she sipped her coffee.

'*Ciao*, Olivia. Are you well?'

The last part she could tell was added on for politeness' sake but she smiled warmly anyway. 'Yes, I'm very well thanks. Looking forward to my son getting here in a couple of days. This is the longest I've ever been away from him. It feels a bit weird.'

Sofia didn't answer and neither did Adele. They simply stared at her as if she were speaking a completely different language. The air in the room began to grow heavy with the awkward silence so that when Nico arrived, looking particularly handsome in pale cream jeans and a dark navy T-shirt, she leapt towards him, forgetting the unease that had existed the day before and in the hours since their argument. She had also forgotten that she was supposed to be quelling any thoughts that veered towards attraction and love and so told herself Nico's outfit was a bit 'meh' and that his aftershave was overpowering and really he'd applied far too much.

'There you are! Brilliant. Right. Let's get going, shall we? I'll wait outside while you say goodbye to Sofia.'

Olivia darted outside leaving Nico staring after her. A minute later, he joined her at the car, frowning.

'What was all that about?'

'All what?'

He pointed back inside the house. 'All that . . . weirdness.'

'What weirdness? I'm just keen to get going that's all.'

'Really?'

He pressed the key fob in his hand and the lights flashed to show the car was unlocked. She climbed in, stuffing her bag down by her feet, but when Nico climbed in, he rested both hands on the wheel and stared in front of him, unmoving.

'Don't worry, my weirdness isn't catching. It just seems to come up when I'm faced with Adele.' He didn't move, or smile, and she worried that the argument of the other night wasn't finished and the day would be spent in awkward and uncomfortable silence. 'Everything all right?' she asked gently.

'No. It's not.'

Great. So he hadn't forgiven her, even though she was trying to forgive him. Suddenly, her heart leapt into her mouth. Was this to do with Giovanni and his concerns about the wedding? Had he said something to Nico? Had he said they were the ones who should get married? Was she in trouble for talking to his father behind his back? She swallowed.

'It's about the other day. Our argument.' Olivia didn't exactly relax, but her worry and tension shifted elsewhere. Nico turned to face her. 'I really didn't mean anything about you. I was just talking in general. I know I've moaned at you before about finding a career, taking time for yourself to discover what you love, but I didn't mean that you coasted. I do know that with Jacob—'

She cut him off. 'It's fine,' she replied, as relief swept through her. 'I know you didn't mean any offence and maybe I was a bit defensive. There've been points when you have disagreed with my choices and I guess it just felt personal at the time.' She had probably been far more defensive because she was spending all her time keeping her emotions in check.

'Even so, it was a stupid thing to say and I'm sorry. Do you forgive me?'

She turned to him, meeting his warm, dark eyes and her heart leapt. *Stop it!* It was a slight palpitation from too much coffee – that was all. 'Of course I do.'

He sagged in relief and before she knew it, his arms

had wrapped around her and he was pulling her in for a hug. She returned the gesture. They'd always hugged it out after arguments. His forehead rested on her shoulder and she could smell the shampoo he used, citrusy bergamot with a hint of spice, similar to his aftershave, which wasn't overpowering after all but tickled her nostrils pleasantly.

Oh give it a rest! she told herself, then the warmth of his hands slipped through the satiny vest top she'd chosen to wear so that it was like he was touching her skin. She assumed they'd pull apart but they didn't straight away, and they stayed there for just a fraction too long until he moved backwards.

'Right,' Olivia said trying to ignore the warmth moving through her body from where his hands had been. *Double down, Olivia. Double. Down.* 'So, where are we going to search for this special cake stand thing that Sofia wants?'

Nico shook his head. 'Nope. Not today.'

'What do you mean no, not today? We need a cake stand, Nico. We need something unique that's still elegant and Insta-worthy and right now, I've no idea where we're going to find anything that fits the bill. Though I've a few ideas I want to talk to you about, but we're not going to be able to just pick something up from the wedding organiser's shop.'

'Olive?'

'Yes?'

'Calm down. We will deal with that tomorrow. Today, we're going to Florence.'

'Well . . . that's good,' she replied, brightening. 'Because they'll probably have antique shops or a market or something where we can try and find this . . . thing.'

'No.' He shook his head again. 'We're going sightseeing.' He looked down at her feet. 'Good, you're wearing trainers. We're going to do lots of walking. And eating and drinking.'

'Sightseeing?' Olivia couldn't keep the smile from her face.

'Yes. We can take Jacob when he arrives, but I wanted to show you the city when it was just the two of us. You and me. You never did get to visit after I moved here.'

'No. I didn't.' She'd been up to her armpits in nappies, bibs and baby bottles. 'Are you sure? Sofia won't mind?'

'Well . . .' He paused, revving the car and turning up the air conditioning. 'I haven't told her. She has enough to worry about and it would only stress her out. We can sort out this strange cake stand thing she wants tomorrow and if all else fails I will tell her we're going to use a table covered in a nice cloth with some flowers around it.'

Rather you than me. 'I don't think Sofia will like that.'

'We can cross that bridge when we come to it. This is my way of saying sorry for being an insensitive idiot. Let's go and have fun. Like old times.'

Olivia's cheeks hurt from smiling. 'It's a good job I

packed a full bottle of sun cream. Come on then, let's get going. There's so much I want to see.'

Gravel spit from underneath the tyres as Nico swung the car around and headed down the drive, out onto the road and on towards Florence. She wondered how much of Tuscany was made up of hills and fields. Most of it, it seemed, but the varying colours of greens and beiges never bored her.

As they reached the city, Olivia pulled down her sunglasses, her mouth hanging open. The tall, pale beige and yellow Renaissance buildings climbed on either side, shutters latched open to let in the air. The streets were full of cars and scooters, the pavements heavy with gorgeous-looking women, stylish men, and shops as far as the eye could see, all framed against the bright blue sky.

When she'd visited with Adele and Sofia, the trip had been rushed and they'd route-marched to the bridal shop – sorry, boutique – and then back to the car and home. Nico was driving slowly, allowing her to enjoy the view and take in everything. The tall tower houses could have been intimidating but the beautiful architecture, the pale white stone of the larger, more impressive buildings gave the city a suave sophistication. Florence had a vibe unlike any other place she'd ever known. Romance seemed to sit on the air in a natural, understated way, almost as if the possibility of falling in love carried in the breeze. Paris might be known as the most romantic city in the world, but she couldn't imagine it ever feeling as romantic as Florence did.

'The Ponte Vecchio,' she shouted, startling Nico a little.

He laughed. 'After coffee, we'll walk along it. And I'll take you to the Duomo and to the Uffizi.'

'And the Palazzo Vecchio. I have to see that too.'

'I'll find somewhere to park then we'll walk along the Arno and find somewhere for coffee and a snack. Did you have breakfast this morning?'

She hadn't. She'd been too nervous about seeing him and after spouting on about Jacob to Adele and Sofia, she'd been quite happy to leg it and put up with being hungry. She was pleased they'd put their argument behind them because, truth be told, there was no one she would rather visit Florence with.

After winding through more charming streets, Nico parked and then they walked along the river bank over wide, grey-slabbed streets and under a tunnel of beautiful smooth cream archways until they reached a café. Occasionally she'd look up and see the archways joining a building, a small window peering out of the tiny bridge-like structure, overlooking the street. How wonderful it must be to live somewhere like this, she thought. She could spend a lifetime in Florence and never get bored of it, or the food.

'Shall we sit here?' Nico asked, pointing to a small café

with a red awning and tables outside covered in dark red tablecloths.

'If the tablecloth supplier falls through, do you think we can run around Florence nicking them off cafés and restaurants?'

'As much as I like that plan, I'm not sure I fancy a criminal record.'

'Good point.'

They sat down and ordered espressos. Nico also ordered *bombolicini*.

'What are they?' Olivia asked, eyeing the menu and trying to make up her mind.

'They're doughnut holes and these ones are filled with cream.'

'Yum. I think I'm going to go for . . .' She just couldn't decide. Everything sounded so good. The handsome Italian waiter smiled at her indulgently but the pressure was on. Her pronunciation was always poor but she wasn't the type to let a man order for her. She had a stab at, '*coccoli e stracchino*' a fried dough served with prosciutto and local cream cheese. 'Sorry,' she added to the waiter. 'I know I'm murdering your language.'

'You sounded like an Italian,' he replied, flashing a smile that she could well imagine would make any woman weak at the knees. It would have her, if her heart wasn't so stubborn. No matter how hard she tried, it wouldn't let go of her feelings for Nico and as she sat opposite him, chatting through plans for what to see next and where to eat lunch, or falling into a perfectly comfortable silence as they watched the tourists go by, the world felt right. Whenever she was with him her heart felt balanced, like it was finally on an even keel. She took a sip of the strong black coffee, trying to shake the thoughts away.

'Is everything okay?' Nico asked. 'You were frowning.'

'Was I?' She laughed, wishing she didn't let her emotions play out so clearly on her face. 'I was just thinking about the wedding and what's left to do.'

'You've done a wonderful job, Olive. All the main things are sorted. We're onto little things now. Little things that don't matter if they don't get done.'

'I just keep thinking that I'm missing something.'

'The only thing you are missing is Jacob.' She smiled and looked over the rim of her coffee cup as his words hit home. 'I'm looking forward to seeing him too. And Jack.'

'No you're not.' Olivia laughed. 'I mean, I know you're looking forward to seeing Jacob but you've never liked Jack – admit it.'

'I did try!' he exclaimed, relaxing into his chair. 'I just knew he was never the right man for you.'

'I remember when you told me that.' She placed her cup down and looked out over the river. The numerous bridges that ran over it were reflected in the still water. It was blue and sparkling in the sunlight unlike the Thames, which was normally a muddy brown colour. 'You were right.'

She'd hated him at the time. For about two weeks. And then they'd begun talking again and all had been forgiven. She knew he was simply looking out for her. She thought again about repaying the favour and spilling her concerns over Sofia, but the wedding was only ten days away. What good would it do? It would ruin their perfect day together. A day that hadn't even begun yet.

'Really?' he asked, sitting back in his chair. 'You've never said that before. Why not?'

Their food was delivered and she was saved from answering, tucking into the delicious doughy cheesy mess. Her taste buds tingled and as Nico, who had always had a sweet tooth, tucked into his quite frankly teenager-on-holiday type breakfast the conversation moved on.

Nico told her about the buildings, about Renaissance architecture, the Medicis and the history of this beautiful city. Before long, they'd left the café and Nico had led them to the cathedral Santa Maria del Fiore with its famous domed tower known as the Duomo. The marble walls of the cathedral and terracotta tiles of the dome glinted in the sun, taking her breath away.

'Can we go inside?' she asked excitedly.

'Of course. A trip to Florence wouldn't be complete without a look inside its most famous cathedral.'

'And then to the Uffizi, yes?'

He laughed. 'If you like. Though I might have to stop for lunch at some point.'

'You've only just eaten.'

'Yes, but you need lots of sustenance for sightseeing.'

By the time they had visited everything she wanted to see, her feet were aching, but it had been one of the most wonderful days of her life. They'd strolled around the beautiful city, not always taking the most direct route, but exploring and enjoying the ambience of Florence, its food and culture.

He'd watched her constantly revelling in her childlike glee at seeing works of art she'd only ever read about, or touching the walls of buildings she'd always longed to visit since the day he'd said he was moving away. At least, that's what she supposed he was watching her for. Occasionally she'd caught him looking when she'd least expected it, assuming she was going a bit over the top. He'd look quickly away, blushing slightly sometimes when their eyes met, and she'd make a mental note to tone it down a bit.

Thanks to constant reminders from Nico, she'd remembered to apply sunscreen so neither her cheeks or shoulders were bright pink, which would make Sofia happy and Olivia too, if she were honest. Pink and orange weren't a great combination, and she was going to look awful enough in that bridesmaid dress.

As they walked back to the car, the evening sun turning

from a bright, whitish yellow to a blazing orange, clouds gathering and the warm breeze growing enough to blow strands of hair into her face, they paused once more.

'I can see why you moved here,' she said breathlessly, looking out at the Ponte Vecchio from the Ponte Santa Trinita, another bridge spanning the Arno. 'It's so magical.' With the sky darkening, the reflected lights made the scene even more impressive.

'I'm glad you like it.' His voice sounded strange, thick and heavy.

They began to walk on, and Olivia's hand caught Nico's, their fingers intertwining and almost instantly releasing. At the same moment, Olivia's heart skipped so violently in her chest, she inhaled sharply. He stopped, as did she, and he suddenly raised his hand to her cheek, his thumb gently stroking her skin. She had no idea what was happening. Her heartbeat was racing at an unhealthy speed, her body tingling.

'Sun cream,' Nico said, as if coming to from a trance. 'You had some sun cream on your cheek.'

'Did I?'

He cleared his throat. 'Um, yeah.' His hand fell away and he dropped his eyes. 'We should probably get going. Everyone'll be wondering where we are.'

Stunned, Olivia mumbled a response. 'Yeah. Yeah, we should.'

They walked on in silence, listening to the chatter

232

of the crowd. She climbed into the car, trying to calm her galloping heartbeat and the fizzing in her stomach. The last time she'd applied sun cream had been in a café bathroom just before they'd left to take a final walk along the Ponte Vecchio, and she hadn't left any on her cheek.

She was absolutely sure of it.

Chapter 17

Olivia watched the arrivals door that she herself had walked through only two weeks before with mounting excitement. She checked her watch. Any minute now she would see her son who she had missed more than words could say. She was also grateful for the distraction from Nico. The way he'd looked at her and touched her cheek made her insides tighten whenever she thought about it. And she thought about it a lot. It couldn't mean anything though, could it? No, that was just her wishful thinking, her stupid heart doing what it had always done, being in love with Nico, instead of putting him and her feelings for him behind her.

Time to move on, Livvy. Time to move on. She'd been saying that mantra to herself over and over again but so far it wasn't really helping.

Nico stood behind her, hanging back but no less excited to see his godson, shuffling from foot to foot like a toddler who needed the toilet. He'd talked on the journey here of all the things he and Jacob were going to do and she'd loved it, though she'd only nodded her agreement, unable to meet his eye. Worried he'd see her longing for him, which had only grown since their trip to Florence, she'd kept her eyes away. Olivia had, however, noticed that Jack hadn't been included in any of these outings and she wondered if some of Nico's disapproval of him still lingered. Whether it did or not, she was absolutely sure Nico would be a consummate host, though she couldn't say the same for Sofia.

The doors finally opened and Jacob walked through, bulky headphones around his neck, his dad pushing a trolley fully loaded with their suitcases. When Jacob saw her, he smiled a genuine, happy smile, and Olivia was transported back ten years to the cheeky three-year-old with a mop of hair and a way of saying 'Mummy' that made her heart melt. That flash of the boy he'd been was enough to bring tears to her eyes but when he launched forwards and wrapped his arms around her, giving her a tight squeeze, the tears began to flow.

'I've missed you so much,' she sobbed, hugging him

tighter. 'So, so much.' After a moment, she let him go to see how he'd changed in the two weeks she'd been without him.

'Don't cry, Mum.' His tone lacked the normal teasing, half-telling-off she'd grown used to in his teenage years. 'I missed you too, but it's been nice being at Dad's.' Though she was glad, she couldn't help but feel a little stab of jealousy. 'Nico!' Jacob rushed forward and into a very manly slap-on-the-back-style hug from his godfather.

'Let me look at you properly,' Nico said. 'Video calls aren't anything like the real thing.'

Olivia could attest to that, given her first reaction to Nico when he'd met her at the airport. The abs, the biceps . . . If she'd have had something to hand she'd have fanned herself. *Get over him,* she reminded herself sternly. *You're not helping yourself!*

'I can't believe how grown up you look.'

As the two began chatting, Jack stepped forward and gave Olivia a kiss on the cheek. It was their usual way of greeting but Olivia was surprised when she caught Nico watching.

'How have things been? Good?' she asked a little nervously.

Jacob had always spent time with his dad – nearly every other weekend in fact – and Jack was a good father, just not a disciplinarian – which meant that whenever Jacob came home, it always took a while to get back into the swing of their normal routine: bedtimes, rules and boundaries. Olivia was always the bad guy: the moaning mum. While Jack got to be the fun one. Perhaps this holiday she'd get to be the fun one a little bit. Especially now Jacob was older and didn't need, or want, as much attention as he had before.

'We've been fine. We even ate vegetables a couple of times. Do tomatoes count as vegetables?'

'Are you talking about ketchup?'

'Maybe.' He gave her the cheeky grin that had made her fall for him all those years ago and, again, Nico seemed unduly interested in their conversation.

'Then no. But it's fine. Did you at least get him to brush his teeth?'

Jack nodded. 'Twice a day. And mouthwash. I was gonna say floss but you'd know for sure that was a lie.'

'Yes, I would.' Olivia relaxed and Nico moved over to them.

'Jack.' He held out his hand for Jack to shake.

'Nice to see you, mate. Cheers for inviting me. Kind of you.'

'My pleasure. Thank you for bringing Jacob out. It's wonderful to have you all here and I – we've – been so glad Olive is here. We wouldn't be having a wedding if it weren't for her.'

'The missus getting cold feet is she?'

It was only meant as a joke. Jack liked to tease

everyone, which wasn't going to go down very well with Sofia, but Nico's bright, friendly eyes grew a little colder. 'No.'

'The venue fell through,' Olivia began. 'So I've been using my skills to get everything back on track.'

'Really?' asked Jacob, approvingly. 'That's cool.'

Nico squeezed Jacob's shoulder. 'I don't know where we'd have been without your mum. She's a genius. She's sorted everything out. And she's going to be a bridesmaid for us.'

'Wow,' said Jack, glancing between them.

'I'll tell you all about it later. For now,' she said, looking at Nico, 'shall we get going?'

'Just a tick,' Jack said, whisking his phone from his pocket. 'Sorry, I need to take this.' He walked a little away from them, towards the corner of the lounge. 'Hello?'

Olivia watched on, concern beginning to build in her stomach. He answered with a lot of 'yeahs', 'nos' and 'no worries', but when he finished with an 'It's all under control,' her stomach knotted disagreeably.

'Everything all right?' she asked when he joined them again a few minutes later.

'Totally.'

'Yeah?'

'One hundred per cent. Now, shall we get going?' He began to push the trolley towards the exit and Olivia worried more than ever he was up to something dodgy.

She just knew it.

Knowing there would be more guests and luggage, Nico had used his dad's car, which was much more suitable than the baby blue sports car. When they pulled up outside the Allegretti villa, Jack was the first to wolf-whistle and run his hands over the bonnet of Nico's baby.

'Wowzers. She's a beauty.'

'Thank you.'

'Must have cost a few quid. You're clearly doing well.'

Olivia watched Nico for his reaction. Since the first time they'd met, on one of Nico's visits to England, by which time she was pregnant, there'd been an undercurrent of dislike. She had hoped it would fade as they'd gotten to know each other and for a while it had. She'd encouraged them to go out without her and had seen them grow a little more used to each other, but now, it was appearing again and she had no idea why. She and Jack had been divorced for a long time, they had no feelings for each other anymore, and Nico was marrying a gorgeous Italian woman. Perhaps he was worried that Jack, with his cheeky demeanour, would chat her up or flirt with the Italian ladies that were everywhere in Tuscany. She was perfectly ready for him to try but had a feeling that a lot of them would be way out of his league and see through his spiel.

'Wow!' shouted Jacob, as excited as a child. 'There's even a swimming pool.'

'We thought you might like a swim and some time to relax before meeting everyone. Does that sound like a plan?'

Jacob nodded and Olivia pulled out the key to the apartment. 'We're just over here. Nico thought we might prefer to be together here rather than in the house with all his and Sofia's family.'

'Does she have much?' asked Jack.

Nico shook his head. 'No, she's an only child. But you remember I have three brothers?'

'I do.' Jack whistled. 'I think one of them threatened to break my legs at our wedding. Said if I hurt Olivia I'd be answering for it.'

Jacob seemed to enjoy this possibility immensely. 'Really?'

'I just hope they don't make good on their threats now.'

Olivia shook her head. 'We've been divorced for almost ten years. I think they're over it by now.' She could hardly believe it had been that long. 'Right, let's get you inside. You need a big drink of water, Jacob, or you'll be dehydrated from the flight.'

'Muuuuum!' Jacob moaned, throwing his head back and letting his hands dangle by his sides.

Jack slapped him on the back and led him forwards. 'Don't argue with your mum, mate. She always knows best.'

Olivia smiled as they made their way indoors, Jack and

Jacob weaving through the open-plan living room towards the bedrooms. She stayed to say thank you to Nico for collecting them from the airport and was surprised to find him watching them all pile in, a look of what could only be described as jealousy on his face.

Chapter 18

Jacob got up to answer the knock at the door, just as the three of them were finishing breakfast. He grunted at Nico who turned to Olivia for guidance.

'That's good morning in teenage speak. It can also mean, "I'm hungry", "Yes, I have cleaned my teeth" or "No, I haven't done my geography homework because I was too busy playing on the PlayStation".' Nico laughed and Olivia's heart coiled. 'Come in.'

Nico edged inside almost shyly. Jack looked up from his phone and flashed him a smile, which he fleetingly returned. The scene must have looked incredibly domestic and happy. But looks could be deceiving. If her marriage had been like this she wouldn't have got divorced. Hera, the cat, who Jacob had taken an immediate shine to, was sat in the corner of the kitchen where the tiles were cool and in the shade.

'I thought,' Nico said, joining them at the table, 'that I could take Jacob out today. There's a brilliant hiking route nearby. It leads to the top of one of the mountains and is great fun to climb. What do you think?'

Jacob nodded enthusiastically. 'Sounds cool. What do I need to wear?'

'Just shorts and trainers will be fine. Do you want to come, Jack?'

Jack's eyes widened in panic at the prospect. He'd never been one for hikes and walks and when he said no, Olivia caught the look of relief on Nico's face, which Jack was oblivious to.

'You don't mind, do you, mate? It's just not really for me and I've got to make a call later anyway.'

'Another one?' Olivia asked, topping up Jacob's orange juice and handing Nico a glass too. 'What about?'

'Just work stuff,' he replied with a shrug.

'The business must be doing well.'

'Yeah, yeah. It is.' He scratched the back of his head, which had always been a tell-tale sign he was lying. Olivia chose not to say anything more, not in front of Jacob and Nico anyway.

'It's not a problem,' Nico reassured him. 'Jacob, I'll

come and get you in about half an hour, shall I? Mathilde will make us a lunch to take and I've already packed sunscreen and water in my backpack.' This last part was directed at Olivia.

'Good planning skills.' She smiled at him. 'And at least I know you'll be fed well through the day. Mathilde is an excellent cook.' She had also taken quite a shine to Jacob who she'd been proud to say had shown impeccable manners the night before at dinner. 'Nico, shall I check in with Peppe and Mario about the food for the wedding? Make sure everything's on track?'

'No, no. Why don't you two hang out by the pool? You've worked so hard. You deserve a day off.'

'Come on, Livvy,' Jack replied, tearing a chunk off his cornetti. 'You said last night there's been a lot to do.'

Internally she groaned, wishing Jack would shut up. Also, if she were going to relax with anyone it would be with Maria or alone.

'I've taken advantage haven't I?' Nico said, his eyes crinkled beautifully. If she could have without looking weird, she'd have screwed her eyes shut. Why was he just so damn handsome?

'No, no, you haven't.' Olivia was quick to reassure him. 'I've enjoyed it. Really.'

'But you do deserve a break.'

'I might ring Maria and see if she fancies spending some time together. She'll be off on her travels again after the wedding and I'm determined we won't lose touch this time.'

That she wasn't going to spend all day with Jack seemed to relieve him somewhat. 'Good idea. So, I'll see you in half an hour, Jacob.'

'Cool. Thanks Nico.'

'Take your phone,' Olivia instructed Jacob once Nico had left. 'Is it charged? Let's put it on charge now to make sure you've got enough signal. I'll text Nico and ask him to do the same.'

'He'll be fine,' Jack replied, shooing away her concerns. 'Hiking's just an uphill walk. What could go wrong?'

***

Maria arrived shortly after Nico and Jacob left, as Jack tucked a towel under his arm and headed for the pool.

'So, how's the happy family?' she asked as they headed away from the villa and weaved their way through the Tuscan hillsides. The grass was short and scrubby, the ground uneven and Olivia watched her step between them as they carried a blanket and a makeshift picnic they'd prepared themselves. Despite Maria's egging on, Olivia was too scared to ask Mathilde to prepare them anything so they'd raided the cupboards and brought with them a hotch-potch of things.

The sky, painted azure blue, displayed remnants of clouds that adorned it like old lace, stretching overhead.

The sun was strong but a gentle breeze eased its heat and the air smelled of herbs and flowers. Cypress trees reached tall, dotted as they were here and there as if someone had decided to fill the wide, patchwork green space by plonking them down wherever they felt like it.

Eventually, they came to a stop on the crest of a hill and spread out the blanket. The food stayed in the basket, but they lay back enjoying the warmth of the sun on their skin, their hands behind their heads as they gazed at the sky.

'We're not playing happy families,' Olivia replied. 'We're just all staying in the same place. There is a reason he's my ex-husband, you know.'

'You've done well to remain so civil to each other.'

'It wasn't easy at first. His roving eye was what broke us up and I was angry. We were young. Too young, I think. But then, after a while I came to realise we just weren't suited to each other. Not really.'

'Sounds like someone else we know.' A moment later, she swung herself up to sitting and poured a glass of chianti for them both. 'Can I ask you something? Has it been worth it? Organising their wedding I mean. Because it seems to me that things could have been a lot different for you two. It must hurt to not only see him marrying someone else but to be helping him do it as well.'

Olivia took a long drink of the chianti, allowing the rich flavours to warm her mouth and light her taste buds. 'Honestly?'

'You can be as honest as you like. I swear I won't say anything. Sofia terrifies me too much to interfere. And there's only you and me here.' She swept her arms in a wide circle. 'Whatever you say will go with me to the grave.'

'I think that . . .' Olivia dropped her eyes to the ground, readying herself for the total honesty she never normally allowed herself. 'There was one night, a long time ago, when we were in Bali, that . . . something nearly happened. Just a kiss. One kiss. And I've always thought that if we'd have actually kissed then, all those years ago, things would have been a lot different. I don't really know why. I don't believe in fate or destiny all that much, but I just feel like our lives took a turn then and if that turn had gone a different way, I wouldn't be organising his wedding to someone else, I'd be organising my wedding to him. In fact, we'd probably be married by now and blissfully happy. Or maybe I'm just dreaming.'

'Wow.'

'Yeah. I know it sounds silly. Our whole lives can't hinge on one single moment like that can they?'

'I don't know,' she said, tilting her head a little as she thought. 'But our lives are made up of millions of decisions we make every day. Who's to say that one wouldn't have sent your lives in a different direction. Perhaps if you had, the knock-on effect would have been he wouldn't have moved to Italy, or you'd have started a long-distance relationship instead of a long-distance friendship. Things could have turned out very different then.' She sat forwards, meeting Olivia's gaze directly. 'So you still have feelings for him?'

She had begun unpacking the food they'd brought with them: leftover cornetti, some slices of ham and bread and a couple of pastries she'd nabbed the previous morning at breakfast. As if doing something at the same time would lessen the impact of the question.

Olivia sighed, releasing the weight of her feelings in that one breath. 'I do. I've tried to get over him, believe me. I thought coming to his wedding would help, then I thought organising his wedding would help but—'

'It hasn't?'

She thought of the moment in Florence. 'No. It hasn't.'

'You should tell him how you feel.'

Olivia honked a sarcastic laugh. 'No way! Absolutely not. Are you mad? Sofia frightens me as much as she frightens you and what if he doesn't feel the same way? Which he can't do because he's marrying someone else in exactly a week's time. He'd hate me for trying to ruin his wedding and rightly so.'

'It isn't rightly so. What if he feels the same way about you? I've been watching him and I'm sure there've been times when he's questioned what he's doing or has been looking at you when he should have been looking at Sofia. Maybe deep down he still has feelings for you but feels it's too late.'

'It is too late! He gets married in a week!'

The feel of his fingers on her cheek, the look in his eyes that she hoped was something more but couldn't believe actually was played in her mind. Was Maria right? The thought sprung a hope inside her that was too much to contemplate, but it still didn't change her mind.

'Not going to happen, Maria. I am not telling Nico I'm still in love with him and ruin our relationship forever more. It's just—'

The ringing of her phone disrupted her monologue and she grabbed it quickly when she saw Nico's name on the screen. She told herself to calm down. He was probably just calling to say they were having fun and for Jacob to show her where they were, but she couldn't stop the nerves mounting in her stomach, making her feel slightly sick after the velvety, rich chianti.

'Hey, Nico, what's up?' She kept her voice deliberately light.

'Olive, I'm so sorry. I'm so sorry. There's been an accident.'

Chapter 19

Olivia's heart leapt into her mouth as she ran into the hospital to find Jacob, Jack trailing behind her.

'Livvy, try and calm down,' he urged, sandals flapping. He was still in his shorts from swimming, a hideous patterned shirt clinging to his back and water running down his legs. But his words didn't even register amongst the tangled thoughts running through her head. She'd known deep down this was a bad idea. Hiking. Hiking! 'Just an uphill walk,' Jack had said. But no, hiking, as it turned out, was dangerous. She should have said no and gone with her gut but instead she'd been far too relaxed in the sunshine, in holiday mode, and now look what had happened. Idiot.

Maria had told her to go as soon as Nico had hung up. She'd tried to listen to his words but panic had overtaken them. She'd heard hospital, his arm, his face, broken bones, something about shock. In her panic she'd managed to latch on to the name of the hospital and while Maria packed up their picnic, she set out ahead, running back to the villa, calling Jack as she went.

Olivia raced through the corridors, past doctors in white coats and nurses in scrubs, willing the tears from her eyes. Like most people she hated the smell of hospitals and as the aroma of disinfectant and bleach filled her nose, her muscles tightened. Her heart was beating so fast her chest felt tight, her stomach heavy. What if he was writhing on a hospital bed, crying for her? What if, at the moment it had happened, he'd wanted her and she hadn't been there? Had he been scared? How bad had the pain been? The situation might have been hypothetical but it didn't stop the very real feeling of guilt travelling through her body, strangling her brain.

'Liv—' Jack tried again, struggling to keep up. His voice grew distant and she turned to see him taking off his sandals and running barefoot behind her. She'd have found it funny if she wasn't so upset, but there was no stopping her. Not when her son needed her. Her baby boy. Her mind was once more replaying the moment he'd fallen as if she were watching a movie in her head. God, she was about to be sick.

But when she rounded the corner to the ward to find Jacob sat on a hospital bed, laughing and joking with Nico, holding his left arm, which was now wrapped in a giant white cast, she felt overwhelmingly angry.

'What the hell happened?' she roared, rounding on Nico. 'You said he'd be fine.'

'We were climbing up a mountain, Mum.'

'A mountain?' She honestly thought she might explode. Veins in her neck and head were beginning to pulse.

'It was only a little one,' Nico added.

'A mountain? You said it was a walk!'

'Livvy,' Jack began, placing a hand on her shoulder. He'd already leaned against the wall and replaced his flip-flops. 'He's fine. Calm down. Look at him.' Jack's laid-back attitude irritated her more than she could put into words but she hadn't expected anything less from him. She clenched her jaw.

'No, he's not. His arm's broken and look at his face.' As she'd grown closer, she'd seen the cuts and grazes on her little boy's cheek. She went to him and wrapped her arms around him. 'Are you all right?'

'Mum,' Jacob protested, wriggling out of her grasp. 'I'm fine. I fell over – that's all. It wasn't Nico's fault. And it was awesome. We had so much fun. There was this one bit where we had to like, jump over a—'

Olivia's head shot round turning to Nico who dropped

252

his eyes, a slight blush creeping up his jaw over the fuzzy dark stubble. Jacob fell silent, but not before she caught Jack signalling to him to shut up from the corner of her eye. His eyes were wide and he was making swiping movements at his throat, telling him to cut it. How could they all be so relaxed? 'You were supposed to be looking after him. How did this even happen?'

'I tripped, Mum,' Jacob said before Nico could answer, his tone wheedling. 'It's not a big deal.'

'Olive, I'm sorry—'

'Don't.' She held up her hand to stop Nico from speaking. 'Just don't. He was supposed to be safe with you.'

Deep down she knew she was being unfair but her anger and guilt were combining into an uncontrollable combination that dominated her rational mind. Something primal had grown inside her. A maternal instinct that had served her well in the past – in those times when she'd argued with doctors over a diagnosis or fought with the head teacher when Jacob had been blamed for something he hadn't done. Even with other parents when she'd had to defend her child. It was a strength that was both powerful and a little bit uncontrollable.

'I think you're being a bit unfair, Livvy,' Jack piped up. 'Jacob could have tripped and fallen anywhere. He's done it on the way home from school often enough.'

'That's because he never ties his shoelaces and it's

entirely his own fault. This time, he was supposed to be on a walk and instead was tripping and falling on the side of a mountain. That's much worse, isn't it?'

Jack didn't answer. Her tone had been sharp and cold. She was in full Mum Mode now. And it was all right for him, he didn't have the worry of being a parent day in, day out the same way she did. He'd grown used to not seeing his son at times but for her the last two weeks had been both wonderful and difficult at the same time. She'd missed Jacob, she'd only just got him back, and when she'd let Nico take care of him, he'd come to harm. She looked once more at the grazes on his face, resisting the urge to cup his cheek like she had when he was little. Some even had dissolvable stitches over them.

'Mum for God's sake—' Jacob hopped off the bed, wincing slightly and clutching his injured arm. 'You're completely over-reacting.'

'Don't for God's sake me and I am not completely over-reacting.'

'Yes, you are. Honestly. It's not that bad. It hurts a bit, but—'

'You've got a cast on. It's broken.'

'I just landed funny, that's all. Remember when I came off my bike and fractured this wrist?' He held up his other arm. 'It's not a big deal.'

Feeling the anger boiling inside but not wanting to shout in the middle of a hospital ward she bit her tongue.

254

'We need to get you home. Giovanni let us borrow his car. Jack can drive.'

'Olive—' She didn't give Nico a chance to speak, silencing him with a tight-lipped angry scowl as she gathered up Jacob's things and, wrapping her arm around him, led him back outside.

As Jack was getting him into the car and helping him adjust his seatbelt, Nico approached her.

'Olive, I'm sorry Jacob fell.'

'You said it was just a hike. You didn't mention mountains or jumping over whatever it was.'

'A crevice.'

'A crevice! In a mountainside? Well that all sounds perfectly safe and reasonable. Yes, I'm definitely over-reacting, aren't I. You said shorts and trainers would be fine. Leaping over crevices must need some kind of safety equipment. A hard hat and those things people stick in mountains.' Nico looked perplexed. 'The sharp, spiky hammer things.'

'Crampons?'

'Yes!'

'Olive, it was just a small gap in the land, like stepping over a stream. It was—'

'You know—' She'd started now and was finding it difficult to stop. All her fears and worries about her son, Nico's wedding, the internal conflict she'd been battling with over her feelings for the man stood in front of her who set her heart alight, her dislike for Sofia, were all mixing together into a maelstrom of emotion like water pressing against a dam, and now the dam was breaking, words leaking then tumbling out over one another. 'It was irresponsible, Nico. You always have been. Why? Why are you so irresponsible?'

'When have I ever been irresponsible?' He threw his hands into the air in defence of himself.

She was about to say that marrying a woman like Sofia was irresponsible but pulled back just in time, changing tack. 'You can't just be the fun godfather when you're in charge of a child.'

'I'm not a child!' Jacob protested from the back seat to be immediately shushed by his dad who muttered: 'I'd stay out of this one, kiddo, if you know what's good for you.'

'I was responsible, Olive,' Nico protested. 'It was an accident, that's all. I love Jacob – I always have. Why do you think I've been happy to help with his trips and school events when you couldn't afford them? I never did it for the praise, I did it because I care and I take my responsibilities seriously. And I did take care of him. It was just one of those things. It could have happened to anyone.'

'It wouldn't have happened if I was looking after him.' She crossed her arms over her chest, turning slightly away.

'Oh no, of course not, because you never do anything wrong.'

'What's that supposed to mean?'

'Nothing.'

'No, come on.' She turned back to face him in challenge. If he had things to say, they might as well get them out in the open. 'What do you mean I never do anything wrong?'

'I mean that you like to pretend like everything is fine and you're happy with your life but you never admit when something is wrong and making you unhappy. You never go after what you want.'

'So you did mean that comment about me the other night?' Remembering the little dig he'd made while they watched the sunset at Castello Chateau, she grew even more defensive, though this time it was for herself and not her child.

'Not at the time I didn't, but after I'd said it and you got upset I realised there was some truth in it, but I didn't say anything because I just wanted us to be friends again. But don't you want Jacob to go for the things that make him happy, that bring him to life?'

'Of course I do. And he will. But you know why I haven't been able to chase every dream that's come to me – I've been busy being a mum and it's something I wouldn't change for the world.'

'Neither would I,' he added though she didn't quite hear him in her anger.

'We can't all just—'

'Just what?'

'Just swan off to Italy when we feel like it and change the entire course of our lives.'

There was a strange silence for a moment as Nico recoiled, the minute he'd announced his move to Florence clear in both their minds. The kiss that could have taken their lives in a completely different direction but never happened playing out on his face.

The sound of sirens filled the air, ambulances arriving at the hospital, delivering patients. There was even a police car, and nurses on breaks, along with patients nipping outside for a smoke.

'I wanted to ask you to come with me,' Nico said quietly, his eyes down studying his hands.

Her breath stilled. The blood pulsed in her ears. She could even feel it pulsing around her body, pounding in her chest. She tried to speak but nothing would come. The world had stopped at his revelation. He'd wanted to ask her to come with him? Everything she'd said to Maria came back at once. All the decisions they'd made that had led them away from each other. How different things could have been if they'd both made different choices. Eventually she managed to speak but her voice was hushed, the words barely audible. 'Why didn't you?'

Olivia could feel her cheeks burning as she stood there. The sun scorched her skin but she didn't care. She was vaguely aware of Jack and Jacob sat in the car. The radio playing to drown out their noise.

'I didn't think you'd say yes. And I was scared. I loved you and if you'd said no, I don't know what we'd have done. It seemed better to not ask.'

He'd loved her. That he had once felt the same way about her as she'd always felt about him sent a shiver down her spine. She'd longed to hear those words and held her breath wishing for more. She wanted him to say that he loved her still, that he wanted to be with her. But he'd used the past tense: loved. Not love. He might have loved her once but he didn't love her now and why would he? She was the polar opposite to Sofia – the woman he was about to marry. She didn't wear the same clothes; she didn't care about the same things. She was loud and friendly while Sofia was quiet and cold. She wasn't really a success at anything, except being a mum. Well, up until today she'd been a success at that. While Sofia was an influencer with thousands of followers, the most successful type of person this day and age.

The heat from the sun suddenly drained away, leaving her cold. Loved. He had loved her once, but not anymore. She felt her love for Nico evaporating, turning from something solid within her to a gas, drifting into the air. It was definite now. There would never be a 'them'. They would never be together in the way she had always secretly hoped.

'We should—' she began, and Nico raised his head a fraction. She wished she could say, *'We should talk about this later,'* and the hope in Nico's eyes was almost too much to bear. But what good would it do? And she didn't want to talk about it. She never wanted to revisit the hurt she was feeling right now. The ending of something she'd always wanted. 'We should get Jacob back. He needs a rest.'

'I think we all do after that,' Jack replied, trying to break the tension.

She took a step backwards, Nico's eyes following her, his expression unreadable, and climbed into the back of the car with Jacob. Nico sat in the front with Jack.

'Right, well,' Jack said. 'I don't know about anyone else but that's all the excitement I need for today.'

She wouldn't exactly call it excitement but he was right about one thing. She'd had enough of today. She'd had enough of weddings and she'd had enough of Italy. If only she could pack their bags and fly home. But there was a wedding to finish organising and bridesmaid's duties to perform. Any escape she hoped for wasn't going to come yet. As quietly as she could she pulled out her sunglasses and put them on. Olivia turned her attention to the window, to the city they were leaving behind and the Tuscan countryside spreading around them. She slipped her hand into Jacob's, expecting him to hold it for a second before pulling away, but unusually, after giving it a gentle squeeze, he let her hold it for the length of the journey home, ignoring her quiet sniffs and pretending not to notice when she wiped an escaping tear from her cheek.

Chapter 20

Olivia woke that night in a cold sweat.

'Damn it!' she whispered to herself, her words echoing in the room. But it wasn't because of nightmares over what had happened to Jacob. In fact, she'd just been having a rather nice dream about Nico. They'd been by the pool, him swimming, all toned and muscular, his olive skin glistening, while she sat in the shade, her pale skin almost luminescent in the sunshine. As the dream faded in the darkness of her room, and she remembered what he'd said the day before, his words filling her with sadness, she squeezed her eyes shut to rid herself of the memory.

She also hadn't awoken because Jacob was in pain. He was sleeping soundly and had only needed a couple of painkillers throughout the day. He'd quite enjoyed reliving the whole experience, embellishing the details every time he mentioned it to her just to wind her up. Instead of it being a small dink in the side of the mountain, as Nico had described, it was now a giant crater he'd had to tightrope walk over. In the end, she'd given up trying to fight and had laughed, relaxing as the adrenalin leached from her system. He was okay, with nothing more than a broken arm and a few cuts and bruises on his face, which was all that mattered. He was still here, still teasing her, still not brushing his teeth when she asked him to.

No, it was the fact that she had woken to Hera, the cat, landing on her bed from the open window and as she'd lain there in the darkness, she had suddenly realised she hadn't confirmed any kind of seating plan with Sofia.

'What am I going to do, hey, furry goddess?' she said quietly.

Olivia had stupidly assumed that the guests would sit wherever they wanted, which was how she would have had her wedding and how they were going to have the ceremony. But this wasn't her wedding. Nico too must have assumed the same thing, or was relying on her to raise these sorts of issues, but Olivia had forgotten and was now acutely aware that Sofia may want a very specific seating plan. She wasn't going to want to end up next to

Nico's brother Aldo with his jokes or next to Olivia for that matter.

'She really won't want that,' she said to Hera's head as she pushed it against her own, almost headbutting her.

Olivia also hadn't had confirmation from either of the two different bands she'd approached to play at the ceremony and reception. Angelo had made some helpful suggestions of local bands and though she'd immediately emailed, none of them had come back to her. What would she do if they couldn't play? How would she find a band then? There were only five days to go. She was most definitely running out of time. Her stomach roiled and then gurgled loudly. She'd been so angry with Nico and upset at Jacob's injuries she hadn't been able to eat all that day. Even though kindly Mathilde had delivered a basket full of food for them in case Jacob couldn't join them for dinner, she hadn't had the appetite for anything, which was not like her at all. She needed food, and then, she had to get on to the bands first thing in the morning.

Olivia glanced at the time and saw it was only half past three. With a sigh, she rolled over, trying to go back to sleep but the cat was pawing at the bedsheets, purring as Olivia stroked her and no matter how hard she tried, sleep just would not come. After half an hour, she gave up altogether.

'Urgh, it's no good, Hera. Might as well make a start on things.'

She grabbed her phone to make some notes. She'd learned in event planning it was normal to start with the big things and as time went on, the tasks became smaller and smaller, but no less important. She should have spent more time updating her lists instead of gallivanting around Tuscany with Nico, letting him touch her face. Opening her app, she went through everything one more time, drilling down to every single action she needed to take and by the time the sun came up, Hera now curled in a ball and asleep on the bed, she was ready to dress and start ticking things off the list.

The only problem was it would mean seeing Nico and she wasn't quite ready to do that yet. She knew that at some point before the wedding she'd see him again, but she would still prefer to put the moment off for as long as possible.

Yesterday he'd told her that he'd loved her once and the thought that he had and they had missed their chance made her want to weep. If she'd have heard that back then, their whole lives would have been completely different, the threads of their futures weaving around each other, together. Instead, they'd run parallel. But she had to keep a stiff upper lip. She might want to run back to England rather than watch him marry Sofia but she couldn't make Jacob miss this special event. Nico was his godfather, and a special bond had developed between them. No matter how painful it was for her, she had to remain strong for her son. With Jack's help he'd flown out for the wedding and she couldn't simply fly them all back again.

Olivia threw on a pair of wide-leg linen trousers and a vest top, pulled her hair into a topknot and brushed her teeth. She hadn't been bothering with much make-up, having to apply sunscreen on the hour, every hour, and her skin had taken on a very pale bronziness that made her look healthy. Even the dark circles from her early morning wake-up weren't that bad and she pulled her shoulders back, pushing down the panic that had gripped her earlier and resolving to rectify her mistakes today.

She walked down to the pool for some fresh air to clear her fuzzy mind and sat on the edge of the terrace, looking out over the hills. The birds were singing as the sun rose slowly, and she watched the changing colours of the sky. The small bright yellow dot on the horizon sent a golden glow over the ground, but all the colours in the peaceful world around her were heightened. The grass was greener from brilliant emerald to lively chartreuse. The sky had lost its inky blackness and between the stripes of gold and honey yellow were slashes of pink and mauve. The clouds were rolling away, as if they'd done their duty overnight cushioning the stars and were no longer needed. It was going to be another glorious day. Weather wise, anyway.

Hera appeared at her side and she began stroking the

lazy feline, who flopped onto her side and stretched out on the warming cobblestones.

'You do like a fuss, don't you, hmm?'

'She definitely does.'

Nico's deep, melodious voice rang around the empty garden. She shivered and wrapped her arms around herself, rubbing her bare forearms. Not now. She couldn't face him just yet. She wasn't prepared. She hadn't thought what she'd say. What he might say.

'Do you want my jacket?' he asked, quietly, as if he wasn't sure what response he'd get. 'It's always cooler at this time of the morning.'

Before she could answer, he slipped it off and wrapped it around her shoulders. It smelt of him, something so familiar and yet so special, her body reacted, her senses tingling. Olivia fought for something to say. After the hospital, they had pulled up in front of the villa and she had helped Jacob out of the car and into the apartment, closing the door behind her. She had no idea what Nico had done, but she was aware of him and Jack speaking for a few minutes before Jack gave him a friendly clap on the arm and then sauntered inside to join them. Nico disappeared into the house and that was the last she'd seen of him.

'Umm, thanks.' She pulled the collar closer around her, less to protect against the cold and more to protect herself from the feelings inside her.

'Why are you up so early?'

She hated the way they slipped so easily back into being together. Had he been her boyfriend, she would have thought it was a sign that he was the one. She had always believed it was a sign that their relationship was special, destined to be. But again, the word 'loved' revolved in her mind like a carousel, rising and falling as if to taunt her. *Loved. Not love.*

'I realised I had some more wedding things to do.'

'Right.'

Silence fell for a moment, and from the corner of her eye she could see the pain on Nico's face. She felt guilty for being so angry with him yesterday. She'd over-reacted, she knew that now, but it was hard for her to ignore the maternal instinct to protect her cub.

'I got a bit stressed about wedding stuff I hadn't done – or thought to do – so I decided I might as well get up, make a list and get cracking.'

Nico chuckled but it was slightly hollow and tinged with sadness. He sat down beside her, resting his elbows on his knees, his fingers playing together. 'Nothing can ever keep you down, can it?'

'You know me.' He did know her better than anyone and yet, he still didn't want her. She turned her head away, staring again at the changing colours of the sky. Hints of pale blue sky were creeping higher and shadows were receding off the blanket of green. 'We need to talk to

Sofia this morning and ask if she wants a seating plan for the reception. I should have thought of it before. I don't know why I didn't.'

'There's been a lot to think about. Too much to think about, really.' He paused. 'You've done an amazing job, Olive. I can't tell you how grateful I am.'

She finally turned to him and smiled. 'I know you are.' She ran her fingers over a small tuft of grass that reached up from under the terrace stones. 'I'm sorry about yesterday. I shouldn't have shouted at you.'

'You were scared for Jacob, and it was a shock. I understand. I was going to ask . . .' He hesitated. 'If you can trust me with him again, do you think I could take him for a ride in my car? I know—'

'Nico,' she began, meeting his gaze full on. 'I've always trusted you with Jacob. I know yesterday was an accident. And I've been in that car with you, remember? You drive like an old lady. So yes, I'm fine with you taking him out for a ride.'

He slipped his hand over hers where it toyed with the grass. 'Thank you, Olive.'

A tingle rose up her arm, lifting the hairs, and penetrated her heart, squeezing it tightly. Her stomach gurgled loudly and they both burst out laughing.

'You need some breakfast,' Nico declared standing up. He held out his hand for her and she allowed him to pull her up to standing. As the sun rose fully into the sky, warming the air around them, they stood holding hands staring at each other, just as he would be with Sofia under the flower altar in a few days' time. Time seemed to stand still until, with a sad smile, Nico let his hand fall away and led the way into the house.

***

'Jacob!' Giovanni shouted loudly as soon as he entered the villa to join everyone for breakfast. 'Come and tell me all about your heroic fall yesterday.'

Jacob grinned and went to join him and the others at the table. Jack was already ensconced eating *cornetti* next to Nico's brother Davide, who patted the empty chair to welcome him over. Jack had made another hasty phone call as he entered, ringing off as soon as he saw Olivia, a guilty look on his face. She was more certain than ever something dodgy was going on and no doubt it would mean the end of his gardening business and him back to being out of work. She sighed, too tired to contemplate what that actually meant right now.

Olivia, sat next to Sofia and opposite Adele and Nico, decided now was as good a time as any to ask the question that had been bothering her since the early hours of the morning.

'Sofia,' she began, smiling to try and put her at ease. The bride-to-be didn't smile in reply but Olivia had grown used to it by now and pushed on. 'I wanted to ask you about the seating plan. Originally, I was thinking everyone would sit where they wanted but then I thought you might prefer to have a set seating plan. If you do, we'll need to get a noticeboard put together to go up at Castello Chateau.' Sofia didn't answer, and Olivia found herself still talking. 'There's more than enough room for everyone with the long tables but a seating plan—'

'Long tables?' Sofia said shaking her head, her voice rising. Down the other end of the table, Nico's family, along with Jacob and Jack, stopped eating, glancing in their direction and then muttering to themselves. 'No, no, no,' she said, her voice rising. 'We cannot have long tables.'

'But—' Olivia looked at Nico. 'You knew they were long tables. I showed you when you visited. We have to have long tables because of the shape of the garden and trying to fit everything into one space.'

Adele shifted, patting her mouth with her napkin and then folding it and placing it on the table. 'I don't remember you ever saying that, Olivia. If you're going to plan weddings you must communicate better with clients.'

'Clients pay,' she replied without thinking, earning a look from Nico that could have been pride or embarrassment.

'Still,' Adele continued, cool as the proverbial cucumber. 'It is a good lesson learned.'

Olivia bit her tongue, refusing to rise to Adele's continued snarking.

'We cannot have long tables,' Sofia said, shaking her head, frantically grabbing her phone and showing Olivia a picture. 'See, this is how Taccarelli has his wedding set out.' She showed a picture of an extravagant ballroom in the venue Nico and Sofia had originally booked. Giant chandeliers sparkled and below them were hundreds of white-clothed tables. Circular, white-clothed tables. 'We cannot have long tables. People will think I'm . . .' She searched for the word, growing animated as she struggled. Eventually, she shouted, 'They'll think I'm basic.'

Olivia attempted to quell the rising panic. 'But you agreed, Sofia. I've ordered long tables. They'll arrive tomorrow, ready to be set up. The garden won't fit round tables like this – it isn't wide enough.'

Sofia looked furiously at Nico, her mouth set into a tiny line. She obviously expected him to back her up. With their years of friendship she felt slightly smug. There was no way Nico couldn't. It was one thing to ask for a particular kind of cake stand (she'd managed to source a huge glass stand that would sit on top of a stone urn; which once decorated with flowers ordered from Giada it would look amazing) but it was quite another thing to demand different-shaped tables just days before your wedding. Nico would surely see how silly Sofia was being.

He cleared his throat. 'I know we've been working on long tables as the plan, but is there no way we can make it work, Olive?' He caught her eye briefly then looked away when he saw her mutinous expression.

So that's how it is. She felt betrayed, and wanted to tell him not to call her Olive anymore, but she bit her tongue, remaining calm, counting to ten in her head. 'You've seen the garden, Nico. You know how much space we have. We planned it all out. Long tables are the only option.'

Sofia stood from the table. Everyone was looking at them now, not even pretending not to. Giovanni's eyes were tight with concern. The brothers all looked like they'd seen this before and were heartily fed up of it.

'Why are you doing this?' Sofia shouted, staring at Olivia.

'Me? I'm not doing anything. You've seen the garden; you've seen the space. Long tables will not only fit but they'll also look better. We—'

'You are trying to ruin my wedding. Why? Do you hate me because I'm with Nico? I know you were "best friends".'

Were? Were they not anymore? Quite possibly given everything that had happened yesterday and her fears over what this wedding would do to their friendship in the future. She was seeing a glimpse of it now. And what was with the air quotes? Surely Sofia didn't know Nico had loved her once or that she loved him still. Still, Olivia felt embarrassed, and worried guilt would be plastered all over her face. She looked to Nico for support and finally, he stepped forwards.

'Sofia, no one is trying to ruin the wedding, least of all Olive. We wouldn't be having a wedding at all if it wasn't for her—'

'This is ridiculous,' she huffed, throwing down her napkin and fleeing dramatically from the room, sobbing as she went.

Adele rose slowly, her eyes pinned and unmoving on Olivia's face. A chill ran down Olivia's spine, as though her life was being drained from her by a Death Eater from Harry Potter. Adele folded her napkin, placed it on the table and strode after her daughter.

'I'm sorry, Olive,' Nico said. 'I – I better—' He stood and left to follow his bride-to-be, leaving Olivia confused, bemused and not a little humiliated.

'This place is mental,' Jack said, chuckling to himself. The band of brothers joined in but Olivia was left wondering what the hell had just happened and feeling, whether rightly or wrongly, that she was, in fact, some way to blame for it.

Chapter 21

As soon as Nico had left, Olivia borrowed Giovanni's car and drove to Castello Chateau, her mind working overtime as she tried to make round tables work. She wasn't sure why she was doing this anymore. The demand was unreasonable, not to mention impractical, but at the end of the day, she had to follow through on her word and it was Sofia's wedding so she deserved to have exactly what she wanted. If there was any way Olivia could make it work, she would, even if she hadn't asked in the nicest way possible.

Before she'd left, Jacob had asked if she was all right, commenting that Sofia wasn't the type of person he'd thought Nico would end up with. All she could do was reply with the usual excuse she'd been trotting out for Sofia, which was that she was stressed with the wedding after having the original venue cancelled. She was sure, she lied, that Sofia was wonderful when she was feeling herself. Jacob hadn't looked convinced but she'd hugged him and told him to get ready for Nico taking him out in the ridiculous sports car, which had cheered him up immensely.

'We're so happy to see you,' Angelo said in his normal, cheerful tones as she arrived at Castello Chateau. He embraced her and kissed her cheeks.

Today was one of the hottest they'd had and sweat prickled her brow. The sun was a glowing disc in the sky, the heat already intense. Planes were leaving trails in the otherwise cloudless sky and she longed to be on one and on her way home, leaving this whole sorry mess behind her.

'Is everything all right?' Francesca asked, her brow creasing in concern. 'You look worried.'

Olivia sighed and pressed a hand to her forehead. 'Sofia has changed her mind and wants round tables.'

'Round tables?' she repeated, concern ringing in her voice. 'I don't think we'll be able to fit round tables. If we do, they will all be in a line too and that would look . . . well, not very nice.'

'I know, I know. I thought we'd agreed long tables but

Sofia's seen pictures of the footballer's wedding set-up and rather than doing her own thing wants the same as him.' She felt guilty for bad-mouthing her and followed with: 'But it is her wedding so . . .'

'Is she here? Perhaps we can convince her otherwise?'

'She ran off upset, so Nico's with her while I—'

'Deal with the problem,' Francesca finished.

'It's a wedding planner's job, I suppose.'

'Come.' She took her arm and led her into the castello. 'Let us have some coffee and *maritozzi*—'

'Ooh, what's that?'

'It's a delicious sweet bread. I learned to make them in Rome. Food will help us figure out what we are going to do. Perhaps if the round tables are smaller, we can fit them in?'

Olivia allowed herself to be comforted by Francesca's maternal warmth. Supplied with biscotti, the delicious *maritozzi* and coffee, she began to relax a little, knowing there must be a solution even if that solution was that Sofia would have to compromise. How could Sofia not be pleased to be married here? The gardens were stunning; the house was enchanting. It even had a turret, which surely she could make use of on her social media, even if she didn't really like it in real life. The orange trees were more fragrant than ever today, in the warmth of the sun. So strong she could almost taste it.

They were just about to go and begin measuring the

garden to see what they could do for round tables when the scrunch of gravel alerted them to Nico's baby blue sports car parking out front.

'Olive?' he called as the three of them went to meet him. 'I knew I would find you here.'

'I've been thinking,' she said, signalling for him to follow her to the garden, 'and if we get smaller round tables, and offset them, we could—'

'We don't need to,' he replied, slightly out of breath.

'I— Sorry, what?'

'Sofia has calmed down. I've explained to her that it's too late to change everything and it doesn't matter what shape the tables are. All that matters is that we're getting married in front of our friends and family and she's fine now.'

Oh, is she? Olivia thought then chided herself for being mean. Sofia was clearly feeling the pressure from her legions of adoring fans and her mother, but still, it riled her. She could easily have done without all this this morning. 'So everything's fine now? We're going to carry on with the long tables?'

'Yes, and if you come back to the villa with me, I said you, me and Sofia could sit and work out the table plan together.'

Francesca smiled. 'See, everything will work out in the end. She is a nervous bride – that's all. She must be handled with care.'

278

Too right. Olivia shook her head, telling herself off again as Francesca left them alone. Olivia's feelings must have played out on her face because, as soon as Francesca had gone, Nico said: 'I'm sorry, Olive. She really isn't a bad person. She's just stressed and when she gets like this she can come across as spoiled.'

'It's fine,' she replied, waving away his concerns.

'No, it isn't. I know you wonder why I'm marrying her.'

Was it her imagination or was there a slight questioning at the end of his tone?

'No, no!' she reassured him. 'I get it. It's fine.' He looked relieved she wasn't pressing him. Or was it disappointment? Did he feel the need to defend himself and was hoping she'd give him the opportunity? It seemed a little late for that. 'I need you to do something for me though and you can't tell Sofia. I need you to telephone the bands I emailed. I've heard nothing back and I need to get something booked because, at the moment, you'll be getting married and partying in silence. I was going to ring them myself but—'

'But you will probably say something rude or accidentally swear at them.'

'Exactly.'

'Give me your phone and we'll do it now.'

She started it ringing and handed it over. After a long and friendly conversation in Italian, the first band, the one she had preferred, was booked for the wedding.

'They got your email but Google Translate made it very confusing.'

For the first time since breakfast she laughed. 'I'll bet it did.'

'They thought you wanted to book them for a wedding in three years' time, not three weeks.'

'I was sure I'd got it right. I copied exactly what it said.'

'It doesn't matter now. They're happy to do the wedding. We just need to email them the times and tell them when they can come and set up. I will do that with you over an espresso when we get back to the villa. I need a break after this morning.'

'I suppose you can have one as you've helped me sort that out.' She exhaled loudly. 'That's one problem sorted at least.'

'The seating plan won't be a problem,' Nico assured her, but after Sofia's reaction earlier, she didn't for a second believe him.

And she was right not to.

***

'I am not sitting next to your father,' Sofia declared, crossing her arms over her chest. 'He will make stupid jokes and encourage your brothers to join in.'

Nico tightened his jaw at the comment. 'I know Dad can be a bit over the top, but he has to be up with us.'

'Why? If I have to have long tables, why can't he go down the other end?'

'Because that's not how these things are done, is it? Family has to be at the top of the table. We could have your parents on one side and my dad and brothers on the other.'

'They'll be giggling like schoolboys. All of them.'

She wasn't entirely wrong there. That's what the band of brothers tended to do when they were together. It had made for some fun Christmases and birthdays through the years. But it was clear Sofia was not willing to have that on her wedding day.

Olivia stuffed another biscuit into her mouth. She'd done her best to resolve Sofia's concerns and suggest a seating plan that spread out the brothers so they wouldn't be near enough to each other to cause too much trouble, but Sofia had looked at her sneeringly as if she'd suggested they dress them in clown costumes and make them the after-dinner entertainment. Now, she was taking a break. Sofia only seemed interested in problems today.

'To be honest, Sofia,' Nico said. 'They'll be giggling like schoolboys if they're next to each other or not.' He smiled in a way that, despite everything, made Olivia melt.

You are hopeless, she told herself. *Hopeless.*

Sofia though was unmoved. 'I have already compromised on the tables, Nico. I will not compromise on this.'

She hadn't compromised on the tables; she'd gone back to the original and only practical arrangement. Olivia resisted the urge to roll her eyes.

'I cannot believe you will not work with me on this one little thing.' Her phone pinged and she grabbed it from the table in front of them.

Immediately, she began typing, responding to comments on the video she'd posted that morning. Olivia had seen it when she'd arrived back at the villa. Sofia was in the garden, pacing and crying that no one had any idea how stressful it was planning a wedding. The thing that made Olivia angrier than that was that her sycophantic followers were all agreeing with her as if no one else had ever planned a wedding before.

'What do you suggest then?' Olivia asked.

Sofia's head spun towards her and she smiled, sweetly. 'I know – let us ask my followers.'

Olivia inhaled her biscuit crumbs in shock, coughing and spluttering. Nico handed her a napkin and she dabbed at her eyes. Whatever she'd been expecting, it wasn't that. 'Sorry! Sorry! It went down the wrong way. What did you say, Sofia?'

'We will ask my followers. They can give their opinion. Family together at the head of the table, or spread out. Let's see what they think.'

'Sofia,' Nico said, his jaw tightening. 'I hardly think a decision about our wedding should be made by your followers who don't know your family or mine.'

'Oh they do. I've told them all about them.' Seeing Nico's face suddenly cloud, she added, 'Nothing horrible, darling, of course.' She took his hand. 'It'll be good for my engagement if I do this. It's important my fans feel like they're on this journey with me. With us.'

'You promise you haven't said anything mean about them?'

'Of course I haven't. Why would I?'

Because you actually don't like them at all? Olivia pressed her lips together. She'd been watching her videos and knew she hadn't slagged off Nico's family. She wasn't that stupid. What she'd said to her mother though . . . that was a different story.

'Great. Okay. And . . .' As his voice trailed away, Olivia lifted her head to see him nodding at Sofia, who, as sullen as a child, widened her eyes in disbelief then turned to Olivia.

'Yes, I'm sorry for what I said earlier. I know you and Nico have only ever been friends. I was just angry.'

'I understand,' Olivia replied, though she was keenly aware of Nico watching her from the corner of his eye. Knowing that he'd loved her once made the situation even more difficult than it had been before. She plastered on a smile. 'As we can't do any more about the table plan until your followers respond (a ridiculous concept in her opinion) I'm going to go and check through everything

283

else. Make sure everything is tip-top. Are you still taking Jacob out?' she asked Nico.

'If you don't mind.'

'Of course not. He's excited to spend as much time with you as possible.'

'Did you want to come, Sofia?'

Sofia smiled, but there was a tension to her eyes and a tightness around her mouth. 'No, thank you.'

Olivia couldn't help feeling relieved. She didn't want her spending time with Nico and her son together. She pushed the jealousy away. 'I'll go get him ready,' she said making her excuses, feeling the need to distance herself from Sofia as much as possible, her worries mounting stronger than they ever had before.

Chapter 22

'Olivia?'

Nico's voice forced her head up from her phone screen where, a couple of days later, she was busy checking and rechecking her event timetable for the wedding. With Sofia proving as volatile as she was, Olivia didn't want to risk missing anything and her having another meltdown. She also didn't fancy being accused of sabotage again. To be perfectly honest, the idea had never crossed her mind. Perhaps she should make clear to Sofia that she had as much riding on this wedding as she did, but she doubted Sofia would care. She only seemed interested in her world and what it looked like to other people.

'What are you doing here?' she asked, shifting her weight, realising her bum had gone numb she'd been sat there for so long. Jack and Jacob had gone swimming, leaving her alone in the apartment to sort herself out. She'd left the door open and Hera the cat was sitting on the warm tiles of the kitchen floor, basking in the rays of the sun that were penetrating her window. She could hear the bees buzzing in the rosemary and smell the scent of it on the air. 'I thought you and Sofia would be spending some time together before the madness of the big day?'

'She's making some reels to post to her followers.'

'Right. So there's nothing specific?' He shook his head and pulled out one of the chairs and sat beside her, unspeaking. 'Are you okay?' she asked. He had inky blue smudges under his eyes and his shoulders were slumped.

'I'm fine,' he replied, running his hand down his jaw, the stubble thicker than she'd seen it before. 'I just didn't sleep well last night.'

'That's not like you. You used to be able to sleep anywhere.'

'I still can normally. Anyway, what are you doing?' he asked brightening, leaning over to see her screen.

'Double-checking my planning. I don't want anything to go wrong on your big day.' She reached out and squeezed his hand.

'My big day, huh?' There was something in his tone that made her wary but then he shook it off, suddenly

286

cheering. 'I have an idea. You've never seen the town where my mum and dad grew up, have you? The one they lived in before they came to England? Where they met and got married?'

'No, I haven't. I remember you told me about it once. The first time you went. You said it was beautiful.'

'We should go.' He leapt off his chair, steadying it as it wobbled in his enthusiasm.

'What now?' Olivia laughed.

'Why not? Where's Jacob?'

'He's at the pool.'

'I'll fetch him. He should come too.' He rushed off, returning a few minutes later with a soaking wet Jacob. 'Go and get changed. We'll leave in ten minutes.'

'Is it far?' she asked, gathering her sunglasses and bag.

'Only about twenty minutes away. You'll love it.'

Jacob appeared, dressed, his hair still soaking wet, making dark patches on his shoulders and water run down his neck. She grabbed a towel that was drying on the back of a chair from her own swim that morning and towelled him off as he moaned and tried to squirm out of her way.

'Mum, stop it! Get off! It'll dry as soon as we get outside.'

'There,' she declared triumphantly. 'Now we're ready. Did you check with Jack if he wanted to come?' she asked, worried that her ex may feel left out, or might get into trouble without her around to stop him.

'Yes, and he's happy by the pool for today. He said he was working on his tan and he had a call to make.'

'Another one?'

Nico raised an eyebrow, reading her tone. She glanced at Jacob who hadn't seemed to notice her concern.

'Gosh, he's busy, isn't he? Anyway, as long as he doesn't go getting his beer belly out I'm sure we can trust him not to get into trouble.'

'Urgh,' Jacob said, pulling a disgusted face. 'Gross.'

Nico decided to use his dad's car as the sports car was only a two-seater. After his mood earlier, Olivia kept glancing at him from the corner of her eye and as they left the gravel drive and turned onto the road, Nico's shoulders relaxed and the tension leached from his face. Worry began to grow in her stomach like a prickly ball and she concentrated on the view out of the window. When they were alone she'd ask him what was wrong, but with Jacob in the car it'd have to wait.

The collage of green fields she'd grown used to seeing passed by as they wound through small country roads. She knew they weren't headed towards Florence, but rather away from it, deeper into the Tuscan countryside. Tractors ploughed their way across the fields and she saw more than one winemaker treading the paths between their vines, checking the grapes for chianti or grappa.

Nico turned on the radio and before long they were all singing along to pop songs that Jacob moaned were lame. She glanced at Nico as he belted out a classic rock song, and saw the man she had always been in love with. It didn't matter that he had only loved her once and didn't anymore, she couldn't just turn her feelings for him off. She wished she could, more than anything. But no matter how hard she tried, the light in his eyes, the kind, considerate, funny man she'd always loved was still there and the grip he held on her heart hadn't lessened yet.

After a while, Nico turned down the radio and pointed to the windscreen. 'Here we are.'

The traditional Tuscan hilltop town rose above them, the city walls surrounding it perfectly intact and, in front of them, stood a matching circle of cypress trees. The tops of the houses were just visible above it as was the steeple of a church.

'Wow,' Jacob said. 'That's pretty cool.'

Nico laughed and glanced in his rear-view mirror. 'I'll take that coming from a teenage boy.'

'Praise indeed,' Olivia echoed.

Jacob replied by rolling his eyes and going back to playing on his phone.

'Do you know the houses they lived in?' Nico nodded, and skilfully manoeuvred the car up the steep road towards the town.

'I'll show you. They lived virtually next door to each other.'

'How romantic.' She couldn't wait to see it. She loved Giovanni as if he were her own father and she knew how much Elenora had meant to them all. She was the reason Nico had changed the course of his life, and the course of hers. The scar her death had left had never really healed for any of them. Even though it was a long time ago it had left its mark on each of them in its own unique way. It had made Davide quiet, Dante quieter still, and Aldo unable to commit. Giovanni it had simply made heartbroken and alone, though he bore it well with the love of his family.

They parked in the shade of an enormous leafy tree and climbed out. The air was dry and dusty but no less fragrant than in the countryside. The scents of citrus trees and herbs carried on the air and the sun burned brightly in the clear, cloudless sky. Nico led them through the narrow streets, the distinctive terracotta tiles identifying the place as wholly and unmistakably Italian. Then he stopped abruptly in front of a very normal, very average-looking house. It was beautiful, as all of the houses were there, but it was exactly the same as the one beside it.

'Here,' he said, gesturing towards it. 'This is the house my mum lived in. And this one—' he motioned to another two houses down '—is where my dad used to live. They were neighbours.' Jacob stood beside him and Nico rested his arm on his shoulder. 'My dad has always said he knew from the first day he saw my mum that she was the woman for him.'

'Really?' That Jacob was genuinely interested put a lump in Olivia's throat and she stood back, watching the two of them together.

She wondered, not for the first time, what family unit they would have made had their paths not diverged to two different countries. He'd make a great dad one day, and she pushed away the guilt forcing its way up that she'd shouted at him over Jacob's accident.

'Did my dad ever tell you how he asked my mum to go on a date with him?' Jacob shook his head. 'Because he and mum had known each other since they were children – were neighbours and had gone to the same schools – he knew he had to do something special. He always said she was the most beautiful woman in the village and everyone wanted to step out with her so he had to think differently to show he was worthy. So one day, he climbed to the top of the church tower and using a loudspeaker he called her name until she came out of the house and then, in front of the whole village he told her that from the first day he'd met her, he knew she was the only woman for him and would she have dinner with him that evening?'

'And she said yes?' Jacob asked.

'She certainly did.'

'Where did your dad get a loudspeaker from?' Olivia asked giggling.

'I have no idea. Somewhere or someone disreputable I'm sure. But from then on, they were never apart. They married a year or two later and moved to England before I was born.'

Jacob scoffed, which wasn't quite as appreciative of the romantic element as Olivia would have liked. 'Why'd they leave here? This place is great. I'd love to go to school here. And the food's lush.'

'The food's lush because Mathilde is amazing,' Olivia said.

'No.' Nico shook his head. 'The food is *lush*—' He said the word comically, emphasising Jacob's teenage language and gently teasing him. 'Because we are in Italy and we have the best ingredients, the best recipes *and* the best cooks. And, speaking of food, shall we find somewhere for lunch?'

They both nodded and made their way back towards the centre of town. Jacob walked ahead of them, peering over the city wall at the view whenever the opportunity arose. She was glad to see him off his phone and looking at the world around him. It made a pleasant change from staring down at screens.

'Thank you for showing me that,' she said quietly to Nico. 'I'm glad I saw it. I can see how much it meant to you to come here.'

'I'm glad I got to show it to you and Jacob. There is something else I want to show you too. Follow me.'

They went to the small churchyard and wandered around the gravestones, stopping behind Nico as he looked down at two well-tended graves. The headstones were clear of moss and fresh flowers had recently been laid.

'These are my grandparents' graves – my mum's parents.'

'They're very well looked after,' she said, stopping by his side. 'They were well loved, I'm sure.'

'We all take care of them. And these—' He signalled to a hand-tied posy of white roses. 'These are for Mum. I lay fresh flowers every month. I know she is buried in England, but her soul is here. Dad and I came last week and he agrees, though he sees things slightly differently.'

'How so?'

'He thinks the part of her soul that belongs to me is here and the part of her soul that belongs to him is with him in England. He says that we all have different parts of ourselves that we give to each other. For some it's as mothers, fathers, brothers or sisters, for others it's lovers and soul mates. We each get the part of the soul we need.'

'He doesn't think we have one soul?' Jacob asked.

'No.'

Olivia willed back the tears gathering in her eyes. It was a beautiful idea.

'Mum, are you crying?' Jacob asked with obvious disdain.

'No,' she lied, wiping her eyes.

Without speaking, Nico engulfed her in an enormous

hug. The feel of his arms around her was a comfort she'd missed. She leaned her head against his chest, breathing in the smell of his T-shirt. His warm, strong hand rubbed small circles on her back while the other brushed the back of her neck. She could have lost herself forever in that moment until Jacob tutted and muttered, 'Get a grip,' making her laugh.

Pulling herself together, she stepped away from Nico and wiped her cheeks. 'I never knew your dad could be so poetic.'

'Neither did I,' Nico replied, laughing. 'I was as surprised as you are.'

'Thank you for showing me all this. I feel privileged to have seen it.'

'It's only a house that none of my family lives in now and a grave for someone else, but I'm glad I could show you. My mother liked you a lot, Olive.'

Without thinking, she pushed her hand into his and squeezed. Nico didn't pull away. 'She really was a wonderful woman. I'm glad I knew her.'

He turned to her, his eyes locking with hers and the clouds that had darkened them that morning returned. 'I don't know if . . .'

'What?'

He checked to ensure Jacob was far enough away. 'I don't know if she would have liked Sofia.' She could see how much it pained him to admit such a thing. 'My dad's tried but I don't know what she would have thought.'

'She would have just wanted you to be happy, Nico. Whoever that was with.' She pushed the last words out over the lump in her throat. Having known Elenora for a while at least, she didn't think she'd like Sofia either, but what good would it do to say so?

Realising they were still holding hands, Olivia removed hers from Nico's. He had loved her once, she reminded herself, but he didn't now and if he was still holding on to her it was in friendship only. The pain in her heart began to rise again and she quickened her pace. 'I'll just see what Jacob fancies for lunch.'

'I can already tell you what he wants for lunch.' Nico was smiling again as though nothing at all was bothering him. 'He wants what any teenage boy wants . . . pizza!'

They ate and wandered around the town some more before returning to the villa. When they arrived it was to find Sofia stalking up and down the front of the house, her heels forcing gaps into the gravel.

'Where have you been?' she demanded of Nico.

'Oh, I . . .' He glanced behind him at Olivia but she had no idea what was happening and therefore no clue how to help him out of whatever spot he'd gotten himself into. 'We – I – wanted to show Olive and Jacob where my mum and dad grew up.'

'You did what?' She crossed her arms over her chest. 'And you didn't think to invite me?'

'I knew you were busy with your videos. You asked me to get out of your hair.'

'I cannot believe that you would do that. You have never taken me there.'

'We've talked about it,' he said, his voice a little firmer than Olivia had heard it before. 'But you've never wanted to go. You've always been too busy with building your brand. You said you'd seen Italian houses all your life and didn't need to see another one.'

Wow, that was a little cold.

'I cannot believe you would do this to me. You'd take her instead of me—'

'Sofia, that's not fair.'

Olivia felt intensely uncomfortable as Sofia narrowed her eyes at her.

'Isn't it? Well I don't care if it is or not.'

Olivia stepped forwards. 'Sofia, we'll be leaving after the wedding. I think Nico just wanted to show us before we went.'

'Really. How nice of him.' She spun on her heel and strode back into the house shouting something in Italian. For once, Olivia was glad they couldn't understand.

'She's mad,' Jacob said before trundling off into the apartment, seemingly unperturbed by the drama.

Olivia stood quietly by Nico's side as they exchanged a glance.

'As you can probably tell, I haven't taken her to my

mum's house yet. She's clearly annoyed I took you instead.'

'Oh.' Olivia didn't know what to say. Had she known he hadn't taken his fiancée there yet, she might have refused. 'Why not?'

'I—' He shrugged, though the movement was forced. As if suddenly realising something he said, 'I don't think she could see how much it meant to me. Perhaps later she will.'

What was she to say to that? Clearly six months wasn't enough time to get to know each other, to bare each other's souls. And it definitely wasn't long enough to know someone inside and out like she and Nico did.

They locked eyes, something significant being shared between them, but she didn't really know what. 'I'm sorry it's upset Sofia,' she said. 'But I'm glad you showed me where Elenora and Giovanni lived. It was nice being near her again. I can see that being in Italy really has connected you with her in a way you couldn't have in England and for that I'm happy for you.'

'Thank you, Olive.' He put his arm around her shoulder. 'I knew you'd understand.' He tipped his head so it rested on top of hers and together they stared at the house. After a second, he said, 'I better go and speak to Sofia.'

'Yes,' she agreed wishing more than anything she could shout no and keep him with her a little longer. 'I've got more double-checking to do anyway.'

Nico's hand slipped from her shoulder and they separated, her walking in one direction and him another, but when she looked over her shoulder, it was to see him watching her, the storm clouds once more gathered on his brow and a look she couldn't read on his face.

Chapter 23

The day before the wedding, Olivia had never been more grateful for the weather. Italian sunshine meant she could set up everything for an outside event without fear it was going to blow away or get rained on and, as she unpacked the chairs, taking one from the top of the stack and placing it against the long table she'd already moved into place with Nico, she took a second to enjoy the feel of the sun on her skin.

'Stop slacking,' he said, nudging her as he placed a chair down beside her.

'I'm not – I'm just enjoying being warm. I checked the weather in England today and though it's August, it's bucketing down.'

'Have you put sunscreen on?'

'Yes.' She stretched the word, aware of how like Jacob she sounded. 'Don't worry, Sofia won't have a bright pink bridesmaid.'

'I was more worried about you.' He sat down and took off his sunglasses, raising his face to the sun himself. The dark circles had grown deeper and were thick, dark marks under his eyes. She was sure now he hadn't been sleeping properly, and it hadn't been a one-night thing.

'Late night was it?' she asked as he put his sunglasses back on.

'Sorry?'

'You look tired.'

'Oh, thanks very much.' She cocked her head at him. 'I – I had things on my mind last night.'

'It's not the wedding is it?' she asked, seeing his eyes widen in surprise. 'I mean, you mustn't be stressed about that. I've got everything under control. You don't need to worry about a thing.'

'Oh, I see what you mean. No, it's not that.'

'Work stuff then?'

'Yes. Yes. Work stuff. Shall we get going? We've got a lot to do today.'

They worked away for the best part of the morning, the sun growing hotter with each passing hour. Francesca kept them stocked with cold drinks and delicious Italian

300

treats while they laid out the tables and chairs and dressed them with tablecloths.

'What next?' Nico asked, wiping sweat from his brow.

'Next up are the candles.' She pointed to the open barn where boxes of them had been delivered and stored. 'And we're waiting for the flowers to be delivered, and the crockery, cutlery and glasses. They're all coming in the next hour.'

'You really do have everything under control, don't you?'

'Of course. Did you worry I'd let you down?'

'Never.'

'Not once?' she teased. 'You know I haven't been doing this for all that long.'

'No, not even once. I knew you could do it, Olive. You can do anything you put your mind to. You know, I think I've been unfair to you.'

'How?'

He sat down, gesturing for her to do the same. As usual they were facing the beautiful vista of fields. 'Some people would have panicked when they found themselves in your situation. Pregnant at such a young age, but you didn't.'

'Oh, I really did.'

'Maybe for a moment, but who wouldn't? No, you faced it head on and you made decisions. I did not always think they were the right ones.'

'Like marrying Jack?'

He smiled knowingly. 'Maybe, but no matter what, you have always done what you believed was right. Even when it is the hardest thing to do, you will always choose right over wrong.'

Except this time, she thought. Her fears over Sofia and Nico's suitability were greater than ever after Sofia's angry words at Nico and their trip to his mum's house. But here she was, setting up for his wedding and though her conscience told her she should say something, she couldn't bring herself to ruin his happiness. If he was sure this was what he wanted, and he'd been at pains to reassure her Sofia was just suffering from the stress of the wedding, then she'd support him. That's what friends did.

As she sat there contemplating his words, she realised that one good thing had come out of all of this that Olivia would be eternally grateful for. She realised now with a startling clarity that every decision she had ever made, for good or bad, had led her here to this moment. To the moment where she had almost single-handedly planned a wedding in three short weeks. Never had she thought she would be capable of such a thing. As a young mum, struggling to find jobs that fitted in with her son's needs, she had never thought she would be envisioning starting her own business. She'd never have had the confidence before, but now she could easily see herself doing it. Not only that, she *believed* she could do it and when she returned to England she was determined to make it happen.

'You're very quiet,' he said as she hadn't answered.

'I was just thinking of how this place is going to change things for me, like it did for you.'

'What do you mean?'

'When I get back to England, I'm going to take the plunge and start my own events business. My mentor, Margot, suggested I think through the financial implications first and if I ask to go freelance with my current job, I can still make sure I've got money coming in, but I can also start to build my own business. It'll take a while, I know, but I'm not in a rush. I don't think I'd have done that if I hadn't had to organise your wedding in such a short space of time. It's given me confidence in my abilities for once.'

'You should always have confidence in your abilities, Olive. You're the most amazing person I know.'

She dropped her eyes. There was no way she could look at him. Not right now. He'd know straight away just how much his words meant to her. He might think she could do anything she set her mind to, but no matter how hard she tried, she still hadn't managed to fall out of love with him. She should have tried harder, maybe listed his faults and repeated them like a mantra every time her feelings for him surged. She'd start that now.

He had hobbit feet.

He sometimes grew a bit of a unibrow if he didn't keep on top of his eyebrows.

Urgh. These were pathetic things and she knew it. He wasn't perfect, a long way from it, but the fact was, he was perfect for her.

Angelo appeared with a tray complete with his usual limoncello. A new bottle, Olivia noticed, and the glasses had been chilled. Francesca followed her husband with a plate of food.

'It is lunchtime,' she declared. 'Can I put this here?' she asked Olivia gesturing to the pristine white tablecloth.

'I'll just cover it with another one so we don't mark it. Hang on.'

'That is the only trouble with white. It is too delicate and troublesome.'

'But it does look nice.'

'It does. Now, you two must eat. There is still so much to do and you must keep your strength up. I have made bruschetta and there is lots of antipasti, so help yourselves.'

'Will you join us?' Nico asked. 'We're so grateful for everything you've done.'

'It's our pleasure,' Angelo replied, his voice booming around them. 'And yes, we would love to join you.'

Francesca rolled her eyes at her husband. 'He cannot think when there is food around. Are you sure you don't mind?'

304

'Of course not,' Olivia added. 'The chateau – castello – is wonderful and we're so thankful to you for letting us hold the wedding here. It'll be magical.'

'It always works its magic,' she replied cryptically, but Olivia didn't ask what she meant. She was too busy filling her mouth with the delicious flavours of Italy.

The fresh tomatoes on top of the bruschetta were juicy and tangy and the artichokes and antipasti Francesca had supplied with it were utterly delicious. She'd definitely worked up an appetite that morning and there was more to do.

As they were finishing lunch – Nico and Angelo speaking in Italian while Francesca and Olivia conversed in English – Giada, the young woman from the flower stall, arrived.

'*Ciao*, Olivia. I have your beautiful flower arch. Are you ready to see it?'

She immediately jumped up in excitement. She'd seen pictures of the work in progress but Giada had refused to send any more over the last few days as she finished it off. In the last one Olivia had seen it was half finished and though she already knew it was going to be beautiful, the gorgeous centrepiece for the ceremony was even more stunning than she'd imagined.

'Where is it to go?' Giada asked as Angelo and Nico leapt to their feet to help her. 'No, no, no!' she shouted as they approached. 'I have it. Don't touch it.'

Olivia smiled. She liked Giada very much.

'It needs to go here,' Olivia said, running to the spot. Giada manoeuvred into place, lining it up perfectly as Olivia instructed, and then tinkering with flowers and greenery here and there. She'd even included some small pearls that reflected the light, making it glisten and glow in places. It was absolutely breathtaking.

Olivia stood underneath it, taking in the details. Soft green ferns poked out between beautiful white and dusky pink roses and fingers of delicate gypsophila settled next to orchids and creamy hydrangeas. It was absolutely wonderful and she couldn't begin to contemplate the skill that had gone into the design.

'It's wonderful, Giada. Absolutely perfect!'

She turned to see Nico, Francesca, Angelo and Giada all staring at her. Giada looked proud, Francesca and Angelo excited, but Nico . . . His expression sent the hairs on the back of her neck raising. His eyes were alight, the smile on his face wide and free, and something seemed to emanate from him. If she didn't know better, she'd think it was love. The type of love that took over your whole body and shined from you like a lighthouse beacon. The only thing she could think was similar was the love she knew radiated from her when she looked at her son. Only this was different. This wasn't maternal or familiar. This was new and exciting. A way he'd never looked at her before. Or had once, on a beach, thirteen years before. Her skin tingled and she cleared her throat.

'What do you think, Nico? It'll look beautiful tomorrow, won't it? When you and Sofia are stood underneath it saying your vows.'

'Yes,' he replied, a tight smile coming to his face. 'Yes it will.' He turned to Giada, thanking her. '*Grazie*, Giada. It's wonderful.'

'Make sure you get lots of pictures of you two underneath it.'

'We will, don't worry,' Olivia confirmed, walking up the garden to meet them.

'The rest of the flowers are in the van. Shall I get them?'

'I'll help.' Angelo stepped forwards and he and Nico followed Giada back round to the front of the house.

'Are you all right?' Francesca asked as Olivia stared after them.

The look on Nico's face wouldn't leave her mind. What did it mean? Did it mean anything or was it something she'd imagined? He'd probably pictured Sofia there and not her all along and his smile, his happiness, was meant for her.

'Yes, yes, I'm fine.' She gave her brightest smile. 'Why do you ask?'

'Oh nothing. Just my imagination, I suppose.'

Olivia busied herself, moving to the barn to make room for the rest of the flowers. It must have been her imagination too. There was no way Nico could have shown any signs of having changed his mind. Of loved becoming love. It just wasn't possible. And with his wedding less than twenty-four hours away, it would have been hoping for the impossible. But still a little piece of her heart, a piece she fervently ignored, couldn't stop hoping she was wrong.

Chapter 24

That evening, a family dinner had been planned. Olivia didn't know if it was an Italian tradition or whether Nico had simply insisted, but while Jack and Jacob were playing on their phones, she was tinkering with her hair, trying to get it to do something that resembled stylish and elegant. Dressed in a long skirt and vest top she was prepared for Adele's sneers and Sofia's curling lip, but she only had to put up with them for one more day. Their flight was booked for the day after the wedding, as she knew she wouldn't be able to stick around and see Nico in the honeymoon stage. It would have broken her heart all over again.

In the mirror, she caught sight of the hideous bridesmaid's dress hanging on the back of the door. She sighed, and rolled her eyes. Tomorrow, she was going to look ridiculous. Tomorrow. A day she was both excited for and dreading. She wanted to see the fruits of her labour, to take photographs of everything she'd organised ready for launching her own business, her own website and social media channels. But tomorrow was the day she would lose Nico for good. No matter what Nico said, she knew Sofia would change the nature of their friendship. It had always changed over time, but in a fluid, natural way. Sofia was an outside force exerting its own wilful pressure. She had a feeling that tonight was a final goodbye. The night she'd have to let him go for good.

'You look nice,' Jack said when she appeared from her bedroom. Slightly taken aback by the compliment she eyed him suspiciously. 'What?' he said in mock offence. 'You do.'

'You don't normally pay me compliments.'

'I do so.'

'You don't, Dad,' Jacob added and Jack threw a cushion at him.

'I do,' he grumbled.

He'd been on the phone again that day, ending the call abruptly as soon as she'd returned to the apartment. She hadn't heard any words but his tone was certainly shifty and she resolved that once they landed back in England she'd have it out with him and find out what was going on.

'Come on, you two layabouts. Let's get to this family dinner.'

'I wish we didn't have to go,' Jacob said and Olivia paused.

'Why not?'

Jacob glanced at her then dropped his eyes sheepishly. 'It's Sofia. I just don't like her. Is that horrible?'

Jack looked to Olivia, clearly stunned by the comment and hoping she'd take the lead in responding. Olivia took a seat near him. 'I know she's not been the friendliest.'

Jack sat forwards. 'Sofia's not that bad, mate. I saw her smile the other day. Like, properly smile. She still hasn't laughed at any of my jokes but—'

'That's because you're not actually funny,' he retorted just as Olivia was thinking the same thing. It brought an unlikely smile to her face.

'I don't think we've seen the best of Sofia,' she began gently. 'Weddings can turn even the nicest people into bridezillas. I'm sure she's lovely when she's not feeling under so much pressure.'

'She's just not very fun and . . . and Nico is, you know?'

'I know.' She rubbed his arm. 'But it's important to respect people's decisions. Now, come on. Let's go. Just stay with Giovanni. He'll look after you.'

'He was trying to get me to try grappa the other day.'

311

'Was he now?' she asked, glancing at Jack who found the idea amusing. 'I'll have to have a word with him about that.'

They walked into the villa to find everyone there, even Maria. She walked over to Olivia, hugging her.

'How are you doing?'

'Good. Everything's ready. I'm pleased. I've got a few bits to do at the venue tomorrow morning first thing, but otherwise it's all good. I'm quite relaxed actually.'

'And?'

'And what?' She sipped her prosecco, pretending she had no idea what Maria was referring to.

'And are you okay with him marrying someone else? You haven't changed your mind about telling him how you really feel?'

She shook her head, her hair loosening as she did so. 'Absolutely not.'

'So you're just going to watch the man you've loved for years and years marry someone else?'

'Yes, I am. That is exactly what I'm going to do and then the day after tomorrow, I'm going to get on a plane and go back to England and get over him once and for all.'

'You mean cry until your tear ducts dry up or you can't breathe anymore?'

'Once Jacob's in bed, yes.'

'Well don't say I didn't try and convince you otherwise.'

Whether out of suspicion or intimidation, Adele came over to them, winding her way through the crowd like a snake slithering across the sands.

'*Buonasera*, ladies. Are you looking forward to tomorrow?'

Olivia worried that she had heard their conversation with her bat-like hearing, then told herself to calm down. The noise level coming from Giovanni and Nico's brothers was deafening. There was no way she could have heard her and Maria's whispered conversation.

'Very much,' Maria replied, followed a second later by Olivia.

'Yes, it's very exciting. The venue looks beautiful. I hope you and Sofia will love it.'

'We've been told the flower arch is particularly special.'

Remembering the moment that had passed between her and Nico earlier that day, her skin began to tingle and goose bumps rose on her arm. Subconsciously she rubbed her forearm. 'It's beautiful. A real centrepiece for the ceremony.'

'Time to eat!' Mathilde declared in her strident Italian accent and Adele stepped to the side elegantly, gesturing towards the table. Sofia and Nico were sat together at the middle of the table. She was dressed in green, an Italian tradition Olivia had read about. Brides wore green the night before the wedding to bring good fortune. She looked beautiful in the pale pistachio dress, decorated

313

with tiny daisies. She looked up, catching Olivia's eye and though Olivia smiled widely, Sofia didn't respond, dropping her eyes to the table, then lifting them to watch her father as he spoke to Nico.

Jack and Jacob were engulfed by Nico's brothers and press-ganged into sitting down that end of the table with them. Olivia sat next to Maria.

'This is going to be weird,' Maria said, pouring a hefty measure of prosecco into each of their glasses.

'Shush! No, it's not. We're going to pretend like I'm just the wedding planner, okay?'

'If you say so.'

Course after course was brought out and conversation with Adele and Salvatore was as stilted and difficult as it had been the first time. For everyone else, particularly for Jacob, Jack and the brothers, and for Maria and Olivia – who drank far more prosecco than they should have – it flowed like water.

'Have you noticed,' Maria said, leaning in and whispering, 'Nico hasn't looked at you once this evening.'

'I know. Do you think I've annoyed him or something?'

'I don't know, have you?'

'I don't think so. But he's been a bit weird over the last few days.'

'He's not the only one,' she replied, nodding in Giovanni's direction.

Normally loud and boisterous, especially when it

came to appreciating Mathilde's wonderful cooking, Olivia became acutely aware that while Nico's brothers were making as much noise as usual, Giovanni had been quiet throughout dinner. Though she was relieved to see Jacob smiling, his unease of earlier forgotten as the brothers told him inappropriate jokes and encouraged him to drink watered-down grappa, her eyes continued to stray towards Giovanni. As Aldo delivered another inappropriate punchline, Olivia gave him a disapproving shake of her head, which he found hilarious and carried on regardless.

Maria topped up their glasses under Adele's disapproving gaze. 'Why put so many bottles on the table if we're not supposed to drink them?'

'True, but I think we are supposed to leave some for other people.'

'Nah, you snooze you lose. You only live once and *you* need to drown your sorrows.'

'I'm not sure there's enough prosecco for that.'

'Why don't they bother mingling with people?' She was referring to Sofia's family who were all down one end of the table, conversing amongst themselves and, occasionally, Nico. 'They might actually like us if they got to know us.'

'Maybe they've seen all they want to see.'

'I heard Adele say something to Giovanni the other day. It was after you and Jack had left for the hospital. I

315

was just about to leave too and I heard her talking to him in the garden, down by the pool.'

'What did she say?'

'I didn't hear exactly. I was too far away and didn't want to risk getting caught listening. But whatever it was, it really upset Giovanni.'

Was that why she hadn't seen him around the villa much? He and the boys had been out most days but Olivia had thought they were just exploring the area, Giovanni reacquainting himself with the places he'd loved in his youth.

As her empty plate was removed, and a delicious helping of tiramisu demolished quicker than was good for her, everyone began to leave the table, dispersing into little groups in the large living room and out onto the terrace.

'I'm just going to speak to Giovanni,' she said to a slightly inebriated Maria. 'Drink some water or you'll have a raging hangover tomorrow.'

Maria saluted in reply and said, 'Yes boss,' before giggling as Adele pinned them both once more with her razor-sharp stare. Olivia left, glancing at Nico who she was now sure was deliberately not looking at her. Perhaps he knew this evening was a kind of goodbye too. The last chapter of their friendship before the story finished and he had his happy ever after. She pressed down her sadness and went to join Giovanni out in the evening sunshine.

At first she couldn't find him, but as she walked round one side of the villa she heard raised voices. Slowing her pace, she rounded the side of the house, away from the large open doors to the terrace to see Adele and Giovanni having a heated conversation. She hadn't even seen Adele leave the room, let alone come out into the garden. Perhaps she'd used another door. Olivia's steps stuttered to a halt as she peeked around the side of the house.

'You cannot be serious about this, Adele,' Giovanni said, trying to keep his voice low.

'I am deadly serious, *Signore* Rossi.'

'But he is my son. I have a right to—'

'Of course you have a right. No one is saying you don't. I am merely being practical.' She crossed her arms over her chest. Adele was a good foot shorter than him, even in her ridiculously high heels, but the difference in stature didn't mean anything. She was a force to be reckoned with and her cold, steely eyes had focused on Giovanni with laser precision. Adele lifted her chin, tossing her hair back from her face with a quick, fierce shake of her head. Worried she might be spotted, Olivia ducked back behind the corner of the wall.

'What are you doing?' Nico's voice made her jump and she almost screamed in surprise.

'Ah! Crap! Nico! What are you doing here?'

'Umm . . . am I really supposed to answer that

question?' He went to peer around the wall. 'What were you—?'

'Nothing!' She grabbed his arm and hauled him back towards the terrace where the light spilled out from the house. 'Nothing. I was just getting some air. I drank a bit too much prosecco at dinner.'

'Not as much as Maria by the look of it.' He nodded inside and she followed his gaze to see Maria dancing with Aldo. 'I'm a little bit worried he's in love. Finally.'

'Oh dear.' Though she smiled, Olivia couldn't stop trying to subtly peer over her shoulder and check that Giovanni wasn't about to come round the bend at any moment.

Clearly, she failed as Nico said: 'What are you looking at?'

'Nothing! I thought I saw an owl, that's all. You have those in Italy, right?' She grabbed his shoulder and turned him back round to watch Aldo and Maria. Realising that she'd never shown any interest in birds in her entire life, she added, 'And I was stretching my neck out.'

'Your neck?'

'Yes. It's sore.'

'You have a sore neck?' He was immediately concerned and guilt flooded her. 'Is it from carrying the chairs and tables today? I knew they were too heavy.'

'They were not! They were fine. It's just a bit . . . stiff . . . that's all.'

'Will you be all right for tomorrow?'

A faint echo of Giovanni's voice drifted on the air. 'Of course I will!' she shouted far louder than was necessary, but thankfully she just about covered it. Everyone in the living room had turned to look at her and now Sofia was giving her the evil eye. 'You should probably go and see Sofia. You must be so excited for tomorrow!'

'Yes,' he replied, his voice losing the happy tone it had carried moments before. 'Very excited.' Once more he didn't meet her eye. 'Thank you, Olive. For everything. You're always there for me. No one knows me like you do.'

He glanced at her from the corners of his eyes and smiled before kissing her on the cheek and leaving to join Sofia.

Olivia felt like she had motion sickness. Either she was unsteady from the adrenalin pulsing through her system or the ground was shifting beneath her feet. She wasn't sure which. A second later, Adele flew around the edge of the building and into the light of the terrace.

'Getting some air?' she asked coldly.

'Yes. I was just chatting to Nico about tomorrow. About how exciting it all is.'

'Yes. It is.' She couldn't have sounded less excited if she tried. It was like she was saying, 'My car requires its MOT,' or 'Can I make an appointment to see the hygienist?' But all Olivia could do was smile. Adele sailed past her and back into the house.

Olivia collapsed against the wall, taking slow deep breaths and deliberately pushing her feet into the ground to steady herself. She tipped her head back and felt the warm evening breeze on her skin. Her chest was tight and weighed down as she took a final deep breath in, then pushed herself away and went to find Giovanni.

Chapter 25

He was stood in the dark, staring out over the fields surrounding the villa. The sun was setting, casting long shadows over the ground. As the darkness drew in, barely anything was visible in this shrouded corner. Sliding her arm into his, she said, 'Hey you,' and smiled up at him.

The last time she had seen him this sad was the day they had buried Elenora and he had cried more tears than she'd thought anyone was capable of for the wife he had loved so dearly. His eyes were dry now, but sorrow marred the brightness of them, the dark irises Nico had inherited, a deep brown, and deep frown lines were etched into his forehead. Even his ever-smiling mouth was turned down.

'What's wrong, Giovanni?'

'Oh, *bella*. You know what's wrong. He should not be marrying Sofia or marrying into that family.' He flicked his head back towards the house angrily. 'She is all wrong for him. They are all wrong for him.'

'What was that with Adele? And what happened the other day? Maria said she saw you two talking.'

He shook his head. 'I cannot believe the conversations that have taken place. She said that after they were married I should not expect them to come to England. Nico is doing well at his firm and Sofia will be busy with her work and raising a family.'

'A family? Is she . . . ?' She couldn't be pregnant, could she? The thought made her feel sick and her belly felt suddenly full of bubbling, swishing prosecco.

'No, she isn't but Adele said that when they start a family, they won't be getting on planes every two minutes to visit us. I said, that's fine, we can come to them and do you know what she said?'

'I've a feeling it wasn't very nice.'

'She said that if, and when, me and my sons visit, they will supply a list of local hotels and *agriturismos* for us to stay in. We won't even be allowed to stay here. They clearly think that after the wedding Sofia and Nico will be moving in with them – either to the house or the apartment you're staying in – and they will have them all to themselves. They plan to cut us off from Nico, I'm sure. And tonight, she said that if I say anything to Nico, she will make it clear I have misunderstood or that I am saying it simply because I hate Sofia. I don't hate her, Olivia. I'm sure she is right for someone, but not for him. Adele is trying to poison Nico against me.'

From what she'd seen of Adele, Olivia could well believe it. 'She won't be able to,' she reassured him. 'Nico wouldn't let her.'

'But what if he doesn't realise she's doing it? The other day, she made him speak to his brothers, asking them to stop making so much noise. He would never have done that before. He was always fun, he knew how to have a good time, but now, he's so serious. She is making him embarrassed of us when they are the ones who should be embarrassed. This is not Italian hospitality.'

The world felt suddenly darker as if the sun had hidden itself completely. Stars were beginning to appear in the darker patches of the sky and the world was slowing down, readying for slumber. Olivia shivered as Giovanni's words sunk in. He was right. Nico had been changing before her very eyes. The fun, vivacious man she'd known was slowly becoming more and more withdrawn. How hadn't she seen it before? She'd put it down to wedding nerves and to the pressure of having their wedding cancelled, then having to organise a new one in such a short space of time.

'I'm going to have to tell him, Olive,' Giovanni said sadly. 'I'm going to have to tell him what his soon-to-be in-laws are saying. In fact, I'm going to tell him not to marry her.' Olivia's throat tightened. 'I know you've done so much for this wedding, and I don't want to ruin it for you, but I cannot let him go ahead. I'm his father. I must stop him making this mistake.' He turned as if to walk away but Olivia grabbed his arm.

'Giovanni, wait! You can't do that.'

'Why not? Will he hate me? Maybe, but better he hates me than ruins his life.'

'Wait, please. I know this is hard, but you have to trust him. Nico would never let anyone push you away. His family is the most important thing in the world to him—'

'And you and Jacob.'

Maybe once, she thought. But not now. 'Giovanni, please. It's the night before his wedding. You're hurt and I understand it's difficult but—'

'Elenora would have said something.' He met her gaze, his eyes swimming with unshed tears. 'She loved him too much to let him be unhappy and I know he will be with her.'

'Maybe you're right. But surely he has to find that out for himself? I can't see that any good will come of telling him what Adele's said. It also doesn't mean Sofia's involved. Adele bullies and pressures her too. For all we know, she has no idea and she might want to get away from her family.' She couldn't believe she was defending her, but also, she did have some sympathy for a woman with such a controlling mother. 'If Nico is in love with Sofia—' the words stuck in her throat '—then he should be allowed to marry her and you saying anything against her and her family will only drive a wedge between you. One that might never come out.'

'And what about you?' Giovanni asked gently.

'What about me?'

'Come now, Olivia.' He took her hand, holding it gently in his giant bear paws. 'I know that you have always been in love with Nico. Why do you think we all thought you would end up marrying him? It isn't because you are friends. It's because you love him.'

She tried to remove her hand slowly without insulting him but the conversation had taken a turn for which she wasn't prepared. 'Giovanni . . . maybe once, but now? Things are different. We're older and—'

'But your feelings for him haven't changed, have they? Come now, don't try and deny it. I can see it when you look at him.'

Caught, her shoulders slumped. 'Even so. He's marrying someone else.'

'Maybe he thinks there's no hope.'

She shook her head, tears stinging her eyes as she thought back to him telling her he'd loved her once. It would have been the perfect time to tell her he still did love her, but he hadn't. Not then, and not since. 'No. I don't think that's it.'

'But won't your heart break?'

'Quite possibly, but Nico can never know. Please, Giovanni? You have to promise me. You can't tell him.'

'If it's really what you want.'

'It is.'

He stared into the distance. 'And you really don't think I should say anything?'

As the blur of a navy and velvety black sky forced the last dying rays of the sun below the horizon, she wrapped her hands around his arm.

'What good would it do? I think all we can do is trust him. Adele might want things to be a certain way, but that doesn't mean they will be. If Nico loves us, we'll always be a part of his life.'

'You're a good person, Olivia. Elenora always loved you.'

She rested her head on his shoulder. Nico's family would always be with him, but as for her and Jacob, she wasn't sure their bond was strong enough anymore. She could feel it fraying and tearing apart, the threads that had held them so closely together unravelling and drifting off into the night. Tomorrow would be her final goodbye. If she hadn't been sure of that before, after Adele's words, she was absolutely certain of it now.

Chapter 26

The morning of the wedding, Olivia awoke from a fitful and difficult night's sleep. Her eyes were gritty and tired because her conversation with Giovanni had echoed around her head. Adele's cold hard stare, not to mention her heartless words, had stayed with her for the remainder of the evening and long into the night, even penetrating her dreams when she had managed to doze off.

When they'd walked back in, it was clear Adele knew they'd been talking and didn't need to guess about what. Olivia had felt genuinely afraid as Adele had watched her, looking like she'd quite happily stab her with a kitchen knife. After gathering up Jacob and Jack and saying goodnight to Maria – who was happily chatting to Aldo – she'd made her escape under the excuse that she had an early start in the morning to finish setting up the venue before slipping into her bridesmaid's dress.

This morning, she made her way to Castello Chateau in Giovanni's car, eager to snap some pictures for her website and to make sure everything was perfect. The last few deliveries were scheduled to arrive shortly and she had the table to lay up for the meal, which, given the hoo-ha over long and round tables, she wanted to make sure everything was show-stoppingly perfect. She'd received a good luck message from Margot already and she'd replied, promising her a picture of the hideous bridesmaid's dress.

Climbing out of the car, Olivia took a second to appreciate the calm before the storm. She normally loved these moments before events began but the whole sorry situation was putting her even more on edge than usual. She took a deep breath of the sweet, scented air and listened to the birds singing. She was wearing her old clothes but her bridesmaid dress and make-up were in the back of the car, ready for later. Francesca had already said she could borrow a room at the castello to change in rather than run back and forth to the villa. She'd tied her hair in a scarf to keep it clear and out of the way, and with a roll of her shoulders, she was ready to get cracking.

The food to be used for decorative purposes on the tables – the pomegranates and fat bunches of grapes – had arrived and Olivia began artfully arranging them along the centre of the table. Next, she placed the plates, cutlery, glasses and napkins that had been stored in the open barn. Checking her watch, she was almost grateful she'd been up even earlier than expected as it was taking longer than she thought to prepare everything, but this was her biggest job of the morning. Once this was done, there were only little things left.

'It looks wonderful!' Francesca clapped her hands together and held them in prayer in front of her face. Olivia had been so lost in her own thoughts she hadn't heard her come into the garden. 'We could not have asked for a more beautiful start to our wedding venture. And look, Angelo, look at the fruit!' Her fingers gently brushed a bunch of juicy black grapes. 'What a wonderful idea.'

'I can't take credit for that really,' she said. 'I saw it online and thought it was a brilliant idea.'

'You still made it happen and arranged it all so it looks beautiful.' Olivia smiled at Francesca, grateful for her support. Next to the flower displays Giada had made the fruits look even more beautiful. It was like all of nature had come together for the wedding. 'You can, and should, take credit for it all. I am going to take lots of pictures so we can—'

Francesca was interrupted by Sofia arriving in a thin-strapped summer dress, her hair in curlers underneath a scarf tied far more elegantly than Olivia's was. As she approached, she was squeaking and squawking like a baby bird. Nico followed hot on her heels though he wasn't smiling at her evident happiness. Far from it. Olivia had never seen him look so serious or so . . . miserable.

'Isn't it beautiful?' Francesca asked Sofia, but she didn't receive an answer. Instead, Sofia was busy flitting around the garden taking close-up pictures of the fruit and table settings, and selfies in front of the flower arch.

When she didn't reply, Nico stepped in, for the first time scowling at his bride-to-be. 'It's absolutely wonderful, Francesca. Thank you to you and Angelo for everything you've done.'

'We were just thanking, Olivia. We couldn't have asked for better pictures to launch our wedding venture.'

Angelo nodded enthusiastically. 'They will be queueing up to book with us once these go online.'

Sofia's voice drifted from the corner of the garden. '*Buongiorno*, to all my followers. Here's a quick behind-the-scenes peek as the venue is being set up. It's going to look wonderful! This is so much more me. I told Nico that I didn't need a massive ballroom or somewhere that was, quite frankly, over the top. I love *him* and that's what this wedding is about.' Olivia couldn't help but glance over to see Nico clenching his jaw. 'A wedding shouldn't be about showing off. It should be about love and happiness and family.'

Love. The word seemed to echo around them, though

of course it didn't, drowned out as it was by the tapping of crockery and the arrival of Peppe. Yet, in Olivia's mind the word didn't stop playing over and over again.

'Nico!' Peppe slapped his friend on the back. 'Mario is in the kitchen, but I'm here with some of the waiting staff and some of the food. And there's a woman with a wedding cake waiting out front.'

'Oh.' Olivia jumped forward. 'I'll see to Renata.'

'No, no, no!' Angelo insisted. 'We will do that. You stay here and take a break for a moment. You haven't stopped since you arrived.'

She felt Nico's eyes on her before she'd even turned her head to look at him. His dark irises met her pale grey ones and for a moment both were transfixed. Then he turned to Peppe, shook his hand and thanked him.

'Is this your bride-to-be?'

'Sofia,' Nico called. 'Let me introduce you to Peppe who, along with his husband Mario, has saved the day with his catering.'

Though she was no longer recording, Sofia remained staring at her screen and held a finger up to pause Nico. Olivia bristled at such a rude, ignorant gesture. She could at least spare a moment to speak to someone who had stepped up at the last minute to save her wedding.

Awkwardly, the three of them waited, but unable to bear it anymore, Olivia started a conversation. 'How is Mario coping this morning? Is everything all right?'

'All right?' Peppe laughed. 'He is in his element! He couldn't be happier, sweating and shouting in his kitchen. Though he only ever shouts at himself. He would never shout at anyone else.'

'I knew that,' she replied with a smile, which Peppe shared. 'As long as this isn't too much work for him.'

'He wouldn't have it any other way. And how are you? When do you get to go and get ready?'

'Once I've got everything sorted out here. I know I can trust you and Mario, and now the cake's arrived I can relax a little.' It was probably a good thing Angelo had gone to deal with the cake given that Renata spoke very little English and Olivia's Italian was non-existent. 'There's just one more thing I'm waiting for.' She checked her watch.

'What is it?' Nico asked.

'Nothing for you to worry about.' Sofia was still intent on her phone, editing videos or something similar, but Nico called her again. Reluctantly, with a narrow-eyed glance over her shoulder, she got up and came to meet them.

Nico had a look on his face that Olivia couldn't read and, for the first time, she wondered if he had reached his limit with Sofia's selfishness. Previously, Olivia had always put it down to Adele, but here she was on her own, acting the exact same way. Clearly the apple didn't fall far from the tree.

'Sofia, this is Peppe. His partner Mario is cooking for

the wedding and Peppe, as well as being a guest later, will be managing the kitchen for him.'

'*Sí*,' he agreed. 'You have nothing to worry about. I can promise everything will go smoothly.'

'Good,' she replied coldly, nodding her head once in acknowledgement. '*Grazie*.'

Another awkward silence descended and Peppe looked at both Olivia and Nico. She was just about to blurt out something – anything – to fill the silence, when Sofia said, 'Excuse me,' and left to take more photographs.

Nico pressed one hand to his heart and placed another on Peppe's shoulder. 'I apologise, my friend. She is distracted by . . .'

Whatever word he was searching for, it soon became clear he couldn't find it.

'It must be nerve-racking for a bride. I will head to the kitchen. I adore Angelo and Francesca and want to speak to them before we begin.'

That left just her and Nico.

'So what are you waiting for?' Nico asked and for a second her heart leapt into her mouth. If this was a movie, this would be where she seized the moment and declared her love. As her courage toyed with the idea, he clarified. 'You said you had one more delivery.'

'Yes!' She shook her head, feeling stupid, though he couldn't have known what was in her head. 'Yes. It should be here any minute.'

'What is it?'

'You'll see soon enough.' He'd always been unable to resist asking on Christmas and birthdays. 'Have you seen your dad this morning?' she asked carefully.

'No. Why?'

'Just wondering that's all.' She could tell he hadn't quite bought it, so she moved the conversation on. 'Are the brothers behaving?'

'As much as they ever do. Though Aldo said something strange to me the other day. He asked me if I was sure I knew what I was doing.'

Goose bumps flew over Olivia's skin. 'Isn't that a question all big brothers have to ask?'

'Probably.'

She was saved by a courier carrying a small box and a large bunch of flowers. Olivia ran to him and signed, taking the parcels carefully. 'I have something for you and something for Sofia.'

'For us? But why? Sofia, come here. Olive has bought us a gift.'

After finishing another shot where she was playfully pouting at the camera, Sofia came over, her gaze suspicious.

Olivia opened the box and took out a card and a small gift-wrapped package, handing it to Nico. Then she took the bunch of flowers and another card for Sofia, handing them to her. Both she and Nico watched her, but Sofia didn't smile. She simply said, '*Grazie*.'

'Aren't you going to read the card?' Nico asked.

She widened her eyes at him in warning, obviously not wanting to, then capitulated and opened it. Her eyes scanned the words and, as she read, a small smile played on her lips. It had taken Olivia a long time to decide what to write. In the end, she had decided to write something she hoped would make her smile as her mum was unlikely to do anything so thoughtful. Inside, Olivia had written that Sofia was beautiful and deserved every happiness. She hoped she'd be able to eat as much cake as she liked now that her wedding day had arrived.

'I will eat a little cake,' she replied, her tone light. 'But not too much. I want to fit into my bikini. It is a gift from a new designer, and I must show some shots of me wearing it on my profiles.' She glanced down at the card and flowers again and suddenly said, 'Excuse me.'

'Olive, that's so, so kind of you,' Nico said, watching Sofia depart.

To be honest, she was glad it would be just her and Nico as he opened his gift. 'Your turn,' Olivia said, holding her breath.

Unwrapping the box carefully, he lifted the lid to reveal a beautiful pair of olive-green cufflinks. 'You don't have to wear them today,' she said quickly, seeing his eyes tear. 'Especially if you don't like them. We can change them. I have the receipt. I just thought—'

'They're beautiful, Olive, and I love them. Thank you.

I—' He cleared his throat, regaining control of himself but as he opened the card, she watched his face fill with a mixture of emotions, each one unnameable but playing out on his face one after the other.

'I mean it,' she said, dropping her eyes to the ground. 'You've always been a wonderful role model for Jacob, especially in the early days when Jack was finding his feet. I don't know if he'd have turned out as well as he has if it wasn't for you.'

'Olive—'

'I was really unfair to you the other day. I shouldn't have blamed you for his accident. It was wrong of me and I really am sorry.'

'I know, Olive. It's forgotten. Please, don't mention it again.'

They stood in silence for a moment, each one not knowing what to say. Then Sofia appeared at Nico's shoulder.

'Thank you again for the flowers, but we must get back to the villa. I need to change.'

'Yes,' Olivia agreed. 'And I need to make sure we're all on track.'

'Don't you need to come back with us?' Nico asked.

She shook her head. 'No, no. I brought everything with me. I'll change here so I can keep an eye on things and make sure we're all ready to go.'

'I can't believe you've done all this for us.'

'For you,' she said without thinking and regretted it immediately, but there didn't seem much point in lying.

She'd done it for him; they both knew it, and it was silly to pretend otherwise. Their eyes met again, and he opened his mouth to speak, then closed it again as if afraid of what he might say. Was he about to remind her subtly that his love for her was in the past? Unable to bear the embarrassment that he might, she made a feeble excuse and dashed away into the house, leaving him staring after her.

Chapter 27

The guests began to arrive and Olivia, in her hideous dress, smiled and greeted them trying not to combust with embarrassment. At least she hadn't been given gloves, or a tiny parasol. That would have been the ultimate humiliation.

Maria was the first of the family and friends Olivia knew to arrive. Looking gorgeous in a wide-leg, strappy jumpsuit, her hair pinned up.

'Oh my God!' She clamped a hand over her mouth. 'Oh my God! You look . . .'

'Horrendous. I know.' Olivia held out the skirt of her dress and twirled. As Maria came nearer, she whispered,

'Isn't it absolutely awful.'

'It's *the* worst bridesmaid dress I've ever seen. And I thought the picture was bad enough but it's actually even worse in real life. Do you think you'll get to change later for the evening?'

She shook her head. 'I can't. It'd seem rude. Nope I'm in this for the long haul. At least I've got low heels on. Sofia's done me that favour at least.'

'And how are you feeling?' Maria asked kindly, catching her eye, the true meaning of her words clear.

Olivia dropped her head and toyed with the ends of her sleeves. 'I feel sort of numb really. Like, I know this is real, but it seems unreal at the same time.'

'I know what you mean. It still seems unreal that he's actually going to marry her. But here we are, on the wedding day itself, so I guess there's no turning back now.'

'Nope. We just need to keep an eye on Giovanni. He has to keep his mouth shut and let Nico get on with it. If he doesn't, I'm worried what'll happen to their relationship. Family feuds are the worst.'

'I'll keep hold of him. Aldo asked me to sit with him anyway.'

'Oh, did he now?' Olivia wiggled her eyebrows as she smiled.

'Don't!'

'What? I'm not doing anything. Though you did look

quite close when you were dancing the other night. Is romance in the air?'

A slight blush came to Maria's cheeks. 'Maybe. We'll have to wait and see, won't we. I'm not cutting my travelling short and he'll be going back to England soon.' There was a sadness to her tone. 'Why are things always so complicated?'

'That's just life, I think. Ah, I better go. More people are arriving.'

The crunching of gravel showed that several cars had parked out front and the familiar voices were growing louder as they made their way round to the garden.

'Olivia!' Giovanni declared, throwing his arms out. 'You look . . .' She waited, raising one eyebrow and holding her arms out wide. He leaned in to whisper, 'What has Sofia done to you?'

'Yes, I know. I'm the same colour as an orangutan.'

He visibly relaxed. 'For a moment I was worried you had chosen this yourself.'

'Unlikely.'

He cupped her cheeks with both hands in such a fatherly manner she almost cried. 'You still look beautiful. And what a beautiful venue. And this—' He gestured around the garden, his smile wide though his eyes were tight with worry. 'Olivia, you have done such a wonderful job! Just look at this place! I just wish—'

'I know,' she replied, stepping forwards and taking his

arm as his tone grew sadder. 'I know. But Nico will be here soon, so go and find a seat. We've reserved spaces for you in the front row.'

The band of brothers followed their father and from behind a bush came Jack and Jacob. They both looked incredibly smart in their suits. Jacob kept fiddling with his collar, which was missing the tie Olivia had laid out for him. Jack too was looking well, tanned and clean-shaven. He was probably going to be flirting with every woman he saw, if she knew him at all. Though, she had to admit he had been a bit more subdued lately, and even on this trip he'd been calmer than he ever had been in his youth. He still liked a good time and to tease and laugh, but there was a maturity to him now that she perhaps hadn't given him enough credit for. Then, he saw her, and his eyes widened, drinking in the monstrous dress, and he started laughing. Within seconds he was doubled over, clutching his stomach. Jacob too, couldn't meet her eye and kept his firmly on the ground, kicking odd stones with his polished shoes and scuffing the toes.

'Yes, yes, all right,' she replied, feeling the hot rush of embarrassment again, but at least everyone had seen her now. Everyone except Nico that was. 'Come on, get it all out. I can't have you disrupting the ceremony by giggling like a child.'

'She really doesn't like you, does she?'

'No. And considering she'd chosen it before she'd even

met me that seems a bit mean.'

'Nico probably talks about you all the time – that's why.'

She doubted that very much.

'You look nice, Mum,' Jacob said, edging forward, his eyes still down.

'Oh, sweetheart.' She embraced him, glad that she'd taught him that sometimes, people just liked to be told they look nice, even when they don't. She wasn't even cross at him for lying. Sometimes social niceties were more important. She let him go and began straightening his collar. 'I don't, but it's fine. I've resigned myself to it. Now go and take a seat.'

There was a slight lull in proceedings, and she checked that the waiting staff they'd hired were preparing the prosecco for after the ceremony. She also stopped in at the kitchen to say hello to Mario who was preparing trays of canapés. Peppe was right. He was absolutely in his element, smiling from ear to ear. After checking in with Francesca and Angelo, who was wearing a bow tie, it was clear that everything was going to plan.

At the agreed time, Nico arrived with Davide, the brother he'd chosen to be his best man. Davide was quieter than the others and she could see immediately how his calm unflappability made him perfect for the role. Her breath hitched as she took him in. The dark grey suit was sculpted to his body, his bright white shirt tight across his toned chest. He was smiling, though still, it didn't quite meet his eyes in the way she'd always thought a groom's should.

When he turned and caught sight of her, the smile faded instantly. Nerves tightened in her stomach, wrapping into a tight ball. Over the years, he'd seen her hungover in her pyjamas, ill with flu, hair unwashed and unbrushed for days, but this . . . this took the biscuit.

'Olive.' He kissed her on both cheeks, and she inhaled the scent of his aftershave as her tummy somersaulted. 'Is this . . . ? Did Sofia choose *this* dress?'

'Yep,' she replied smiling, hiding her hatred for it. 'She and Adele, I think. It's very Seventies, isn't it? In a good way!' she added quickly.

'Olive—' He cocked his head. 'It's horrendous. I told her you were a redhead, and she knows all about fashion and style. I described you to her. I can't believe this is what she chose.' His jaw was tightening again as he clenched his teeth in anger.

'What did you say about me? You didn't say I was a hippy who loved Solero ice lollies, did you?'

'I told her you were tall and beautiful with a smile that—' He suddenly looked at her and she couldn't drag her eyes away from his, aware that for the first time in days they were finally shining how she'd hoped they would be. To break the spell that seemed to be binding around them, she laughed.

'Well that might be why I've ended up with this then. You should have said I was miserable and grumpy and—'

'And had a wicked sense of humour. Perhaps she thought that meant you'd see the funny side of this.' He motioned to the dress.

'I'm trying. I think I rock it quite well, actually.' She twisted so the dress turned about her ankles. She'd removed the scarf that had kept her hair out of the way and now wore it loose, the waves landing on her shoulders. She'd leaned into the Seventies vibe and was making it work as best she could.

'You look beautiful. Truly.'

He adjusted his cuffs, and she could see he'd worn the cufflinks she'd given him earlier that day. Olivia's body felt suddenly warm and heavy as though it had filled with love that had no way of escaping. She was still as in love with Nico as she had ever been. Perhaps more so as they'd spent so much time together over the last few weeks. She'd seen him with Jacob, him guiding her son, helping shape him into a responsible adult. She'd enjoyed seeing him with his family, laughing and joking. Most of all, she'd seen that the move to Italy had been right for him all along, and that reconnecting with his roots had made him the person he was now, just as she'd become the person she was thanks to the choices she'd made in her life.

'I'd better—' He signalled to the garden after checking his watch.

'Yes, yes. Sofia will be here soon and you mustn't see her. You have to be waiting for her at the end of the aisle, under the flower arch.'

He flashed her a small, unsteady smile and as he passed, he suddenly stopped, grabbed her arm and placed a kiss on her cheek. His lips almost stung and she couldn't help but gasp at the contact; but before she could right herself, or say anything in reply, he'd gone. She looked to the sky, staring upwards, eager for the tears pooling in her eyes to dry. For her heart rate to decrease.

The moment he looked into Sofia's eyes and said I do, her heart was going to break. She'd bite her lip and think of her business. If nothing else, she could be proud of all this, of everything she'd achieved in three short weeks. The wedding she'd put together brought out the best of Italy. The beautiful Tuscan garden, pretty and welcoming, was perfect for the ceremony and would change with the sun and the twinkling fairy lights when the band began to play. She had done all this and for that she was proud.

She ran her hands down her hideous dress as a beautiful vintage car arrived, and Adele, Salvatore and Sofia climbed out. Adele was fussing with the train of Sofia's dress, the veil and her hair. Sofia barked something in Italian at her and she stepped back before replying angrily with a barb of her own. Salvatore shushed them both.

This was not how a wedding party should be. No one seemed to be happy, but no one could do anything about it without hurting or humiliating someone else. Olivia went to meet them, a smile plastered on her face.

'Where do we go?' Adele snapped.

'Into the castello. Francesca and Angelo have prepared a room and as soon as you're ready, I'll signal to the violinist to start playing when Adele has taken her seat.' Salvatore smiled and nodded, Adele stared as if she were an idiot and Sofia nodded blandly. 'This way.'

She led them inside through the front door. Unsurprisingly, Angelo and Francesca looked as if they were preparing to meet royalty. Angelo even bowed a little as he shook Salvatore's hand while Adele sneered at everything her cold eyes settled on.

'We are so excited to have your daughter's wedding here,' Angelo said to Salvatore.

'Hmm,' Adele replied, her eyes roving around the room with obvious disdain.

Olivia's heart broke as she saw Francesca's face fall under Adele's snobbishness. Still, Francesca remained the consummate professional. 'If you'd like to come this way. I'll take you through to the anteroom.'

The small room was complete with a table laden with water and snacks and comfortable chairs. They'd even set up a beautiful full-length mirror so Sofia could check her appearance before leaving. The frescos on the wall gave the room a sense of solemnity fitting to its purpose. They depicted scenes of love and merrymaking. How a wedding should be, but the party inside could not seem less happy to be there. She tried to remember how she'd felt on her own wedding day to Jack. She'd been nervous, of course, but at the time she'd been sure it was the right thing to do. She'd been happy to marry him, even though it hadn't worked out.

Sofia reached out for a biscuit and Adele slapped the back of her hand.

Without thinking, Olivia said, 'Was that really necessary?' Adele looked murderous, her eyes narrowed and mouth pursed. 'It's her wedding day!' she said with a small laugh, trying to ease the tension. 'Surely one wouldn't hurt. You don't want her fainting through the ceremony.'

'Yes,' Salvatore agreed to his wife's obvious displeasure. 'She must eat something. You wouldn't let her have breakfast.'

Sofia took up the biscuit again and nibbled like a mouse, but her eyes lifted for a moment to meet Olivia's and there was gratitude there. Pretty sure that Adele would have happily stabbed her if there'd been a sharp object to hand, Olivia stepped nearer the door that led to the garden.

'I'll be outside if you need me. And I'll come back in ten minutes or so. I'll just make sure the celebrant is here.'

She headed out into the garden, the warm air making her cheeks feel even hotter. She was definitely red in the face, which meant she looked even more ghastly. Oh well, there wasn't much she could do about it now. She surveyed the garden once more. Her eye ran the length of it from the semicircle of chairs, all covered in white with cream bows on the back in front of the show-stopping flower arch to the long table a few feet away overflowing with flowers and fruit, sparkling glasses and glinting cutlery.

She lingered at the back, watching Nico speak to his dad and brothers. Aldo was talking to Maria who had half an eye on Giovanni. He was clearly putting on as good a show as he could, but Olivia could see the tension in his neck, the slight slump of his shoulders. Nico and Davide were rocking from side to side – Davide with his hands in his pockets, Nico tugging down his suit jacket. He was biting his lip, then his nail. Something was bothering him. He looked up and saw her and she smiled, giving a double thumbs up.

She'd thought he'd grin back. Maybe laugh a little. But instead, his eyes darted to Jacob, to his dad, and finally back to her and to everyone's utter surprise, none more so than her, he ran out of the garden to the front of Castello Chateau.

Chapter 28

Without hesitation, Olivia took off after him, like an orange version of that superhero Jacob liked so much. What was he called? The Flash, that was it. Except even in her low heels she turned her ankle and fell into a row of chairs, nearly ending up on matronly Mathilde's lap.

'Sorry! I'm so sorry! Hello, Mathilde.'

'You're a strange woman,' she said in English, immediately following it with something in Italian that was probably a more forceful version.

They pushed her up to standing and she chased after Nico, wondering what the hell was going on now.

'Nico? Nico!' She charged after him, hiking up her dress so she could run more easily. She caught up with him at the front of Castello Chateau, staring at Sofia's wedding car. He ran his hands over the wide cream ribbon tied to the front of the black vintage Jaguar.

'Where's Sofia?' he asked, breathlessly.

'In the anteroom waiting to walk down the aisle. Why? What's wrong?'

He didn't answer her and instead ran into the house, calling her name. She'd never seen Nico like this. He was always calm and controlled. This wilder version of him was worrying. Was he unwell? Did he think Sofia was? Olivia was about to follow when Giovanni, and all the brothers, as well as Jack and Jacob called her.

'Olivia?' Giovanni said, his voice tight with emotion. 'What's going on?'

'I don't know. I—' She shrugged. 'Can you all go and try and keep things calm for the other guests? I need to find out what's happening. Maybe he's poorly or has forgotten something? Davide, do you have the rings?'

He nodded and tapped his pocket just as she heard a scream from inside.

'Go!' she ordered them all before diving inside, weaving her way around the waiting staff, all as perplexed and confused as she was. She pushed open the door to the anteroom to find Adele staring furiously at Nico while Sofia, ashen-faced with a blotchy red neck sat unmoving, like a statue.

Salvatore paced back and forth in the small space, his hands on his hips. 'What do you mean you cannot marry my daughter?'

Olivia gasped as did someone behind her. She turned to see Giovanni, his eyes wide in shock and with a hint of relief dancing in them. They both moved into the room, closing the door behind them. Nico's eyes followed her, but she was too scared to look at him. Relief mixed with shock and a paralysing fear that she had somehow brought this about by not liking Sofia as much as she should have.

'Sofia,' Nico began, crouching down in front of her and taking her hands. 'You are a wonderful person and I wish I'd been brave enough to do this before now. I hate to hurt you.' Adele scoffed and Nico shot her a warning glance. 'I'd never want to embarrass you, but I can't marry you. It wouldn't be right, and I don't think we'd work out. And I think, maybe, you feel the same way?'

Adele gasped and replied before Sofia could: 'Of course she doesn't. Do you think she would have done all this if she didn't want to marry you? You fool!'

'Hey!' Giovanni said, stepping forwards.

'It's all right,' Nico said, stopping him with his hand. He turned once more to Sofia.

She'd been staring at her hands, where his thumbs had gently brushed her skin but now, she lifted her head. Olivia had expected tears. Had it been her, they would

351

have been flowing down her cheeks, but Sofia looked relieved. A small smile was playing on her lips and Olivia suddenly glimpsed the woman Nico had fallen in love with, albeit briefly.

'Look at my daughter,' Adele commanded. Her small stature didn't stop her being intimidating and somewhat terrifying as she squared up to Nico, pointing at Sofia. 'How can you not want to marry her? She is beautiful. You won't get anyone better than her. Than this—' She ran her hand up and down the length of Sofia's body. She then turned squarely to face Olivia. Embarrassed, Olivia dropped her head.

Nico's voice, harder and stronger than Olivia had ever heard it before, cut through the silence. 'Sofia is more than just beautiful, Adele. She's kind, generous and intelligent. Perhaps if you saw more than her superficial qualities, you'd see the amazing person she is underneath, as I did.'

Adele stiffened, a redness creeping out from under the neckline of her dress and crawling onto her face. 'How dare you—'

Just then, the door burst open, and Jacob and Jack came in along with all Nico's brothers and Maria.

'No! This is not acceptable! How many more people need to witness our embarrassment?' Adele shouted, throwing her hands in the air.

Olivia caught Maria's eye and she gave a small wave, then a thumbs up from behind Aldo's back. Jacob's eyebrows had pulled together in one long unibrow of confusion.

'You don't love me,' Sofia said calmly, drawing everyone's attention back to the drama unfolding before them. It wasn't a question; it was a fact.

'No. I'm sorry. I don't regret a single moment of our time together, but my heart belongs to someone else.'

Sofia looked to Olivia just as Nico turned around to face her too. 'Ah,' she said, breathily. 'I thought it did.'

'Who's she talking about?' Jacob whispered to Jack, earning a playful cuff around his head from Giovanni.

'She's talking about your mum,' Nico's dad said, smiling widely, the happiest she had seen him for days.

As all eyes fell on her, Olivia's throat tightened. She couldn't breathe. Her heart rate was increasing far too quickly for her not to have a coronary. Her skin felt hot and prickly, perspiration dripped out of every pore, and the stupid dress was sticking to her armpits.

'I truly am sorry,' Nico said to Sofia.

'Don't be. It's—' She suddenly laughed. 'It's all right.'

Adele gasped. 'Sofia! What are you saying?'

She ignored her mother and remained focused on Nico. 'I was starting to think it wasn't such a good idea too.'

Light-headed and faint, Olivia pulled the high neck of her dress away from her throat. No matter how hard she tried she couldn't breathe. She needed air. Her lungs were crying out for more oxygen. Stumbling, she ran into the garden, taking tracks that led away from the house and the guests. The sun was dazzlingly bright and scorchingly hot. What little breeze there was seemed to freeze the sweat on her forehead. She couldn't move fast enough in the heels and kicked them off, leaving them where they lay on the ground behind her. She must look a fright, bright red and sweaty in the hideous orange dress.

'Olive!' Nico's voice carried on the air towards her, but she continued on. She just needed to catch her breath. To inhale some huge gulps of air. 'Olive, wait!'

She slowed her pace but couldn't turn around to face him. She couldn't believe any of this was real. Couldn't believe that he had stopped his wedding to the beautiful Sofia because he was in love with her. The world around her was still and quiet, a strange contrast after the noise and madness of the anteroom. She was in the middle of a field. She had no idea how far away from the house she was but all around her was the vibrant green of Tuscany. The undulating hillsides escaping away into the distance, the world scented and bright in a way she had never known before.

'Olive,' Nico said again.

She had no idea how close he was behind her, but still, she couldn't bring herself to look around. This was going to be the most romantic moment of her life and here she was, looking like a sweaty orange lollipop. Far from ideal.

'Please turn around.'

'No.'

'Why not?'

'I look hideous.'

He chuckled. The deep, joyous sound piercing her heart. 'You look beautiful. As you always do. You always have.'

Reluctantly, she turned on the spot, her arms hanging limply by her sides. 'I look like a Calippo.'

He took a step towards her, smiling, placing his hands on her shoulders. 'You are, and always will be, the most beautiful, wonderful woman I have ever met. That's why I am, and always have been, in love with you.'

She looked up. His eyes were swimming with tears, and they glistened in the sun.

'Do you mean it?' Her voice shook as she spoke, emotion after emotion crashing into the words as she said them.

He nodded. 'I love you and Jacob, and I'm so sorry that I dragged you out here to watch me marry someone else and then asked you to organise my wedding.' He dropped his head, pressing his fingers to the corners of his eyes. 'I am so embarrassed.'

'At least you didn't go through with it.'

'How could I when the woman I have been in love with all my life was standing right in front of me?' He stepped forwards, cupping her cheek and raising her head so their eyes met. 'I love you, Olive. I don't know why it's taken me so long to tell you.' His lips met hers so gently, she felt like she was dreaming.

'I love you too,' she murmured. 'I always have.'

As she returned his love, wrapping her arms around his neck and pulling him in closer, they both finally let free all the emotions they'd been holding back for so long.

He was hers and she was his.

Finally.

Chapter 29

'So what happens now?' Olivia asked, trying to regain her breath.

She'd been waiting years for that kiss, and she had to admit, it had been worth the wait. Being with Nico made her feel alive in a way she hadn't for a long time. Her heart had always belonged to him, and it was as though it had been lying dormant, waiting for the moment when he would bring it to life.

'I don't know,' he replied, brushing a strand of hair back from her face. He was looking at her as if he'd never seen her before and as his eyes roved over her face, her stomach twisted in a surprisingly pleasant way.

'I guess someone will have to make an announcement.' She suddenly panicked, pulling away from him. 'I have to find Jacob and tell him.'

But Nico pulled her back for one more kiss and she was eager to oblige. She was more than happy to stay with him, in the middle of this field away from the mayhem that would greet them when they got back. Eventually, there was no putting it off any longer and, hand in hand, they walked back to the garden. Most of the guests had gone. Sofia's parents sat together, angry and hunched at one end of the long table. Giovanni and the brothers were all laughing and tucking into the prosecco, Maria huddled with them, Aldo's arm around her shoulder.

They made their way first to Jacob and Jack.

Jacob met his mum with a hug, wrapping his arms around her. 'I was really worried when you ran off like that.'

'I'm sorry,' she replied, grateful for the kind, caring boy she'd raised.

'I thought you must have diarrhoea or something.'

Olivia rolled her eyes.

'So, you two are finally making it official?' Jack said jokingly, handing Olivia a glass of prosecco. She drank it eagerly, the bubbles tingling her tongue. 'About time you did. He's always been in love with you. I knew it back when we were together.'

Nico laughed and held out his hand for Jack to shake.

'I'm sorry, Jack. I hope we can forget about the past and think about the future now.'

'No hard feelings here, mate. Actually, umm . . .' He shuffled his feet and glanced at Jacob. 'Liv, can I have a quick word?'

She frowned in confusion. Jack was never normally bashful. He usually said exactly what was on his mind without hesitation, often forgetting that there might be consequences. They took a few steps away and from the corner of her eye she saw Nico hold his arms out and Jacob, who moved into the embrace with a smile on his face.

'What's up? You're not going to tell me I should steer clear of Nico, are you?'

'No, it's umm—' He scratched the back of his head. 'I've been meaning to say something for a while but what with one thing and another there hasn't been the right time.'

'Is something wrong? Are you ill?' The panic was clear in her voice. She may no longer be in love with her ex-husband, but he was a good man, and she couldn't bear the thought of anything happening to him.

'What? No! Don't be daft. Fit as a fiddle, me. No, it's – well – I've kind of met someone.'

'Oh.' She took a sip of her prosecco to try and hide the smile appearing on her face.

'Her name's Shelley and she's an absolute diamond.'

'Wow, it must be getting serious.' Jack had had girlfriends on and off through the years, but she'd never seen him like this before. 'Wait! All those phone calls? Were they to Shelley?'

His cheeks flooded a vibrant pink.

'They were, weren't they?'

'So? I'd said I'd stay in touch and mention her to you because, well, I'd – I'd like to introduce her to you and Jacob, if that's all right.' After a few mis-starts, Jack had kept his love life completely separate to that of being a dad. They'd agreed the disruption wasn't good for Jacob and since then he hadn't brought anyone home or even mentioned anyone to Jacob. 'Do you think when we get back we could – I don't know – all go for dinner or something?'

'I'd love to.' She stepped forwards and wrapped her arms around him.

'Hang on.' He gently pushed her away. 'Did you think I was doing something dodgy?'

'No!' She'd answered far too quickly. Then over his shoulder she saw Sofia walking past, scrolling on her phone. 'You'll have to tell me all about Shelley later, but she sounds brilliant and I know I'm going to like her. Right now though, I think I better speak to Sofia.'

'Good luck.' He kissed her cheek. 'I'm glad you're happy, Liv. You deserve it. You've always been made for each other, you two.'

She felt the tears well in her eyes and could do nothing but nod for fear that if she tried to speak, they'd run free.

'And if he's going to love you in that dress then it must be the real deal!' Jack darted away from her before she could bash his arm.

She smiled as he went and caught up with Sofia in the corner of the garden, near the door to the anteroom, speaking into her phone. She lingered, shifting from foot to foot, toying with a flower, trying to stop the cape part of her dress flapping about annoyingly.

'So there you have it,' Sofia said to the camera. 'I'm not getting married today after all. In fact, today is my break-up day.' She wiped her eyes and suddenly frowned, her tone growing harder. 'No, no, no! I won't have hateful comments about Nico. He has done me a favour. I wasn't sure about marrying him and my doubts had grown over the last few days. I do not hate him. I love him as a friend. He is one of the only people who has stood up to my mother. And you all know what she can be like but shhh!' She pressed her finger to her lips. 'Don't tell her I said so.' She looked up to see Olivia and smiled a genuine happy smile that lit her eyes and showed her true beauty. 'I must go now, but I'll speak to you all again later. *Ciao*.'

She waved, stopped recording, and stood up.

'Sofia, I—'

'It's all right. Really.'

'I feel terrible.'

'My mum will be glad to hear it.' She laughed and Olivia joined in. 'I meant what I said, Olivia. Nico and I, I do not think we would have lasted. He never wanted to be in any of my videos and I don't think he really liked me being so public about our lives. If someone wants to be with me, they must support my career too.'

Olivia smiled. 'I couldn't agree more.'

'I will share my photos of the event so you can use them for your business. Nico told me you were hoping to set up your own?'

'I am and they'll be useful. Thank you. I feel for Angelo and Francesca though. They were hoping this would launch their wedding venue business and I worry I've ruined it before it's even begun.'

Sofia shook her head. 'Nonsense. My father will still pay for everything, and we'll still serve the food and cut the cake and do all those things, just for photos for their website. No one needs to know that the wedding didn't go ahead, and I am beautiful enough to be a model, am I not?'

For the first time, Olivia saw the sense of humour Nico had talked about but that had always been missing.

'It will annoy my mother even more if we get a picture of me eating cake.'

Olivia laughed at this and nodded. 'We'll get one of both of us.'

'I am sorry about the dress. My mother . . . I think she

worried about the way Nico spoke about you. So when he asked for you to be a bridesmaid . . .' She held up her hands in surrender.

'I can imagine. I think I wear it rather well anyway.' Sofia scowled, clearly not convinced and Olivia laughed again.

'There she is!' Giovanni boomed, looming towards her with arms outstretched. 'My daughter-in-law.'

'Not quite yet, Giovanni.'

'Ah, but it won't be long, I'm sure. You two have wasted enough time already.' He saw Sofia and blushed. 'Ah. *Scusa*, Sofia. I'm sorry.'

She playfully rolled her eyes as she walked past, pulling out her phone to record another video. Olivia felt some of the guilt drain from her system. Sofia was fine, Jack and Jacob were fine, and she and Nico were finally going to live the life together she'd always hoped they'd have. She made her way to him, realising too late they were stood just in front of the flower arch.

He pulled her towards him, his hands nestling in the curve of her waist. 'One day we will get married in a garden like this and watch the sunset as husband and wife.'

'Are you proposing to me already?' she joked, her body fizzing with excitement at the prospect.

'In a way. My dad always said he and my mum were two halves of the same whole. It's the same for us. Thank you for waiting for me.'

He pressed his lips to hers in a kiss she knew she'd never grow tired of, only to hear Jacob tutting behind her. She and Nico separated just enough to open their arms and welcome him in. He joined them for a moment before squirming away murmuring that it was embarrassing and going back to his dad.

Her life hadn't turned out quite the way she'd thought it would when she was eighteen, sitting on a beach on the other side of the world, but she wouldn't trade the winding roads she'd been down for anything. They'd made her who she was, taught her lessons she might never otherwise have learned and given her gifts like her son. She was exactly where she needed to be and, this time, Nico was right beside her.

Epilogue

One year later

'Can you put that table over there please?' Olivia asked directing the staff hired in to Castello Chateau for the wedding due to take place the next day.

Her wedding. Hers and Nico's.

Olivia raised her head to the sun, feeling the warmth on her skin, the breeze on her face. She inhaled the familiar scent of Italy: the citrus trees, the herbs and flowers that grew all around her. She couldn't believe tomorrow was actually happening, or that this was where she now lived. Her language skills were coming on slowly while Jacob was already fluent, loving life. He was happy, which meant she was too.

In the days after he had almost married someone else, there had been numerous discussions about how they were going to make things work. She and Nico had taken things slowly to begin with, trying a long-distance relationship as they had managed a long-distance friendship, but when Jacob said he'd love to live in Italy, Olivia had spoken to Jack, and everyone had agreed that a move was doable. In some ways it would be hard, but so many things in life were. Jack was happy to video-chat, to travel to Italy when he could, and she and Nico had agreed that they would come over at least every couple of months for the weekend.

Now he was settled with Shelley and she was sure Jacob would have a half-brother or sister soon. She was probably more excited at the prospect than Jacob was, especially as she and Nico had no plans to have any more children. Her career was finally going from strength to strength and, with Nico by her side, she felt her family was complete. As ever, her life wasn't taking the easiest of routes, but she was enjoying walking those paths and seeing where they led.

Sofia's pictures had been shared and Castello Chateau had become a must-use venue in Tuscany. Olivia had got on so well with Angelo and Francesca they had recommended her to everyone. She'd been lucky to get the date for her own wedding, given that she was having to fit everything in whilst also running her own international wedding-planning business. After starting out running different types of events, she'd decided to specialise in the one that gave her the most joy. Everything was going well so far, and she was building a name for herself with client recommendations making up the bulk of her business. Her work often took her to different parts of Italy, sometimes all over the world, and she finally felt she had found her calling.

She looked around at the beautiful gardens and the rolling hills falling away in the distance. The set-up for the wedding was basically the same, with an area for the ceremony and a long table for the wedding breakfast, though this time she hadn't ordered a flower arch. Giada had instead made two beautiful displays that stood on plinths either side of the spot where they would marry. The stone urns overflowed with flowers, greenery and trailing ivy. It was simple and elegant – the same as her dress. There was no looking like a traffic cone tomorrow.

Their families were already there, as was Maria, whose relationship with Aldo was progressing nicely. Giovanni couldn't be happier at the prospect of having Olivia as his daughter-in-law and had even cried when they'd shared the news that a date had finally been set for the wedding.

'Are you ready to become Mrs Olive Rossi?' Nico pulled her in and kissed her, distracting her from her thoughts.

'I am. Are you ready to become my husband?'

'I couldn't be more ready. I feel like we've waited long enough for this. Too long. But there is one thing we haven't talked about.'

'Oh?'

'You've been so busy organising this wedding we haven't sorted out where we'll be having our honeymoon. Jacob is going back to England with Jack for a week so we can go wherever we like. How about Greece?'

'So you can laugh at my terrible language skills there? No thank you. Can't we just stay here?'

'Your language skills are still terrible here.'

'Hey!' Before she could protest too strongly, he kissed her again. 'I'll have you know I am actually getting better.'

'You are. I'm only teasing. So Greece?'

'Greece will be wonderful.'

'Will there be a chateau in Greece do you think?' he asked, turning to look at Castello Chateau, the most romantic chateau in Italy.

'Maybe. We can hope.'

He kissed her again and she melted into his embrace, ready to spend the rest of her life with the man she had always loved, in the country she was beginning to love just as much.

THE END

Acknowledgements

I can't tell you how much joy this book brought me! I absolutely loved writing it and I hope it makes you just as happy: making you laugh and smile at the end of a long day. Thank you to everyone who has read one of my books or has decided to pick up this one for the first time. It's thanks to you that I'm able to keep writing and I appreciate you spending time with my characters. If you have time to leave a review, that would be amazing as it does so much to help us find new readers.

Thanks, as always, go to the wonderful team at Avon, especially my incredibly talented editor, Elisha Lundin, and to the rest of the team. It's a real pleasure working with you all and your commitment and enthusiasm makes the days when the words won't come more than worthwhile.

Thanks also go to my agent, Kate Nash, of the Kate Nash Literary Agency who is such a supporter of all things romantic fiction. I feel blessed to have you in my corner.

Finally, to my family and friends, thank you for always being there. I'd particularly like to thank the Romantic Novelists' Association. Life as a writer can be lonely, but it's through the RNA that I've made some amazing friends. I cannot thank current chair Jean Fullerton enough for her always sound advice, especially when it comes to raising daughters!

If you enjoyed *A Wedding at the Chateau*,
you'll love the first book in the series,
Summer at the Chateau.

**A newly single woman.
A handsome stranger.
A chateau that keeps
bringing them together…**

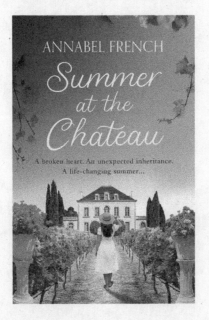

The perfect feel-good romantic comedy that
will leave you falling head over heels!

Available from all good bookshops now.

Life has gone a little bit downhill for Naomi Winters...

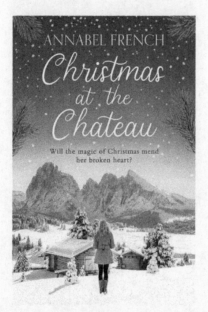

Escape to the Swiss Alps with this festive, feel-good novel!

Available from all good bookshops now.